COLD DECK

Cold Deck

Gordon Donnell

Writers Club Press
San Jose New York Lincoln Shanghai

Cold Deck

Writers Club Press
an imprint of iUniverse, Inc.

For information address:
iUniverse, Inc.
5220 S. 16th St., Suite 200
Lincoln, NE 68512
www.iuniverse.com

ISBN: 0-595-22434-2

Printed in the United States of America

CHAPTER 1

Bernie Cohn clamped a fresh Havana between his teeth. An impatient glance at Scott Birmingham accomplished nothing. He had to use his own monogrammed lighter.

"You said the Judge was waiting?"

Birmingham glanced around to warn against speaking in front of witnesses.

Cohn ran his fingers through his hair, like a politician making sure the thin spots were covered before a public appearance. His fingers were meaty, dimpled. Diamonds twinkled on two of them when he removed the cigar.

"Well, let him wait!" he bellowed, and made the clot of people around the roulette table stare.

Cohn was dressed to be stared at. Blue suede accents set off his black patent leather shoes. Blue trousers fit the lower curve of his belly like an egg holder. A paisley tie squirted out from under the stiff white collar of his pink shirt and cascaded down the folds of his stomach. A pink display handkerchief fanned up from the pocket of his burgundy sport coat.

Birmingham ignored the spectacle and feigned interest in his surroundings. Off-reservation casinos were illegal in Florida. The house where this one hid from the law was left over from an age of long-tailed coats, billowing crinolines and unquestioned privilege. On the parquetry where silver-mounted slippers had once moved in stately rhythm, fat-soled shoes now shuffled as rows of people worked slot machines. The dull clink of falling coins had replaced the tinkle of musical laughter.

A snicker brought Birmingham's attention back to the roulette table. "I think I'll just make me a little bet while the old fart's waiting," Cohn declared in a Manhattan snarl.

He surveyed the layout grandly and put five one hundred dollar chips on twenty-eight. The performance was wasted. The other players had quit staring.

"Bets down, ladies and gentlemen." The croupier's voice had a Brooklyn edge as distinctive as a stale roach. "No more bets."

The wheel spun. A chromium ball whirled and clicked. Presently it stopped clicking.

"Twenty-eight. Black."

Cohn took the cigar from between his teeth. "Should've bet a grand," he complained loudly.

"How long are we going to be at this?" Birmingham inquired.

"Hold your water!"

Cohn's furtive words created only a fleeting disturbance in his smug expression. He gathered his chips. No traditional winner's tip remained on the cloth. He jerked his head for Birmingham to follow.

The room was filled to capacity. Cohn had to squeeze his bulk between gamblers who had been jostled too often to notice any more. He was just a face in the crowd, and he didn't like it. He dumped the chips at the cashier's cage and turned to vent his displeasure at Birmingham.

Birmingham wasn't there. He had paused to exchange earnest words with a cocktail waitress. Cohn had to wait while the younger man oozed through the crowd to rejoin him. Blood pressure made a thermometer of his moon face.

"The thing you got to learn," he snarled around his cigar, "is there's one heavyweight in every deal. One dude that plays the game smarter than everybody else."

"I'll have it on the tip of my tongue, if Ruellene Kingman or her Chief Criminal Deputy ever ask."

Bernie Cohn called loudly for thousand dollar bills. They made a bulge in his wallet.

"C'mon. Let's go see what old Judgy Wudgy wants."

"Judge Picaud will meet with you privately," Birmingham said.

"So what do you tell the cocktail broad when she asks why you weren't in with the big boys?"

"The Judge is waiting upstairs, Mr. Cohn."

Cohn paraded out into a two-story entry hall. Ornately railed stairs rose past the shadows of paintings that had once graced the rose damask walls. The doorman watched Cohn climb, as if he found the sight only slightly more amusing than paring his fingernails with a switchblade.

The balcony at the top formed the central segment of a dim and disused hallway. An ambiguous glow fanned out under a door at the end. Cohn fumbled briefly in a pocket then went quickly along and opened the door.

The room was poorly lit by a sagging floor lamp. As if late August were not hot enough, a gas mantle burned with an asthmatic hiss in a clouded marble fireplace. Luminous blue tendrils wavered out across a massive desk behind which, oblivious to the flickering minuet of blue light and bluer shadows, an old man sat and stared. The smoldering fixity of his dark-rimmed eyes was the only sign of vitality left to him.

Bernie Cohn strutted to the desk and looked for a chair. He found only a bar-top jukebox; a filthy relic of some failed and forgotten enterprise. He suppressed a scowl and thrust out his belly.

"Evening, your Honor," he said with hugely exaggerated familiarity. "Getting any on the side these days?" His laugh had an echo like bats up under the high ceiling.

"You are late, Counselor," the old man lectured in a voice as brittle as the parchment they kept under glass in the Confederate Archives. "I summoned you twenty minutes ago."

"Must be something wrong with my hearing, your Honor. I thought you said summoned."

"Summoned," the old Judge repeated. Purple veins bulged in the bony hands he clasped around a fragile teacup. The palsied rattle of cup and saucer had the jittery quality that turned family dinners into knife fights.

A pitying smile formed around Cohn's cigar. "We're partners, Judge. Partners don't summon partners. They ask them to take a meeting. Politely."

"You were my agent, Mr. Cohn. Never anything more. Even in that, you have failed me. You were to have had a man killed. He is still alive."

"Some wimp bookkeeper," Cohn recalled contemptuously. "He's in the hospital, crippled for life."

"The man was to die. Without heirs and without executing a will. You were to arrange it so."

Cohn snatched the cigar out of his mouth. "My end of this deal is the processing and distribution. I been kissing up to the meanest gang bangers in the South Bronx to sew up the connections we need, figuring you'd get the merchandise in on schedule. Harvey Ricks tells me hasn't seen snowflake one."

"You have defaulted on your responsibilities, Counselor. You will remove yourself from my affairs. Your Mr. Ricks will be free to join you as soon as he has discharged the last of his duties here. That is my decision."

Cohn's voice got cagey. "Seems to me that decision could be your last, if a certain Congressman gets the juice on you."

"You are in the Everglades, Counselor. Nothing is as it seems to be in the Everglades."

Profound weariness weighed down the old man's words. The teacup ceased its rattle. The Judge's eyelids drooped until they shut off the smoldering glow. His head slacked until his chin touched his chest. It gave a spasmodic jerk, and then subsided. He was as still as he soon would be on the white satin of his coffin.

A taxi was idling when Bernie Cohn clumped down from the veranda of the old house. An African-American driver held the rear door. His head was bald on top. At the sides black hair was slicked back as hard and shiny as tile. A freshly pressed black suit with a white carnation in the lapel didn't fit a life of heavy luggage and sweltering boredom.

Cohn brushed blindly past and plopped his bulk onto the seat. The driver closed himself in front.

"Where to, sir?"

"Sheraton Beach," Cohn ordered irritably.

The gravel drive made a wide curve, ran the length of a seedy grassplot where private cars were parked end to end in two ranks then curved back to give him a last look at the old mansion. Shaded lower windows gave off a subdued glow, like diamonds at the throat of a faded courtesan reduced to living on the half-remembered desires of a final, patient admirer. Gnarled cypress trees stood as hags in waiting, wearing drippy shawls of Spanish moss. The perpetual mist of the Everglades seemed a swirl of whispered gossip.

Cohn clamped a fresh Havana between his teeth. His lighter reflected in the cloudy plastic that covered a driver's ID fastened on the seatback in front of him. Lost in the flare was the will-o-the-wisp aura of Miami, filtering through the swamp from an invisible horizon far off to the left.

The driver turned right at the end of the gravel drive. He went fast along two lanes of asphalt. They met no cars, passed no lights. The high beams bored a tunnel walled in by unbroken vegetation and roofed over by a black planetarium sky.

Cohn blew a plume of smoke toward the front seat. “Won big tonight,” he announced.

“I am pleased to hear that, sir,” the driver said.

“‘Course,” Cohn conceded, “owning a piece of the action didn’t hurt my chances.” He sounded drunk when he laughed.

The driver turned sharply onto a secondary road and spilled him sideways on the seat. Tires slithered and bumps hammered the suspension. Cohn flailed and caught the top of the front seatback. He pulled himself up coughing unexpected smoke from his lungs.

“Where the hell do you think you’re going?”

They came to a field where fog drifted in stringy clumps and random patches of standing water shimmered under a bright moon. The driver took his foot off the gas and let go of the wheel, content to let the taxi slog to a stop.

Cohn peered at the moonlit ID for a name to call the man. Surprise made him blink. He ripped away the plastic cover and yanked the ID out of the frame for a better look. The man in the small photograph was African-American, but he had a broad, blunt face and a whiskey grin missing two teeth.

The driver turned his long face, showing a full set of large teeth in a solemn smile. He brought up a hand with shiny nails cut square. Something glowed softly against the pink insides of his fingers. He moved a forefinger and a blue steel blade pivoted up from a pearl handled straight razor. He brought his arm over the seatback. His movements held Cohn’s eyes like the hypnotic waving of a cobra.

“Rip off?” Cohn asked in a clogged voice.

“I’m afraid not, Mr. Cohn.”

“You know my name?” Sudden rage bloated Cohn’s face. “That Goddamn Judge! Listen, Boy, I’ve got connections that old fart never—!”

The driver’s arm made one stroke. Quick, light, precise.

Words stopped coming from Bernie Cohn before his lips stopped moving. He put a hand to his throat. Meaty fingers came away dark and slippery with blood. His mouth went slack in horror. The cigar fell into his lap and smoked forgotten. He groped and caught the door handle. The door swung open and he tumbled sideways. His head slacked an inch from the ground. His eyes were wide open. They did not see the driver open his door and step out.

The man caught Cohn beneath the armpits and pulled him free of the cab. He retrieved Cohn's cigar from the floor mat with fastidious care and dropped it. It hissed in half an inch of water and went out. The rear door made a firm click closing.

A nearby swamp bird sang three shrill, startled notes that died away into the quiet idle of the taxi.

There was no sound when black fingers opened Cohn's wallet, just the satisfied flash of white teeth. The driver took only the fat sheaf of currency. He replaced the wallet and closed himself behind the wheel.

Adjusting the carnation in his lapel, he guided the taxi away at the solemn pace of a funeral procession.

CHAPTER 2

A Miami cab deposited David Sinclair on a shaded street of flamboyant art deco homes built during the nineteen twenties, when land promoters and rum runners and tourists had left South Florida awash in its first tidal wave of money. The stifling suburban afternoon brought perspiration to his face, like condensation on the ghastly petals of a rain forest orchid. He planted a cane to stabilize his balance.

His driveway held a visiting Buick in a shade of gray that slid between silver and smoke as he passed it on his way to the front door. Oiled hinges silently admitted him to a dim vestibule. From there he could see into a sunlit living room.

Scott Birmingham stood beside a thickly upholstered club chair. A white polo shirt emphasized the perfectly defined wedge of his back. White tennis shorts hugged his lean hips. White athletic socks molded themselves to the taper of his tanned calves. Against the cream color of the walls, the white had an unreal purity.

"I've taken the chicken shit long enough, Cindy," he said in a voice thickened by its own fervency. "I'm ready to make my move. I want you with me when I make it."

Cindy Rivendahl stretched languidly in the chair. She considered Birmingham with cobalt eyes, where doubts lingered with the persistence of radioactivity. He set a half finished highball aside and put a supporting hand on the chair. His fingers pressed deep furrows into the upholstery. He bent at the waist and pressed his lips onto hers. Their kiss was sultry.

Sinclair set down a suitcase, pivoted the door noiselessly to within a foot of being closed then slammed it. He went into the living room, using his cane as sparingly as possible. Trying to hide his clumsiness only made it more obvious.

There was no languor in the movement that brought Cindy out of her chair. High impact aerobics had left a pliant dancer's body instantly responsive to her moods. She crossed the living room in half a dozen mercurial strides and confronted Sinclair.

"David, you promised you'd stay in the hospital until you were completely well."

He caught the fragrance of Jasmine and a fond smile tugged at the corners of his mouth. "I need the taste of freedom," he said in a voice as gentle as Indiana springtime, "a lot more than I need to improve my white blood cell count."

"You're going back."

His smile flickered out. "Hello, Scott," he said, a hint of early winter in his voice.

Ice clinked lightly when Birmingham raised his highball in a half-hearted salute. "How are you feeling, David?"

"Bored stiff."

"Sure, but how are you physically? Are you up to fending for yourself at home?"

"Actually, I thought I might stop out for a last look at the casino. I heard the old place was closing for remodeling night after tomorrow."

A note of strangled laughter escaped from Cindy.

Birmingham crossed the carpet quickly and stood beside her. "It's nothing to me, David. Harvey Ricks might object, though."

"I was sort of hoping you'd introduce me, Scott."

"David, whose gunmen do you think put you in the hospital?"

"I just want to talk to him. I can introduce myself, if you're not comfortable with the idea."

"Well, it's up to you." Birmingham drained his glass in a swift gulp and put it on the corner of an upright piano. "Think about what I said, Cindy," he urged in his thick, fervent voice. "We can talk about it later."

The doubt in her eyes spoke more eloquently than words.

Birmingham nodded formally at Sinclair and left, closing the front door with a firm quiet that said he knew its idiosyncrasies.

Beneath the perspiration on Sinclair's face lurked the bloodless white of impending collapse. He sank down on the piano bench and put his back against the keyboard cover. Aluminum under a dozen coats of black lacquer, the piano was one of only a few built between the World Wars to fly on the great Zeppelin airships. It stood at the focal point of a room as sterile as a museum exhibit. Art deco furniture predated both Sinclair and Cindy, favoring neither and putting no emphasis on the generation that separated their ages.

She came and stood over him. "You're going back to the hospital, David."

"I'm okay. Just a little light headed. Not used to being on my feet, I guess." The cane slipped from his fingers and made a quiet thud on the carpet.

Cindy stooped quickly to recover it. She frowned at the intricately carved ivory handle, the elaborate low relief twining down the teak stem. "Where did you get this fancy thing? The hospital didn't give it to you."

"Cute, isn't it?"

"It looks like it belonged to one of those pompous jerks in an old British Empire movie."

"I'm fair itchin' to have a go at those fuzzy wuzzies, M'Lady."

She gave him a worried look. "I'm going to call your doctor. If you won't go back on your own, he'll send an ambulance."

"Not if he wants to keep his license. He can't drag people out of their homes and practice medicine on them without their consent. It's not legal."

Cindy gave her head a petulant toss. She left the cane beside him and collected a frosty gimlet from a side table. The furniture was briefly alive with her movement, mirroring it in expanses of lacquered wood as she crossed to a bay window. She curled onto the cushions like a pampered cat withdrawing to warm herself in the sun.

Sinclair took out a handkerchief and patted perspiration from his face. He planted the cane, regained his feet and made his way across the room. Leaded diamonds of glass fragmented his reflection when he came up behind Cindy.

"I guess I should've called," he said contritely. "Let you know I was coming."

Her reflection remained motionless, her face as smooth and pure as a cameo. Outside the bay window lay a flagstone patio ending at the concrete bulkhead of a canal. A taut-rigged sloop floated past with the peaceful slowness of fading summer; a suggestion of far horizons and fresh beginnings.

"Yeah," he said. "I should have called."

He went into a den where sunlight slanted through an octagonal window, pollinating the air and spreading a lopsided swatch of brilliance over a large desk. Sinking into a swivel chair, he unlocked a credenza and dialed open a safe fitted inside. From one of the pigeonholes he took a sheaf of fifty-dollar bills, folded several into a clip made from an Army parachute badge and replaced the rest.

"How much have you got left?" Cindy had come quietly into the den.

"How much to you need?"

She perched on a corner of the desk next to a computer monitor. An array of accounting texts confronted her from shelves in the opposite wall. This was Sinclair's world and it made her visibly uncomfortable. She picked up a framed photograph. In it she and Sinclair posed together before a single engine Cessna. Across the lower corner straight feminine handwriting with a downbeat of suppressed emotion read *David—solo at last.* She put it back on the desk, face down.

"I didn't say I needed money. I asked how much you had left."

"I don't know."

"You mean you won't tell me."

"I mean I don't know."

"You never told me the bank made automatic mortgage transfers. The first couple of days you were in the hospital, I didn't dare spend a nickel for fear I'd have to make your stupid house payment."

Sinclair conceded the point with a conciliatory shrug. "I thought I was probably dull enough without reading you the fine print in my loans."

"You never involve me in anything. You're afraid you'll have to compromise your precious way of doing things."

"You know my story," he said. "My career wound up in the dumpster after a corporate reorganization. Now I'm breaking a few rules to prove I'm not just another dinosaur. I don't want you hurt if turns out that I took the wrong risk."

Cindy's stare was cold and relentless. He turned his chair back to the open credenza.

Cindy said, "I took the LSAT." She said it very quickly, to Sinclair's back as he pressed the safe door closed.

"The what?" He twirled the knob.

"The LSAT. The Law School Admissions Test. I took the Law School Admissions Test."

"How did you do?"

"David, I'm trying to talk to you. Do you want to look at me?"

Sinclair secured the door that hid the safe. He palmed his key case away and brought his chair around to face her.

"I said," she repeated earnestly, "that I took the Law School Admissions Test."

"And I asked how you did."

She flushed and glanced at her toes. "I didn't want to tell you before I knew. That I took it, I mean. I wanted to be sure I scored high enough to get into a decent school before I said anything."

A congratulatory grin warmed his face. "Have you picked the lucky school yet?"

She shook her head, a tiny shiver of anticipation. "I just got my results yesterday. They were in the mail when I got back from visiting you."

"You'll need money," he decided.

She lifted her shoulders; let them fall. "Cocktail waitresses work nights. I'll go to school days and work nights."

"That sounds all right to talk about, but three years of it will be a grind."

"You worked your way through graduate school," she reminded him.

"An MBA takes only eighteen months. And you won't have the GI Bill to back you up."

She shook her head vigorously. "I don't want any more of your money, David."

"Call it a loan. You can pay me back on a schedule like you would a bank, if that'll make you feel better about it."

"I don't want any more of your damned money!" She stood down from the desk, startled by her own outburst.

Sinclair made his gentle voice solemn. "Maybe I'm a dreamer, Cindy. I convinced myself that a few years difference in age didn't matter between us. If I had thought for a minute I was buying you, I would have called it off right there."

Her words came quickly and low. "David, all my life I've been a slave to someone else's expectations. I can't be smothered any more."

She touched his sleeve and cobalt eyes pleaded for understanding. "I'm sorry. I just can't."

"Tell me where I'm crowding you. I'll back off."

Her shoulders moved aimlessly. "Anyway, you have to leave Miami. Scott is only a Deputy State Attorney. I don't think he can protect you any more. Even if he wanted to."

"Are you sleeping with him these days?"

Red spots appeared below her cheekbones. Sinclair closed his eyes, tightly, and then brought the lids up slowly, a millimeter short of fully open.

"I guess I got in a little over my head when I started playing house with you."

"It's not just me, David. It's everyone you deal with. I know your intentions are good. You want to take care of your own problems. You don't want to be a burden on anyone. But it's not that simple. Everything you do touches someone else's life in some way. You can't isolate yourself. You have to make allowance for other people's hopes and plans."

"I'm sorry if I'm in anyone's way," he said. "I'll try to impose as little as possible."

He opened a shallow drawer in the desk. White spotted green dice made straight rows in the felt lined indentations of a wooden tray. He worked out a pair, put them together between a thumb and forefinger and held them to the octagonal window. They were transparent to sunlight, to persuade the gullible they could not have been doctored.

Cindy watched him load dice from the tray into his coat pocket. "Are you going to try to get money? Because of me?"

A wistful smile touched his lips, but he shook his head. "There's no price on lost dreams. Once they're gone, they can't be bought back. Not for any amount."

"What are you going to do?"

"I once saw a bumper sticker that read *Life is what happens to you while you're busy making other plans*. I've never liked that idea. There's not much point in making plans if you don't see them through to some kind of conclusion."

Skin at the base of Cindy's nostrils whitened. "Harvey Ricks will kill you this time."

A reassuring smile came automatically to Sinclair's face, and remained for the moment it took conscious thought to remind him it was no longer appropriate. Its departure left only strained pallor.

CHAPTER 3

Night had cooled Miami to a slow oven. The bus lumbered away and left Sinclair at a deserted stop. Across the street stood a boarded-up hotel. A street lamp illuminated a billboard with an architect's rendering of an intersection soon to be, dominated by gleaming towers of aluminum and glass.

Kitty corner loomed the eleven story mass of the old Lloyd Building. Three stories of neon script sizzled ominously, threatening to extinguish the word *Parisian.* Gone from the theater marquee below were the glittering names of Hollywood and Broadway. Block capitals now summoned the lonely, the sick, the frightened and the feeble to take refuge in the living Word of the Lord. Smaller letters identified the Reverend Vernon Granger as pastor, promised services in English and listed the hours when faith would be dispensed.

Sinclair crossed and used a master key to enter the empty building lobby. Ornate elevator doors shimmered in dim light. He made his way back to a blank wooden door and passed unseen into the lobby of the Parisian Theater.

Mildew formed an oppressive backdrop to the silence there. Fluted columns rose twenty feet to frosted capitals illuminated at random where an aging bulb was still waiting to sputter into darkness. Pulp religious tracts spread on the concession stand bled to ghastly shades in the satanic aura of sconces flanking the grand staircase. Sinclair climbed to a landing where the stairs divided and disappeared on their way to separate balcony entrances above.

Bright light lay in a tight wedge across threadbare carpet, spreading from the crack of a door not quite latched. The door pivoted soundlessly at his touch, rotating into a cramped office. A plastic fan turned on the kidney shaped desk where Vernon Granger worked. Sinclair spoke quietly over the asthmatic whir.

"Good evening, Sergeant."

The word, "David?" began as a drill instructor's resonance in Granger's diaphragm and died in a surprised gust an inch beyond his lips. A swivel chair drifted backward in a lazy spin as disbelief brought him to his feet. "David, God bless you for coming." He came around the desk and intercepted Sinclair with a powerful handclasp. "How are you? How do you feel?"

"Pretty good." The shortness of his breath said otherwise. "A little tired, I guess."

"Here, David, sit down. Sit down and rest."

Granger installed him in a chair beside the desk and stepped to the doorway. He swept the staircase and the dim lobby below with the expert glance of a man who had not forgotten how to scan hostile places, then closed the door and turned the deadbolt. Retrieving his own chair, he unlocked a drawer and removed a bulging manila folder.

"The Lord has spared you, David, as he has spared few mortals." He handed Sinclair a news clipping.

> BUSINESSMAN INJURED IN SHOOTING
> Real estate investor David Sinclair was shot by unknown assailants shortly after two AM outside a Coral Gables bank. Sinclair, who recently purchased Miami's Lloyd Building for an undisclosed sum, was reportedly making a deposit in connection with church activities. Police declined to speculate on whether the shooting might have been a robbery attempt. Sinclair is listed in stable condition following surgery.

The clipping was dated two weeks previous. Sinclair handed it back without comment. Granger replaced it and locked the folder away again.

"What happened, David?"

"I'd just put the soft count from the casino in the deposit chute. Whoever it was caught me under the light. The whole thing was over before I knew it had started. I was down and my leg wouldn't work and my rib cage felt like someone had used it for karate practice. I caught five rounds in all. My armor stopped four of them."

"But you were paying for protection. Weren't the police covering you while you made the deposit?"

"They only drove escort once in a while. Just enough to let anyone watching know they were around."

"Why didn't you call on me?"

"You took enough chances for me in Vietnam. Kid lieutenants didn't last long without good platoon sergeants."

"David, this concerns me, too. You've used my Church to launder your gambling money. You conducted casino business through the Church's bank account, and took your profit by paying rent to yourself for the Church's use of the Theater."

"I've told the building management company to send you an eviction notice," Sinclair assured him.

"Eviction?"

"A church may not have to pay taxes on its business activity, but it does have to report it. The casino is gone, and the IRS is certain to notice your banking activity went from six figures a week to nothing overnight. If you can't prove you lost your lease, you'll be conducting Bible study in Club Fed."

"The Bible tells us to render unto Caesar the things which are Caesar's," Granger rumbled with more indignation than logic.

"What does it say about sitting in a nightclub in Cheo Reo with a twelve year old B-girl on your lap, singing *Love Potion_Number 9* at the top of your lungs?"

Granger blinked and spoke with solemn, resonant candor. "I was lost then, David. I truly was."

"The way you told it then, you were lost when you were a gigolo in Fort Lauderdale. You joined the Army and found your sense of direction. What did you do after that, Vernon? You were studying to be an insurance adjuster toward the end of your tour in Vietnam. And you told me once you'd been a private investigator since then."

"I have followed many false prophets, David. Through many wastelands."

"I didn't come for the sermon. I only stopped by because I wanted you to hear about the eviction from me before the notice came."

Granger found a squat cognac bottle and two glasses in a drawer. There was an air of ritual in the way he decanted the liquid. He set a glass before Sinclair and drained his own in a single pass.

"What are you planning to do, David?"

"Resurrect the Lloyd Building. The Latin American banks have pushed a lot of pinstriped suits off Brickell Avenue. This part of Miami is getting respectable again. That means big money. Legitimate money."

"You are an outsider in Miami," Granger reminded him. "Outsiders are no longer stoned, as they were in biblical times, but the Pharisees still prefer to deal within their own small circle."

"Crofton Lloyd was an outsider himself. He was a marine architect who came to Miami rather than spend his life designing bilge vents for the old boys' network in New England. He made enough money building fast offshore boats during Prohibition to put up an art deco skyscraper."

"That was during the depression, David, when any money was welcome. Lloyd was even able to buy himself a society bride. When he dropped dead, his widow, Opal, got everything. Her pedigree gave it instant respectability."

"Well, it's gone now. Scott Birmingham arranged for me to take over the mortgage on this building the day before the bank was due to foreclose on the old man's grandson."

Granger frowned sharply. "Opal owned the building."

"Not according to the bank. Or the Dade County records."

"The grandson is totally irresponsible. He's forty something, and he's been on and off drugs since he was fourteen. Mostly on."

Sinclair dismissed the subject with an impatient shrug. "I needed a business front. The Lloyd Building was available. With funding from the casino to stall foreclosure, I could turn it into a viable asset."

"David, the Lloyd Building is worth millions under capable management. Why would anyone just give it to you? And your experience with casinos was in the head office. Accountant. Auditor. Controller. Why recruit a bean counter from the executive suite to set up a working operation? Why not a pit boss? And why go all the way to Atlantic City? There are plenty of gamblers in Miami."

A vague, wordless gesture was all Sinclair had to offer.

"David, have you never wondered about Birmingham's motives? Or the motives of that Rivendahl woman?"

"I've spent the last two weeks wondering about damn little else," Sinclair confessed.

"But when they put the deal to you…didn't you ask?"

"How many questions did you ask when I offered you the Theater for your Church?"

"The Lord had sent succor to his flock," Granger protested. "I acted out of faith in Him."

"I acted out of frustration. A lot of years working long hours until a corporate re-engineering put me out on the street. Scott Birmingham came along with a franchise and I signed up."

"David, it wasn't Birmingham who offered you that franchise. He hasn't the influence. He was fronting someone."

"Of course he was. Scott's kind of insulation is how respectable people stay respectable."

"Have you met the people behind him? Do you know their names?"

"Not yet," Sinclair said cheerfully. "But the night is young." He regained his feet without resorting to his cane. The accomplishment surprised him, and fortified his resolve. "I guess the casino is still running taxis from the Gold Coast?"

Granger was on his feet instantly. "Most of your crew is gone, David. There are New York people there now. You'll be about as welcome as Jane Fonda at a VFW picnic."

"I can't devote my time to the building until I've got my other potential problems contained. And I can't be sure there won't be blow back from the casino until I get some insight into this Harvey Ricks, and what he's doing out there."

"Harvey Ricks is the man who had you shot," Granger objected. "So he could take over the casino."

"My friends," Sinclair said, "were the only ones who knew my schedule the night I was ambushed."

Granger's face became very still. "God has warned you, David. Just as He warned the sinners of the Bible by the betrayal of His only begotten Son for thirty talents of silver."

Biscayne Bay was rippled velvet beneath the Causeway, reflecting the night lights of Miami Beach like second hand diamonds on the cloth of a pawnbroker's window. Sinclair rode between a flashy black whose cologne blended badly with the stale atmosphere of the old taxi and an immaculate, fiftyish Jew who studied Sinclair's elaborate cane with knowing eyes.

"That sort of piece is very rare," he ventured in a tactful voice that wondered at its origins. "Not for many years have they been made."

"The old gentleman I shared a hospital room with didn't need it any more. He had his grand daughter bring it for me."

"She did not know what it was, of course."

"I don't think so." Sinclair's tone was polite without inviting further conversation.

Biscayne Bay fell away in the rear window. The driver found a sparsely traveled boulevard and made speed past commercial outlets that stood dark behind empty parking aprons. A smugglers' moon hung low over the Everglades.

CHAPTER 4

Men subdued by intense concentration crowded around a twelve-foot dice table. The stickman's chant was Puerto Rico by way of Spanish Harlem.

"Shooter's point is five."

The flashy black who had ridden out with Sinclair bet a hundred he could make it. Most of the black money around the table got on the Pass line behind him. A waspish black loan shark concessionaire did a slow prowl for a preliminary look at watches and rings. A thickly larded white houseman passed a plastic tray piled with quarter sandwiches. Sinclair took one and chewed hungrily.

A rattan stick whispered across white lined green felt. It snicked white spotted green dice together and whisked them under a brown hand. A flourish of the stick invited more bets while the hand slipped behind the padded rail, out of sight. The stickman's eyes jittered on the dregs of a cocaine high. Play was for cash. Sinclair put fifty dollars on the Don't Pass line.

"Five to stay alive," the stickman chanted, and returned a pair of dice.

The black ran a pink tongue over his lips, flashed a smile. The dice made a surging run. Stricken sighs told the story.

"Eleven is craps. Pay the No Pass."

Sinclair palmed his winnings into an inner pocket. He had accumulated considerable money in half an hour's rapid play, but kept only a few bills visible in his hand.

"New shooter coming out," the stickman chanted.

It was Sinclair's first turn in shooters' rotation. He threw efficiently, without emotion or flourish. The green cubes ricocheted together, stopped dead in front of the stickman.

"Shooter's point is six."

Sinclair bet fifty dollars he would make it the hard way, with two threes. The table paid ten for one if he did. True odds against him were ten to one.

The houseman hustled even money side bets that Sinclair would show seven or eight in two rolls. Honest dice would have favored the house six hundred seventy one to six hundred twenty five. The stickman returned the table dice.

"Shooting sixty days."

Dice rebounded from Sinclair's first roll with three white spots showing uppermost on each green cube. A murmur of disbelief went up. The stickman's eyes hung in glistening stillness, like two sweating chorus boys poised on a sudden crescendo.

"Six. Pay the Pass. Pay the Hard Way."

The stickman raked money off the Don't Pass line and paid winners. His eyes were wide with innocence for the houseman's benefit.

The houseman thrust a thick arm through the crowd and snatched the dice off the table. He held them up to the light and peered through them, tilting his head this way and that, glowering and not seeing anything. Inspiration lit his face. He waddled out of the room, drawing pocket doors closed on the deserted entry, and on the glitter of chromium and glass in the crowded gaming room on the far side.

"Shooter's point is four," the stickman announced at Sinclair's next roll.

He permitted himself a tiny smirk when Sinclair put his winnings back on the Hard Way. The smirk grew when more money crowded the Pass line. Nothing like a fluke to loosen the bankrolls. The rattan stick made a quick sweep. He palmed the dice off the felt, released white spotted green cubes from the curl of his little finger.

"Four to score."

Sinclair palmed the dice and cocked his wrist. Green cubes ran the length of the felt, broke cleanly off the far bank and stopped short with two white spots showing on each.

Soft, eager profanities rippled around the table.

The stickman said, "Four," in a shallow voice with no breath behind it. "Pay the Pass. Pay the Hard Way."

Powerful fingers closed around Sinclair's arm before he could pick up his winnings. The voice in his ear was as chilly as the frost on a convenience store six-pack.

"Police officer, Mr. Sinclair. Someone wants a word with you."

The man wore street clothes. Broad and not quite Sinclair's height, his blue eyes had the personality of a pair of reflective sunglasses. He plucked Sinclair's winnings from the table and put them into the pocket of a dressy leather jacket. Then he tried to draw Sinclair back from the table.

The crowd of gamblers hemmed them against the padded rail. The most prominent obstacle was a three hundred pound black with a small derby hat on his huge head. He grinned, like a cannibal chief being introduced to a pair of plump photographers from *National Geographic.*

"You goin' somewhere wif mah fren'?" he asked the blond man in a drippy falsetto.

There were a few snickers.

The officer opened his leather jacket to expose a shiny badge and a glimpse of a stainless steel automatic.

The big black decided he didn't need that kind of trouble. He moved, very slowly and delicately, just enough to let the man steer Sinclair past.

"That shit bum's the goddamn heat we pay our tax money for," came the nicest of several redneck drawls.

"Muvvah huckin' riyup join'," a black voice muttered.

There was some unpleasant Spanish.

The stickman said, "New shooter coming out." His voice was as thin as last month's welfare check. The game resumed as if nothing had happened.

The officer opened a door and steered Sinclair into a narrow servants' passage between the living areas of the old house and the outer wall. A bare bulb dangled from a frayed strand of black wire. Incandescence dribbled down rough-hewn wall studs and puddled on a worn plank floor. The two men stood inches apart.

The sustaining intensity of gambling drained out of Sinclair's system and left his face as gray as cold ashes. "I don't think I've seen you before, have I?"

"My name is Roland Jardine." The frosty voice carried a faint scent of wintergreen. "Officer Jardine to you."

He pushed the door closed, released Sinclair and began to pat him for weapons. Wood scraped lightly behind an open plank staircase. A shaft of light shot into the dimness there. The old house had been equipped with a dumbwaiter, originally installed to lift meals from the kitchen to the upper floor. A heavy iron box was pushed onto the platform.

"You know what's in the box, don't you?" Jardine asked.

Sinclair leaned on his cane for support. "I built the security system here."

An electric motor made noise overhead. The dumbwaiter platform rose slowly until it disappeared. An unseen panel made noise sliding open. Slivers of light showed through chinks in a plank floor one level above. The light flickered as a prolonged scraping announced that the box was being dragged off the platform. The panel closed and the light vanished.

Jardine snatched away Sinclair's cane and grinned when Sinclair clutched the door frame to keep from toppling over. "All right, we can go on up now."

Sinclair released the door frame and tested his balance. It was none too steady. "There's no way I'll make those stairs without my cane."

Jardine put the crook into Sinclair's stomach, hard enough to hurt. "Another time, another place, you'd crawl. Except you just ran out of other times and other places."

A door at the top let them into one end of the dim second floor hall. They went along past closed doors, crossed the balcony that overlooked the lighted entry and walked along more dim hallway to the door at the far end. Jardine rapped once with hard knuckles, pushed it open and steered Sinclair into the office.

The derelict bar-top jukebox waited to greet them, hulking on a drop cloth on the desk. Electric current infused its horn-shaped pilasters with a cloudy amber glow. A ragged orange spark sizzled behind the filthy glass that looked into the changing mechanism, leaving a tang of burnt insulation on the sultry air. Behind tiers of crooked selection tags, a robot arm freed itself from decades of dirt and hardened grease with the spark and sputter of impending overload. Low, scratchy noises began in the dried-out cardboard of the speaker cone. The volume grew by fits and starts as amplifier tubes heated gradually and unevenly, with the odor of time burning away. The noises resolved themselves into the old Negro gamblers' lament, *Lavender Coffin.*

A great long cadaver of a man rose to six and a half feet behind the machine. His shirt and tie were an identical shade of green. Heavy silk emphasized narrow shoulders with no depth to them, like the folded wings of a prehistoric flying reptile. His thin face was acne-ravaged and lusterless.

"Your name Sinclair?" His voice had the rasp of carrots on a grater.

"Yes, Harvey. You are Harvey Ricks, aren't you?"

The rhythmic scratch of the Wurlitzer trailed away. Ricks ignored Sinclair to peer into open back of the machine while a sequence of jerky movements retracted a stubby tone arm.

A second man sat on a dilapidated sofa, trim and middle-aged, in a blue suit. He held a zipper case on his lap and studied Sinclair through gold-rimmed spectacles.

Sinclair's lips moved in a wintry smile. "Hello, Captain Hewitt. Nice to see you again."

"Good evening, Sinclair."

Sinclair leaned on his cane and watched Ricks cycle relays with a long screwdriver and needle-nosed pliers.

"I had a pretty good slot mechanic look that Wurlitzer over, Harvey. He told me to write it off, so I left it to gather dust with the old Mercedes in the tunnel."

"I know a Nigger who used to fix the jukes in Harlem."

Ricks set the tools aside and cut the current to the machine. He began wiping his fingers on a silk handkerchief, as if it were a grease rag. His fingers were hard and hooked and thin, like talons.

"That was a pretty stupid play downstairs," he remarked.

"Always change the dice when you take over a casino," Sinclair said cheerfully. "I had a drawer full of mercury loads my crew took off the local sharpies. All exact duplicates of the bricks downstairs."

The revelation produced only a fleeting irritation in Ricks' lusterless features. "What good did they do you?"

"They got me up here."

"That's not good for either of us."

"What should I have done, Harvey? Sandbagged my rotation and bet your stickman's switches until I paid for the equipment you took over from me?"

"If you're that cool, why didn't you?"

"I was curious, Harvey. Did Captain Hewitt tell you the FBI raided this location?"

"I may have heard about it," Ricks rasped.

"Why would a man as shrewd as you agree to operate in a known location?"

Ricks tossed the handkerchief aside and turned starched French cuffs down over skeletal forearms, fastened them with diamond-studded links. He checked Sinclair's urbane tailoring for accessories and didn't find any.

"I'm stupid. What's it get you?"

"What does it get you, Harvey? You're no boss gambler. Your dice crew is a joke. I had to do the chicken dance all over the table just to get noticed."

"So?"

"So this place barely pays the graft when it's properly run. I was given a sweetheart deal on some prime real estate for my trouble setting it up. What do you get for running it? How do you make out here?"

Ricks put on his suit coat and shrugged his shoulders in a hopeless effort to duplicate the flawless drape of Sinclair's quiet glen plaid.

"Talk about making out, let's have the cash you ripped off my table."

"That's like everything else here, Harvey." Sinclair moved two awkward steps sideways, away from Jardine, and sank down on the arm of the sofa. "I did the work, the police collected."

Ricks shot a disgusted look at Jardine. "You can put it on the desk, Sweetie."

Jardine didn't move.

"No hurry. Any time in the next ten seconds will do."

"When I work, I get paid."

"The Captain picks up the envelopes Monday night," Ricks said.

"Sinclair is overtime."

"You want to talk about time, Sweetie? Let's talk about the time you and Hewitt spent up here making eyes at each other, instead of down watching the crowd. Side betters took my table for ten times what Sinclair picked up. Any of that action you collect, you can keep. What's in your pocket now is mine."

Jardine leaned back against the door and folded his arms. He studied the remote ceiling while he whistled a few succulent notes.

Hewitt lectured, "This isn't New York, Mr. Ricks. Back alley bums don't talk to Dade County Police Officers that way."

"Whatever blows your dress up." Ricks winked at Sinclair. "Personally I never figured out how two queers knew who was supposed to do what to who."

Sinclair curtailed a surprised glance at Hewitt. Since coming in, he had made a point of not looking at the plastic intercom box fastened behind the desk.

Jardine straightened away from the door. He moved in a loose fighter's crouch until he stood in a space of open floor, his weight balanced on the balls of spread feet, his face as grim as a batter stepping to the plate in the high school championship.

"Maybe you'd like to come here and give me some of your shit, Stringbean?"

"I'm scared to," Ricks said sourly. "Your case of the stupids might be catching. Come on in, Mal."

The door pivoted across the patchy carpet where Jardine had stood a minute earlier and bumped the wall. A stoop shouldered man took a cautious step inside the room, peering through plastic rimmed bifocals. Perspiration trickled on his pouchy face. Humid confinement had stained the outline of his undershirt through the white Dacron of a cheap dress shirt. He held a black assault rifle in damp hands. An irritable expression warned that he would use it on short provocation.

Jardine remembered a training academy lecture on steely presence. "I guess you didn't hear the Captain say we were police officers."

"The dog food factory in Jersey won't hear him either," Mal said through a bad case of adenoids, apparently unaware that it wasn't just a hot night in lower Manhattan.

Hewitt cleared his throat lightly; spoke in a clear, strict voice. "Someone will hear something. That is a loud rifle, and this is a crowded building."

Harvey Ricks slipped a hand under the drop cloth on the desk and brought out a .22 automatic, a worn Colt Woodsman.

"Shut the door, Mal."

The stoop shouldered man hooked a scuffed loafer around the door and got it closed without moving his eyes or the rifle from Jardine.

Ricks brought the pistol smoothly up to shoulder level and discharged a single round. The report echoed like an M-80 firecracker in an empty oil drum. Across the room one of the tassels dangling below the lamp shade exploded to dust. The shade turned a lazy half-revolution, squeaking to a stop.

Tension became a palpable presence, as prickly as the Florida heat. Hewitt fixed a meaningless smile on his face, waiting for the inevitable curious crowd and embarrassing questions.

A small fan turned on the floor. Silence amplified the whir of plastic bearings. No sound came from the stairs. Nothing stirred out in the hall. Muted noises of gambling drifted without interruption from below. It began to seem possible that the stagnant air had smothered the shot completely.

A daring smile formed on Ricks' lips. "You want quiet? Okay. We got quiet."

Jardine was still looking for someone to stare down. "Think that popgun will stop me before I wring your buzzard neck?"

"Don't be crude," Ricks rasped. "We're civilized in New York. I'll whack Hewitt, and break your heart."

The oscillating breeze carried the fragrance of Mimosa, floating from Hewitt like some cloying messenger of fear. Hewitt curled his hands over the edge of the case on his lap. He had small hands, beautifully kept. Plump fingers began kneading the case.

"Roland and I would be missed," he told Ricks pointedly.

"Not by me. You two are set to whack my ass out the minute I get the processing running and you think you don't need me any more."

Hewitt stared blankly through his spectacles.

"Don't fish-eye me," Ricks said. "You and me are going the limit and we both know it. The shipment is due in an hour. No later than tomorrow, one of us is history." Ricks lined the pistol carefully on Hewitt's head. "And so long as it's you, right now is fine by me."

Jardine threw a swift, uncertain glance at his Captain.

Ricks slipped the safety. "On the desk, Sweetie. Yeah. That'll do it nicely."

Jardine moved wooden legged and emptied wadded bills from the pocket of his leather jacket. Hewitt and Sinclair began to breathe again. Jardine stepped back, stood squarely in Ricks' line of fire.

"I won't forget this," he said with tightly restrained fury.

Ricks lowered the pistol. "You badge-flashing airheads give me a pain. I'm running on empty trying to set up a twenty million dollar a year plant in a dirt floor basement, and all you can think about is chiseling nickels."

"How long do you think you can operate in Dade County without police protection?" Jardine asked.

"How long did Sinclair operate with it?"

Sinclair used his cane to stand. "It could be a short romance, Harvey, depending on what you're doing for them."

"As little as possible," Ricks rasped. "The in-crowd gets the Benjamins. You get the nooky. What's left for me but pick up a few crumbs off the floor and hope nobody screws a gun in my ear?"

Hewitt took out a handkerchief and patted his face dry of perspiration. He stood up, tucked the zipper case under his arm. He looked as prim as a school master in his gold rimmed glasses.

"We have to see to Sinclair now," he told Ricks. "Just you be ready when we bring the shipment back."

"Take him out by the main stairs. I don't want any of you assholes back near the cash boxes."

CHAPTER 5

Down in the entry it became clear why the report of Ricks' .22 had gone unnoticed. Gaming rooms on either side were packed. Players fortunate enough to have table space or a slot machine bet with fierce concentration, fearful they would be elbowed aside at the first sign of slack interest or a short bankroll. No one noticed Sinclair and the two officers.

Hewitt opened a door and Jardine steered Sinclair through a kitchen where a phlegmatic woman constructed sandwiches with the efficiency of a welding robot. Marijuana smoke and stale profanities drifted from a half-hearted poker game. The back door was guarded only by a spring lock.

Spongy stairs took the three men down into ankle-high, sopping grass behind the house. Moonlight shimmered through the tangle of a cypress tree, turning gossamer mist into a luminous shroud around a Jaguar coupe. Jardine jerked Sinclair to a stop.

"If Stringbean really is running on empty, he can't be making the monthlies on this ride."

"The shipment is due in a few minutes," Hewitt reminded him.

"I've got friends in motor division."

"I know," Hewitt said icily.

"Cycle jock pulls him over and reads that chassis number into the East Coast hot net. If it clicks, we've got him by the short curlies. If it doesn't, we'll know he's skimming."

Hewitt went on around the Jaguar, picking his way as carefully as a slumming debutante. "Bring Sinclair along, will you please, Roland."

Jardine concentrated his fury in the fingers that imprisoned Sinclair's arm. A loose stone skittered out from under his shoe. It rattled down a steep embankment that lifted the old house out of the blackness of the swamp and found shallow water at the bottom. A solitary bird beat its wings at the noise, a meaningless flurry that ended when Hewitt opened the rear door of a sedan standing up to its hubcaps in pulpy sedge.

"Get in, Mr. Sinclair. Slide across."

"Where are we going?"

Jardine bent Sinclair's arm into a vicious compliance hold and forced him down into the rear seat. A feint at his head sent him scrambling across the seat. Hewitt got in and Jardine shut the door. The scent of Mimosa grew strong. Jardine closed himself under the wheel and fired the engine.

The car idled forward. The tires made sloppy noises in the wet grass. Sinclair rubbed circulation back into his arm.

"Do you know what's underneath you back here?"

"Stringbean shored up the tunnel," Jardine said. "If it's safe for that two ton baby carriage of his, it's safe for us."

The sedan idled around the side of the house. Light from a sliver of window down at ground level filtered through the weeds.

"Twenty million is a lot of money to make in a cellar," Sinclair remarked. "What's Harvey Ricks doing down there?"

"Digging his grave," Jardine said in a voice that liked the idea. Tires crunched on gravel and he let the sedan pick up speed past the ranks of cars on the grassplot. Snapping on the highway beams, he turned right at the end of the drive and went fast along two lanes of deserted blacktop.

Hewitt put on the dome light. He opened the zipper case on his lap to reveal a manila folder. Block printing identified it as Dade County Police property and listed the punishment provided by the Florida Administrative Codes for anyone who removed it from an authorized records depository. Typewritten on the tab were Sinclair's name and an alphanumeric file designator.

Topmost of the papers clipped inside was a recommendation from the United States' Attorney that Sinclair be prosecuted on gambling conspiracy charges. A three-line endorsement indicated that action had been deferred pending further investigation, over the conformed signature of Ruellene Kingman as State Attorney for Dade County. Hewitt clipped a field interview blank on top of that and entered Sinclair's name in delicate linear script.

"Is there anyone you'd like us to get your personal effects to?"

"You make this sound like a one way ride."

Oppressive silence filled the sedan.

"If this is a scare, you're wasting it. I'm through with the casino. I have other priorities."

"You have a girl friend, don't you, Mr. Sinclair? It seems to me you're keeping house with a nice looking cocktail waitress from the casino."

"Talk to Scott Birmingham," Sinclair said with uncharacteristic bitterness.

"Stole your girl friend while you were in the hospital, did he? And him married with two little children. I'll tell you the truth, Mr. Sinclair. I've never liked the man. Too much the aristocrat for my taste. Too quick to let others do the work while he takes the landlord's share of the bounty."

"I guess I've been hoping Scott would be the one to sell me out," Sinclair admitted.

"Beg pardon?"

"I made sure only three people knew I'd be coming to the casino tonight."

"Who were the other two?" Hewitt asked.

"Neither of them is a Deputy State Attorney. It would take at least that much clout to use the police to kidnap me."

"We don't kidnap people, Mr. Sinclair. You are under investigative detention."

"That has a nice, official ring. Would I sound silly asking if there's anything substantial behind it?"

"An anonymous caller alleged that you murdered the man who took over your casino." Hewitt sounded like he was rehearsing the statement for an inquest.

"Harvey Ricks looked pretty healthy to me."

"Ricks?" Hewitt bit the name off short.

"Ricks is just window dressing?" Sinclair asked.

His only answer was the rush of velocity.

"What's the plan, Captain? Kill me now and Ricks after the casino closes for remodeling? Pretend justice has triumphed then re-open under new management after the FBI has gone on to greener pastures?"

Jardine emitted a sarcastic laugh. "We get all the bright ones, don't we, Captain?"

"Call in and report Sinclair's apprehension, will you please, Roland? The time sequence on the dispatch tape needs to support our testimony during the shooting review."

"There's got to be a smarter way to do this," Jardine grumbled. "Both of them could just disappear. No bodies—no investigation."

"You know the orders, Roland. There can't be any question that Sinclair is dead. Or any unanswered questions about the circumstances of his death."

"I know whose butts will be flapping in the breeze if that bitch State Attorney doesn't like the answers."

Jardine put the microphone to his lips. His words were too low to be audible. The dispatcher's replies were cryptic, broken by static.

Hewitt made entries to the effect that Sinclair had been advised of his constitutional rights, declined legal counsel and offered to show the location of the body to investigating officers. He added a note that Sinclair appeared increasingly agitated as they approached their destination.

Jardine swung the sedan off the blacktop. The tires slithered on a film of muck. Rough ground hammered the suspension. Highway beams sprayed among spindly alders. The trees ended abruptly and there was only thin, luminous fog. Jardine braked to a sliding stop, killed the lights and motor.

Captain Hewitt rolled his trouser legs up two fastidious turns, taking care not to disturb the creases. Jardine opened the door and Hewitt got out.

"Come out this side, Mr. Sinclair."

Slimy ooze found its way in under the tongues of Sinclair's wingtips. His balance was none too steady, but he did not use his cane for support. He held it low across his body, one hand at either end, like a majorette holding a baton just before the band struck up. Nervous fingers played on the carved ivory handle.

"Is this where we settle it?" Shallow words and no heart behind them.

"Quiet," Hewitt ordered.

A small gasoline engine idled, not far off. High tension electric current sizzled briefly. Tight cylindrical beams of light shot up out of the ground like jets from a high pressure fountain, imprisoning swirls of blue fog. The beams stood at intervals of a hundred feet, two lines of them. The lines made a corridor, fading away into the distance to meet somewhere on the far side of infinity.

"Air strip," Sinclair said in a low voice full of unquiet memories.

Jardine caught his arm. "Do you hear the plane, Captain?"

"Give me the flashlight, will you please, Roland?"

Hewitt started toward the engine noise in a precise, angry walk intended for hard ground. His street shoes slipped and slid in the muck and made him look like a penguin.

"Niles, where are you?" he called out.

"Come see what I found, Captain." The voice was deep and coarse, with a careless slur of intoxication.

"Niles, you turn those lights off. Do you hear me, Niles?"

The blue cylinders vanished. Moonlit fog enveloped Hewitt and made him as fuzzy as a picture of the Loch Ness monster. Jardine plunged into the haze after him, hauling Sinclair along like a forgotten puppy at the end of a leash.

Hewitt's flashlight found a high-slung compact pick-up truck nosed in against the tree line. A portable generator idled on the tailgate. Beside it slouched a man.

As they drew nearer, the man took shape; an ironworker's shoulders, a belly the size of a beer keg and bandy legs too short for his height. A faded denim vest hung on his hairy torso; a swastika sewn on one side and a skull and crossbones on the other, except that the bones were crossed motorcycle pistons. Small eyes shone smugly in a big flat face with a hard anvil of flesh for a nose. He made a production of glancing down at his feet.

Hewitt put his light on filthy motorcycle boots. Next to them was a pair of men's dress shoes. The shoes had feet in them. The heels were spread a few inches in the soft muck and the toes pointed up. A man lay on his back. His clothes were soggy; his face a lifeless moon, sallow and reflective in the light. Porcelain teeth glittered between colorless lips parted as if to disclose some tawdry secret. Hewitt concentrated the beam on a thin, dark line that ran the width of a bloodless throat, edged in dried-out droplets.

"Goddamn Smoke did a straight razor job," he swore in a soft, passionate voice. "Now just how the hell is it going to look to put a straight razor job off on a white collar like Sinclair? You want to tell me that, Roland?"

"What Smoke, Captain? What gives?"

Sinclair peered down with the sudden revulsion of a stranger passing an accident, and seeing himself lying in the victim's place. "Who was he?"

The hairy man let out a disgusted snort. "Big-rich son-of-a-bitch New York lawyer."

Hewitt shone his light into the man's eyes. "Put it all on the tailgate, Niles."

Niles squinted against the brilliance, but otherwise didn't move. "You ever stop and think it's brothers like me that does all the work, while you lord it over us in your fancy suits and get all the gravy?"

Jardine released Sinclair's arm. He edged around behind Hewitt, behind the light, where the big man had no chance to see him. "The Captain told you to put it on the tailgate, Niles."

"That you Roland?" Niles pushed his bass up to a cracked falsetto. "That the Captain's good boy Roland?"

Niles was six inches taller than Jardine, at least sixty pounds heavier. Jardine wasn't impressed. He stepped in fast and hit the big man; a short, straight drive with compressed fury behind it. The knife edge of his knuckles took Niles just below the floating ribs. The impact had a clean, solid sound, like a butcher's blade trimming fat. A sudden rush of air choked Niles' throat. His coarse face filled with sick, incredulous surprise. He folded to his knees in the muck.

Hewitt stepped back smartly, before the big man's stomach could erupt all over his shoes. "You've got a murder victim's personal effects in your pockets, Niles. One credit card could put you in the back seat of a squadrol with a couple of heavyweights who get their confessions with the butt end of a flashlight, and like it."

Niles' only answer was a thick, bubbling noise. Hewitt said, "Get him on his feet, will you please, Roland?"

Jardine flexed down and patted the big man for weapons. He fished a heavy revolver out of a belt holster. Wrapping the fingers of his free hand into shaggy hair, he rose like a power lifter putting his legs into two hundred fifty pounds of deadweight iron. Niles' features contorted in pain. He staggered up. Bandy legs supported his weight, but he depended on Jardine for balance.

Captain Hewitt focused the light into one of Niles' eyes then the other, probing for signs of responsiveness. His speech was the upbeat patter of a hospital orderly getting a moron ready to see the doctor.

"All right, Niles, here's what we're going to do. Officer Jardine is going to put an envelope on the tailgate of your truck. I want you to put everything you took from that man's body beside the envelope where we can see it. That's beside the envelope, Niles. Not in it. Not on top of it. Beside it. Do you understand me, Niles?"

"Ud-udder-stad."

Jardine released the big man and took a quick step back, as if he expected him to topple over and send up a geyser of mud. Niles swayed precariously, but managed to stabilize. Jardine stowed the revolver in a jacket pocket. He unfolded a clear vinyl envelope on the tailgate. Hewitt put the light on it, on the stamped legend: *Police Evidence.*

Niles dropped a wallet with an unceremonious plop. A pink handkerchief unwadded on impact. It spilled diamond rings and an assortment of coins. A gold wafer watch followed, then a gold lighter, a roll of breath mints, a shrink-wrapped condom. Last was a microcassette recorder.

Captain Hewitt shook the handkerchief loose and used it to lift the recorder. He tried to eject the tape. Heat and humidity had jammed the plastic mechanism. He put down the recorder and tucked the flashlight under his arm so he could use both hands to extract the blade from a small folding knife. The forgotten beam flitted around his feet. He stood an inch from one of the corpse's outflung hands. The light reflected briefly from something in the rigid curl of dead fingers. Hewitt focused his light back on the tailgate.

Sinclair squatted awkwardly and unnoticed next to the corpse. Careful to hold his cane clear of the muck, he worked a wad of soggy paper loose, pushed it up his sleeve and stood again.

The other three men remained intent on opening the recorder.

"That tape's been run," Jardine observed. "What do you think, Captain? About ten minutes worth?"

"You going to play it, Captain?" Niles asked.

Hewitt closed the recorder and stowed it in a coat pocket.

It was Sinclair's turn to be curious. "What's on the tape, Captain? Something about me?"

Jardine stepped over the body and put his face an inch from Sinclair's. "How would the Captain know what's on the tape? He just found it. He hasn't heard it himself."

"He knew the body was here. And he seems to be the only one who knows who put it here."

"That's why he's the Captain."

Hewitt said, "We'll need the straight razor too, Niles."

"Maybe he was cut with a straight razor, Captain. Wasn't no straight razor on him." The big, shaggy man had recovered most of his breath, none of his bluster.

"Did you bother to look under the body?"

"You want to try moving that thing?" Niles asked sullenly.

"Roland, give him a hand, will you, please?"

They took the corpse, one under each arm, and lifted. It rose as stiff as a timber. They got the shoulders high enough to clear the span of an outflung arm and pivoted the body around one foot. A sodden shoe came apart under the stress and the weight got away from them. The dead man plopped face down, one stiff arm stuck straight out, like he was signaling for a left turn.

Hewitt and Sinclair wiped splatters of mud from their glasses. Hewitt ran his flash carefully over the pressed down muck. Patterns of wrinkled clothing were clear where the corpse had lain. There was nothing else.

"Tell me exactly what you saw when you found the body, Niles."

"Wasn't nothing but them tire tracks. Just like you see."

Hewitt put his light on parallel ruts curving through the soft muck. He lectured Niles without bothering to look at him.

"Mr. Sinclair is going to sit on the tailgate of your vehicle, Niles. You are going to watch him for us. Just watch. Keep your fingerprints off him and off his personal effects. Do you hear me, Niles?"

"I hear you, Captain."

Jardine pushed the items on the tailgate into the envelope, pushed the envelope into his pocket without sealing it. He found a flashlight in the bed of the truck, clicked it on and wagged the beam at Sinclair. Sinclair boosted himself onto the tailgate beside the generator and put his cane across his lap.

Hewitt and Jardine started off in opposite directions from the body, following the curving ruts and sweeping the ground in wide, patient arcs with their lights.

Niles watched after them with the helpless, disbelieving fixity of a pedestrian looking after a car that had just gone through a puddle and left him dripping.

"They ain't gonna find shit," he said with glum satisfaction.

CHAPTER 6

The officers vanished into the mist. Niles rummaged in the truck bed and found a bottle of beer. He twisted off the top and chugged down half the contents. A satisfied belch arose. He swirled the bottle to dissipate the mist that separated him from Sinclair.

"Know why I took it?" His bass was a condescending sneer.

"The dead man's property?" Sinclair asked.

"The crap!" Niles snapped. "From the pigs."

"What did you expect to gain arguing with the police?"

"A man's got to be able to take the crap," Niles said solemnly. "It's part of being a man. Part of being your own man. Some day we'll bring the storm troopers down. But for now we take the crap."

"We?" Sinclair glanced around.

"The People, man. The Goddamn People." Niles waved his bottle at the corpse. "Bring them down just like him."

"What did you say his name was?"

"Ber-nard Cohn. That's what his plastic said. Big-rich son-of-a-bitch New York lawyer."

"What was he doing in Florida?"

"Ask the fucking pigs."

Niles drained the bottle and gave it an angry heave. It landed with a muddy splat. Swamp birds responded with a brief flurry of noise.

Niles liked that. He had shown them who was boss. A couple of swaggering steps brought him close enough to loom over Sinclair. He hooked his thumbs into his belt loops and peered down.

"What's your story?"

"That's what I was trying to find out when the police picked me up."

"What do you do for work? You don't look like you do man's work."

"Bean counter."

"What did you do? Cook the books for some big-rich corporation? Find out something you wasn't supposed to know?"

"I'm not sure why Hewitt was told to bring me here," Sinclair conceded, "but it hasn't anything to do with the pablum they spoon out on prime time television."

"Went to college, didn't you?"

"Yes," Sinclair said.

"You sit on your skinny rich ass in college while the poor boys got their shit blowed away in 'Nam?"

"I was a rifle platoon leader."

Niles hawked and spat. "Was you one of them ROTC boys?" He pronounced it rot-see.

"What unit were you with?"

"Back then the real men was on the road."

"Excuse me?"

"You ever hear of the Outlaws, Man?" Niles sounded the name importantly, as if anyone who knew anything would have heard it.

"No."

"Bikes. Harleys. Choppers. Outlaws was ready to fight. Some of the Brothers was ready to volunteer for 'Nam, if they could take their cycles. They just didn't take no crap. Not off the Man. Not off no rot-see boys."

"Is that who is at the other end of the field?"

Suspicion crept into Niles bass. "What makes you think anyone is?"

"You've got about fifty lights and a mile of connecting cable," Sinclair observed. "That, and whatever is being flown in tonight, is more than this one little truck could carry away."

"Think you're smart? Think because you went to college, that makes you smarter than me?"

"I didn't learn about aerial resupply in college."

"Well, you're not," Niles declared. "You're stupid."

"I'll take your word for that." Sinclair put a sarcastic edge on his voice. "Anyone who hangs around in a swamp after the police have beaten him up and taken his revolver ought to know stupid when he sees it."

"What's that supposed to mean?"

"Why do you think a Police Captain is looking for a straight razor in the middle of the night? Why not just secure the area and get a search team out tomorrow?"

"Suppose you tell me."

"Hewitt and Jardine have been told to kill me for resisting arrest," Sinclair explained. "To get away with that, they will have to convince the State Attorney they had probable cause to believe I killed Cohn. They want to be sure of their evidence before they risk anything."

Niles let out a coarse laugh. "You wouldn't be scared, would you?"

"Of course I am."

"A man wouldn't say he was scared. Not even if he was."

"You're a witness. Your testimony could send them to prison. And they wouldn't have taken your revolver if they trusted you."

"That piece is a low number Smith and Wesson," Niles recalled bitterly. "The first model .357 they made. Three and a half inch pipe, ramp sights, worth eight bills, easy."

"It's not worth your life," Sinclair argued. "Let's get in the truck and leave. While we still can."

"I'm getting my shit back."

"From Jardine? Try any roughhouse with him and you'll wake up in intensive care. If you wake up at all."

"I got plenty on good boy Roland," Niles confided. "On both them pigs. And my old lady knows right where I'm at, if they try any real heavy numbers."

"You still have the truck keys, don't you?"

"This what you want?"

Niles pried the keys out of his jeans and dangled them just out of Sinclair's reach, daring him to snatch. The throb of the generator muffled a tiny click. The tip of Sinclair's cane came away in his hand. He pointed the cane at one of Niles' bandy legs.

A voice chose that instant to break squelch through an unseen radio. "Ground, this is Twin Piper."

The words rode a rip tide of adrenaline. Niles pushed the keys into his pocket. He rummaged in the truck bed again and found a handset that displayed a lighted aviation frequency.

Sinclair blew the tension out of his body and fumbled the tip of his cane back into place.

The voice came again, an insistent echo of itself. "Ground, this is Twin Piper. Ground, this is Twin Piper."

Niles struck a pose, like a television game show host getting set to welcome all the wonderful folks at home to another half hour of fun and surprises. He cleared his throat and keyed the set.

"Twin Piper, this here's Ground," he said importantly.

"Twin Piper. I need landing lights."

"Uh-huh. Yeah. That's a ten-four on that."

Niles started for the generator. Hewitt waddled up, blowing too hard to speak. He touched Niles' hairy torso with the tip of one finger. A gun muzzle couldn't have stopped the big man any more effectively.

"Pilot wants them lights on, Captain. You hear him just now?"

"Half the Everglades heard him," the Police Captain wheezed. "Give me that Goddamn handset."

Hewitt scanned the night sky. The moon was an empty hole in the mist. A few stars made hazy dots. Nothing moved. His breathing settled back to mild asthma. He keyed the set.

"Twin Piper, this is Ground. What's your ETA?"

"Zero five minutes. Confirm landing lights, please."

"You were told to stay off the radio until you were over my location. You'll get lights when I hear engines."

"That won't work, Ground."

Hewitt set the radio aside without responding. He removed his gold-rimmed glasses and began wiping off the steam of exertion. Niles eyed the handset like a man who wanted to answer a ringing telephone. He didn't move. Passing seconds were ticked off by the slow throb of the generator. The voice came again. Ice replaced adrenaline.

"Ground, if you don't feel like making conversation, that's fine, but you will have to make a decision. That is a small strip. I need to see the lights to set up my glide path. It's either that or a landing at Opa Locka, and a lot of embarrassing questions. We need to resolve the situation in the next two minutes."

Hewitt hooked his spectacles over his ears and retrieved the handset. "That wouldn't be a threat, would it, Twin Piper? I wouldn't like to think you'd snitch on your friends."

"I had some friends once, Ground. A few of them died trying to shoehorn C-rations into dirty little airstrips in Vietnam. The rest came home and put their hearts into a country that wasn't sure it wanted them back. I wouldn't put them in the same class with lizards who'd sell their souls to the first creep with a weekly envelope."

Moonlight glistened in a fine film of perspiration on Hewitt's cheeks. The delicate line of his jaw stood out hard and sharp, a controlled rage under the softness of his jowls, hardly moving when he spoke.

"Hear that, Mr. Sinclair? You're a creep. The man says you're a creep."

"He's liable to say the same thing to some honest police if he doesn't get his lights."

Jardine stepped out of nowhere and hooked an arm around Sinclair's neck. He exerted just enough pressure to let Sinclair know his windpipe could be closed off at will.

"Goddamn airplane driver. You'd think he wants to get caught."

Hewitt keyed the set. "You could land yourself into a long term in the Federal Penitentiary, Twin Piper."

"I don't think so, Ground. I've done a little contract litigation for the US Attorney. He doesn't like to go to court without a pat hand. Immunity shouldn't be hard for a talkative witness to negotiate."

Hewitt tossed the radio back onto the rags. "Give him his Goddamn lights."

Blue cylinders rose into the mist. An engine caught at the far end of the field. A distant glow appeared in the haze and grew brighter. A second pick-up truck materialized. It bounded over ruts and slid to a crooked stop beside Niles' compact, dwarfing it. The driver cut the engine and headlights. The interior light winked on briefly while he climbed down. A dirty tank undershirt showed off tight little muscles pumped up by day labor. He was an insignificant shadow swaggering over to stand beside Niles.

"Heard you dudes on the monitor," he announced in a loud, familiar voice. He nudged Niles and indicated the body, curious to hear about the impact it had. That only made Niles sulk. The little man glanced curiously at Sinclair. Nobody said anything. Aircraft engines had become audible.

Captain Hewitt checked his watch. "Where's the rest of your crew, Niles?"

"What rest?"

"Jesus Christ! With just two people loading the cargo and the lights, you're going to be here all night. What were you using for brains?"

"What was you using?" Niles shot back. "You don't give no freebies. You don't give nobody around here no distribution. How many dudes you think are going to work their butts off this hard for chump change?"

Jardine inserted himself between Hewitt and the big man. "Is that a complaint, Niles?"

"Little sugar'll get you a lot more than a sucker punch in the gut."

"If we were looking for a lot, you wouldn't be here. Now quit bitching and get ready to earn your keep."

Niles squirmed, said nothing. The drone of aircraft engines grew louder. Sinclair shifted uneasily.

"Before things get too busy, Captain, how about telling me who signed my death warrant? It can't hurt anything now."

"Maybe you did, Mr. Sinclair. Maybe you signed it yourself."

"I don't understand."

"It could be as simple as respect," Hewitt said. "Maybe you didn't show somebody enough respect. I know you never showed me any. In all the months I protected you, it was just, 'Evening, Captain. Here are the envelopes. Good-bye.' No acknowledgement of my contribution, not even that I was on the team."

"I didn't know about you and Jardine, if that's what's chewing on you."

"Nothing is chewing on me."

"Look, Captain, in a hundred years I couldn't begin to imagine what it means to feel the way you do. But I do know you can't be a victim unless you choose to be. It's your decision, no matter how people treat you."

Hewitt gazed upward, silent and unmoved. A red tail beacon flashed in the foggy sky. Red and green wing tip lights appeared. Mooncast formed a fuzzy silhouette as backdrop. The silhouette settled slowly, crabbed over in a clumsy attitude relative to its apparent glide path. Niles and the little man watched the precarious descent like fence crowders at a stock car race, salivating for a wreck.

Birds rose out of the swamp, wheeling aimlessly in the face of an unfamiliar threat. The plane cleared the last of the trees at the far end of the field. The pilot dropped one wing several degrees, stepped hard on the opposite rudder to swing the fuselage into line with the field. A nose light glowed momentarily, then blazed brightly. Its beam ran fast over rutted ground, glittering in bits of stagnant water. The birds took off in terrified flight, massed without formation, straight across the field.

The plane tore into them with soft, savage explosions, like rapid-fire flak charges. The blue glow resolved it into a squat two and a half ton Piper Aztec. It came down heavily on one main wheel, throwing a long rooster tail of mud. The pilot fought velocity and rough ground to keep it between the lights until the second wheel came down. The nose wheel settled and the aircraft slogged to a stop as it drew abreast of the trucks. Twin Lycoming engines emitted a deafening racket. Slimy water flew in the propeller drafts.

Hewitt waddled out into the brilliance of the nose light and drew a finger across his throat. The light went out and Hewitt vanished. The engines coughed out. The wind and thunder died. The stillness was perfect. The blue field lights wore shrouds of mist that swirled as slowly as galactic nebulae.

A door swung open from the plane's fuselage.

CHAPTER 7

A man climbed stiffly out onto the Piper's wing. He let himself down and walked away from the plane. When he had gone fifty feet or so he stopped and stood spread legged. A stream of liquid made noise in a puddle.

An agitated waddle brought Hewitt back to the trucks. "Niles, you put those lights out. What's the matter with you? Another plane could fly over any time."

Niles plunged the airstrip into darkness. The pilot turned on a ruby flashlight. He returned to the plane and opened a cargo access.

"Don't be bashful," he called out, and went around to the front to inspect for bird strike damage.

The little man swaggered to his pickup and started the engine with a roar. Niles guided him backward with a series of hand-signals, importantly, as if the signals were the secret fraternity handshake.

Jardine watched them transfer bundles from the plane to the truck. "There's no way we can make probable cause against Sinclair," he told Hewitt. "And Niles has got a mouth."

"As soon as the plane is empty, you and Niles put the body on board."

Jardine slogged off obediently.

Sinclair wiped the last of the propeller-thrown water from his spectacles and put them back on. "Captain, I don't claim to be anyone's innocent child. I came to Florida knowing what I was doing was contrary to the law and to my own upbringing. But I was fed up and frustrated, and I didn't see how anyone could lose anything except a little money they'd drop at the jai alai fronton anyway. Tonight is different. This is strictly for hard-core desperadoes. I don't belong here. Neither do you."

"We seem to be here anyway."

"Why don't we talk this through with the people in charge? Maybe we can find a way out of whatever it is."

"It's a little late for that, Mr. Sinclair."

"Maybe it's not too late for Jardine. That hardcase attitude of his could land him in real trouble."

"It's just a phase," Hewitt said. "I've been there. I can see Roland safely through it."

Jardine's phase bared its teeth. He barked at Niles and the little man until they finished transferring the load then closed the cargo access and ordered the little man to move his truck.

Jardine and Niles carried Bernie Cohn to the plane, facing each other across the ponderous corpse like cats across a fence, cursing each other's lapses, neither man willing to be the first to allow his strength to fail. Jardine counted and they heaved Cohn shoulder high and pushed him head first onto the wing. Jardine shooed Niles up into the plane, into the cargo area behind the seats. Niles leaned out and took the rigid body under the shoulders, tugging and turning, working it through the doorway inch by inch.

Hewitt called Jardine over and lifted Niles' revolver from his jacket pocket. "Call in and report that we've released Mr. Sinclair, will you please, Roland? We checked the informant's report. There was no evidence of crime. Pick up the lights and get the shipment to Ricks. No trouble tonight. We'll settle with him after the processing is done."

"Let me take the plane, Captain. Isn't that what I'm here for? To handle the rough stuff?"

"I have to answer personally for this situation, Roland."

"Answer to who, Captain? Who the hell can push you around like this?"

"Pick me up at Opa Locka. I'll change the paperwork and do the reports."

"I thought we had a relationship here."

Hewitt patted the younger man's shoulder fondly. "This isn't the time or the place, Roland." He left Jardine to sulk and switched on the field lights. "All right, Mr. Sinclair, let's get aboard the aircraft."

The struggle to pull Bernie Cohn into the plane had left Niles against the rear bulkhead. He was trying to crawl out over Cohn's rigid corpse when Sinclair climbed in awkwardly over a folded down seatback. The pilot got in, pushing the seatback upright and trapping both men. Hewitt climbed in and shut the door.

Claustrophobia put some of the bluster back into Niles' voice. "Hey, Captain, you forget about me?"

Hewitt pulled the harness across his chest and fastened it.

"I'll take my piece and go now, Captain. No hard feelings or nothing."

"I can't possibly dump this much weight on my own."

"What about the shipment, Captain? And the lights? And my ride?"

"Roland will see it all safe."

The pilot ignored a headset hung over an air inlet. Instead, he pushed tiny sound valves into his ears, plugs that would cut the low frequency engine noise while still letting him hear conversation. He turned in his seat. In the red glow from the instrument panel he had a satanic profile.

"Let's everyone sit back against the bulkhead. We need an aft center of gravity to keep the nose wheel from digging in."

The airframe trembled briefly as he cranked one engine to life. Terror sent Niles scrambling to the rear of the plane. Sinclair moved awkwardly and squeezed beside him. They had to sit shoulder to shoulder on top of the corpse. The pilot started the second engine. He increased the manifold pressure in the left engine, turned the plane in its own length then equalized the engines to begin the half-mile journey back to takeoff position.

Sinclair listened to the oleo struts creaking over the rough ground. "Not much better flying conditions than Vietnam, but I guess the pay is better."

"Do I know you?" the pilot asked.

"Just a grunt from one of the dirty little airstrips you and your friends used to shoehorn C-rations into."

"We'll make a nice feature on the evening news. Crazed veterans in dope and murder ring. Film at eleven."

"Vietnam is ancient history," Sinclair said. "The important thing now is that we all get out of this in one piece."

"We will," the pilot said with more assurance than the situation seemed to warrant.

The regular parade of blue beacons stopped. They had reached the end of the airstrip. The pilot reversed direction and brought both engines to full power. The parade of lights began again, slowly at first then flickering past faster and faster. The pilot drew the nose up. The landing gear jitterbugged briefly then lifted free. The nose came back down and they were flying level, a few feet off the ground, gaining speed rapidly. The black mass of the approaching tree line materialized at the periphery of the nose light. It grew and loomed and filled the wind screen, accelerating relentlessly toward the plane. The pilot drew back the nose for maximum angle of climb. The rush of the tree line slowed almost to nothing and the plane rose like a kite. Treetops sank out of view. Fog disappeared. The sky filled with stars. A climbing turn showed the lighted sprawl of Dade County under a lowered wing.

Residual nerves put a hush in Hewitt's voice. "Head directly out to sea. We need to get rid of our embarrassments as fast as possible."

The pilot leveled the plane on a northward heading instead.

"Didn't you hear me?"

"You still don't get it, do you, Captain?"

"Get what?"

"You've been scammed, Policeman. This ride is sponsored by the Federal Government."

For a moment there was only the noise of the engines.

"I don't think so," Hewitt said irritably.

"The little party back on the strip was videotaped through night vision optics. Every word was caught by a parabolic microphone. A Blackhawk surveillance helicopter is making wide orbits. Federal Agents are waiting at Opa Locka, which is where we'll be landing in ten minutes."

"You've had your one bluff for tonight," Hewitt snapped.

"The control tower can put you in touch with the FBI. Or you can put the bottom radio on one two six point four. The Blackhawk's call sign is Ghost Rider One Three."

Hewitt pressed the muzzle of Niles' .357 against the pilot's ear. "Take us out over the ocean."

"You may have the gun, but this plane is fifteen hundred feet in the air, and I'm the only one who can get it down safely."

"Mr. Sinclair is a qualified pilot."

"My certificate says student," Sinclair corrected. He gave the tip of his cane an unobtrusive quarter turn and slipped it off.

"We'll just have to make do."

Hewitt drew back the hammer of the revolver until it clicked perilously on the sear. He had picked the wrong time for theatrics. The plane was crossing out of the relative cool of the Everglades into the sky over built up areas, where the stored heat of day rose off expanses of paving. A thermal current shook the airframe. Hewitt tensed reflexively. The revolver discharged with unexpected thunder. The pilot seemed to implode. Every fiber in his body jerked taut in the same spasm. Then he fell slack in the restraint of his harness. The engines droned under a blanket of stricken silence.

Hewitt's face turned ghastly in the red glow from the panel. "Mr. Sinclair!" was the only sound he could choke out through the horror coagulating in his throat.

The fear that had frozen Niles against the bulkhead thawed into panic. He lunged toward the revolver in Hewitt's hand, pinning Sinclair where he could not see out the window.

One of the terrors drummed into student pilots was the graveyard spiral; a catastrophic corkscrew descent in which centrifugal force replaced the pull of gravity and left a pilot who had lost his reference to the horizon with a complacent sense of normalcy. In less than a minute pilot sense no longer mattered. Dive velocity would be so high that the force required to pull out would exceed the stress limit of the airframe. Sinclair squirmed until he could press his cane against the back of Hewitt's seat, turned his face away and applied finger pressure on the carved ivory handle.

The cane jerked violently. The thud of a shotgun reverberated. Niles' .357 emitted a harsh cough, a knee jerk reaction to the blast. The big man sighed heavily and fell back against the bulkhead. Sinclair caught the top of Hewitt's seat and pulled himself up to his knees.

A glance at the horizon told him the plane was drifting away from straight and level. He reached between the seats and unbuckled the pilot's harness. The man slumped forward. Sinclair grabbed his shirt to keep him from falling against the control wheel and sending them into a dive.

"Help me get him out of the seat!" he yelled over the noise of the engines.

Hewitt moved feebly in the constraint of his own harness, as ineffectual as a fly with one wing pulled off. Niles sat back against the bulkhead. He made small, hurt noises. Sinclair prodded him with his cane.

"Pull him out or we'll crash!"

The big man came to life in another violent lunge. He bumped Sinclair aside and seized the pilot by both shoulders. He dragged the body over the seat and fell backward with it. The nose of the plane pitched upward with the sudden weight shift.

Sinclair pushed the control wheel forward as he wormed himself into the empty pilot's chair. Air whistled loudly through a bullet hole in the Plexiglas next to his ear. The rapid-fire radio traffic of a control tower frequency rattled down from the roof speaker. Below, Dade County was a sea of lights that swallowed any possible landmarks.

"Okay, Captain, where are we?"

Hewitt burbled unintelligibly.

Sinclair's only hope was to spot something in the relative dark of the Everglades. He focused on a road intersection off one wing tip. His hand was trembling when he took the microphone from the panel hook.

"Opa Locka tower, twin Piper Four One Tango. Krome Avenue and the Trail, inbound for landing. Student pilot with an emergency."

"Four One Tango, ident. Say type aircraft. Say emergency."

Sinclair pressed the transponder button that would light up his blip on the controller's radar screen. "Four One Tango is an Aztec. Student pilot has no instruction in multiple engine or complex aircraft. No night flying time. Limited familiarity with local landmarks. Gunshot injuries on board."

"Enter on a right downwind for Two Six Right. Number three for landing. Wind three one zero at eight. Altimeter three zero zero two. Report the Bend in the Bypass."

The tower was already talking to another aircraft before Sinclair could acknowledge. The controller didn't seem concerned about clearing other planes out of his way. Student pilots were an industry in the clear skies of South Florida, and a day without one in trouble was probably rare. Sinclair tried to put the microphone back on its hook, and found Hewitt groping for it.

"Give me some room, Captain. The instructions may have sounded simple, but what they mean is that I have to fly over a specific wiggle somewhere in that maze of roads down there, locate a two mile strip of asphalt in those two thousand square miles of lights, then negotiate three precise turns while maintaining an exact glide that will set an airplane three times as heavy as any I've ever flown on a pair of numbers I won't see until I'm right on top of them."

Hewitt heard neither Sinclair's words, nor the taut nerves that drove them. He put his hand to his mouth, as if he didn't know it had come away empty.

"Officer needs help," he said feebly. "Officer down. Shots fired. Any unit on this frequency respond."

Sinclair banked the plane into a tentative right turn, getting a feel for how much pressure it took. He keyed his microphone. "Four One Tango. Over the Bend in the Bypass."

"Any unit on this frequency," Hewitt repeated. Blood bubbled under his voice and dribbled from the corner of his mouth. "Somebody's going to have to reply by endorsement in his personnel file if I don't get a response."

The tower was talking to Sinclair simultaneously. "Four One Tango, we're going to bring your propellers to full advance and your manifold pressure to twenty one inches. You have six levers on the quadrant. The center two control propeller RPM. Push the levers full forward. That's all the way toward the control panel."

"Full advance," Sinclair repeated, and pressed the propeller levers as far as they would go. The plane began to descend, and he had to divide his attention between easing the control wheel back and listening to the tower.

"The left pair of levers control your manifold pressure. Locate the manifold pressure gauge. It'll be a split needle presentation. Bring the throttles gently toward you until both needles read twenty one."

Sinclair pulled the throttles back gingerly. "Manifold pressure twenty one inches. I'm losing altitude pretty quickly. Over five hundred feet a minute."

"Relax and say airspeed."

"One two five," Sinclair said.

"Trim for one one zero. Then we need to lower your landing gear. The control should be a knob shaped like a small wheel. Push it down. That will increase your descent rate again."

Sinclair tried to follow both instructions at once. The gear went down with a heart stopping series of thumps and thuds. The altimeter started down alarmingly. Sinclair put more back pressure on the control wheel to try to regain a five hundred foot per minute descent rate. Too much put him into a climb and sent the airspeed plunging dangerously toward a stall. Too much release put him back at eight hundred feet per minute. He began rolling the trim wheel to stabilize the control pressure. To complicate things, the tower was talking to him again.

"Four One Tango, chase aircraft reports your gear down, but he doesn't like your flight attitude. Are you out of limits aft on your center of gravity?"

"I'll see what I can do about that."

Sinclair's voice was leaking pressure like a bad steam line. Things were closing in faster than he could deal with them. He set the microphone on his lap and tried to rub the sweat off his palms. His trouser legs were still slimy from the swamp.

"Niles," he called.

"We're going to die," the big man blubbered.

"Not if you move as far forward as you can."

"Tell him to get us the fuck down."

"Just move forward. Do it now."

Niles crawled forward. "The Brothers wouldn't take this crap. Outlaws don't take no crap. Not off the Man. Not off nobody. Just fucking tell him to fucking get us the fuck down."

Two closely spaced parallel runways passed a thousand feet below the right wingtip. Moving lights marked planes on final approach to both. Sinclair put down the first ten degrees of wing flap, rolled the trim wheel to stabilize his descent. At eight hundred feet, he gathered his nerve and tipped the airplane into another right turn. He rolled level perpendicular to the lighted ribbons of runway and glanced at the glide slope indicator lights beside the threshold.

"White over white—high as a kite," he repeated from memory and put down another notch of flap.

Airspeed fell toward ninety knots, where too steep a turn would reduce the vertical lift component of the wings below that required to support flight. He tipped the airplane gently to turn to his final approach. His bank was too timid, the turn too shallow.

The tower came on immediately. "Four One Tango, come right. You are encroaching on the parallel approach. Traffic on final."

Sinclair had to bank with terrifying steepness to avoid a plane he could not see. He realigned himself. He was still high. The last increment of flaps failed to steepen his descent enough. He cut power and pushed the nose down to aim for the oncoming threshold numbers. His airspeed rose alarmingly.

The tower could see Sinclair's mistakes beginning to compound themselves. "Four One Tango, go around. Do not try to salvage this approach. Full power and go around for another try."

"Negative," was all Sinclair could manage to blurt before a wave of ground induced turbulence startled the microphone out of his sweaty hand.

The tower came back, demanding that he go around. Runway numbers flashed beneath the plane. Sinclair drew the control wheel back, flaring the nose up to bleed off speed. The heavy airplane simply floated, refusing to sink to the runway. It began to drift sideways.

He dropped one wing into the cross wind and stepped on the opposite rudder to bring it back to the runway center line. His first try wasn't enough. Then he over corrected. One turnoff passed, then another. The end of the runway was in sight. The lowered wheel touched asphalt and bounced clear. Sinclair applied power to ease the next touchdown. It was still jarring. He cut power and the second wheel jolted down. He held the nose wheel off as long as he could. When it finally touched, he stood on the toe brakes. The plane slewed. He released the brakes, cramped the rudder full right to make the last turnoff and clamped on the brakes again to bring the plane to a lurching stop.

The tower said, "Four One Tango, go to ground point niner," and went back to his other traffic.

It was a minute before Sinclair could control his trembling enough to switch the radio frequency. He found the microphone again. "Opa Locka Ground, twin Piper Four One Tango. Request taxi instructions."

"Four One Tango, secure the aircraft in place. Assistance is on the way."

Sinclair pulled the mixture levers to idle cutoff to kill the engines, turned off the ignition, cut the electrical master. He blew the air out of his lungs and closed his eyes. When he opened them again, hypnotic flashes of crimson and orange emergency lights made the windscreen look like a traffic warning at the gate of hell. The plane bounced as someone climbed onto the wing. The door opened.

"Mr. Sinclair?"

It was a woman's voice, cool and clipped, Radcliffe class of not many springs ago. She wore an armored vest under a military combat harness, and under that camouflage fatigues limp and brackish from hours of wear and time in the swamp. There was an L-shaped flashlight taped to the harness at one shoulder, a UHF radio handset taped to the other. A blue steel machine pistol hung from a neck strap. A black woolen cap concealed any hair she might have had.

Her face was sweat streaked under several shades of camouflage stick. She looked, in the syncopated flashes of colored light, like she had arrived to deliver the ending monologue of World War III.

Sinclair put his head down and lost the contents of his stomach.

CHAPTER 8

❀

Sinclair woke suddenly from a fitful catnap. He straightened in a chair beside a desk. Brightening a sound absorbing partition next to him was a chromium framed print of a cheerful yellow concoction that was half chicken, half 1930's racing monoplane. It was titled: *Sunny Side Up*.

"It's sort of a trademark."

A blonde woman not yet thirty seated herself gracefully behind the desk. Neither a tailored suit bare of accessories nor the patrician composure of her face could stifle the impish energy in her eyes. A buoyant laugh put music into her cool, clipped Radcliffe voice.

"Everyone has called me Sunny as long as I can remember."

Morning brilliance slanted through a window as if she had arranged for it and fell across a routing box with correspondence on Department of Justice letterhead.

"Are you a Police Officer?" Sinclair asked in a voice still fuzzy with sleep.

"I'm with the Federal Bureau of Investigation."

The name on her Special Agent's credentials was Sonia Tearoe. A law degree on the wall had been issued to Sonia Marie Hastings. Her wedding set was poetry in white gold and diamonds.

Sinclair gripped his cane and brought himself to his feet. He managed, by careful shuffling, to execute a clumsy about-face. Experimental steps took him to the window. A disheveled apparition floated in the double glass, a slim man in a rumpled suit with hair caked into ludicrous cowlicks. The angular aluminum and reflective windows of a nearby office tower told him he was downtown, many stories above street level. He pulled back a coat sleeve and shirt cuff caked with dried mud. Only an outline of his watch remained in the dirt caked on his wrist.

"What time is it, please?"

"It's six in the morning, David. Do you mind if I call you David?"

"May I have my personal effects, Mrs. Tearoe? I'd like to go home now."

The request left her staring at him. "David, people were killed last night. One was a police captain."

"I'd like to call my attorney. I'd also like to know what specific charges I'm being held on."

"There are no Federal charges against you at this time. Your eventual status depends mostly on you."

The faintest possible amusement touched the corners of Sinclair's mouth. "I used to supervise accounting for a large casino in Atlantic City, Mrs. Tearoe. From time to time I caught people doing things they shouldn't. A few tried to fix their troubles by cutting deals with Federal law enforcement. They all wound up wishing they'd taken their chances in court."

"What does RICO mean to you, David?"

"Edward G. Robinson's character in *Little Caesar*?" He mimicked a nasal twang. "Nyah, and the Big Boy ain't what he used to be, neither. Pretty soon he won't be able to take it n'more. Then watch me."

"RICO is an acronym for Racketeer Influenced and Corrupt Organizations," she explained patiently, melting a light coat of sugar over the dire consequences. "It provides severe penalties, including prison and seizure of assets, for anyone who participates in or conceals a criminal enterprise."

Sinclair went back to staring out the window. "I was teasing you, Mrs. Tearoe. There isn't an accountant in the country who doesn't know what RICO is. Or hasn't wondered when some ambitious civil servant might use it to ruin him. According to my attorney, I could be criminally liable if I phoned my mother in Indiana twice within ten years and fibbed about reversing the charges."

"David, you are trying to sound terribly cynical. Trying too hard, I think. Like a little boy whistling his way past a cemetery."

"I'm tired, Mrs. Tearoe. I'd like to go home."

Sunny rose from her chair, came around the desk and stood close to him. His nostrils twitched at a subtle hint of gardenia and he shuffled around to face her. Three-inch heels brought her eyes level with his.

"David, how did a man with your background get involved in something like this?"

"Like what, specifically?"

"After last night, don't you think denial is pointless?"

"I'm not sure what I'm denying."

She studied him, perhaps to see if silence and scrutiny would make him nervous. When they didn't, she said, "You're a quiet person, aren't you? Independent. Self reliant."

"I know that's not very trendy, but I wasn't aware it was a Federal crime."

"You don't make friends easily, do you?"

"No, Mrs. Tearoe. I don't."

"Yet you've spent the last eight months running a casino that depends on cronyism for its very survival."

Sinclair admitted nothing.

"David, you don't even own a cell phone."

Sinclair put his wrists together to accept imaginary handcuffs. "Take me away."

"You needed connections in the local power structure," she insisted.

"It's your fairy tale. Tell it any way you want."

"I think you were recruited. Brought to Florida by people who could provide those connections. By people who used you for their purposes they threw you away like trash when they were done with you."

"Do you have someone in mind?"

"I've never seen Lucinda Rivendahl, but I've heard she's spectacular."

A light updraft from the perimeter air conditioning duct sent a shiver through Sinclair. "She was way out of my league. I always knew it and never faced it."

Sunny put a gentle hand on his sleeve. "You know, David, sometimes it's the people who seem most against us who are really the ones in our corner. Did you resent the students who marched in the streets against the Vietnam War?"

"Everyone did. Everyone who went. Whether it's fashionable to admit it now or not."

"Did it perhaps not occur to you later that those long haired freaks might have shortened the war and saved the lives of some of the young soldiers who hated them?"

"Public opinion didn't turn against the war because juvenile neurotics paraded their frustrations in front of television cameras. It turned when eighteen year old girls came home too shaken to cry and told their parents the boy who had taken them to the junior prom had returned to a closed coffin funeral. People are only moved by things that strike close to home."

"A police Captain was killed last night," she reminded him. "That is very close to home for the County authorities."

"You people tried to sic Dade County on me once before," Sinclair recalled. "You handed Ruellene Kingman a casino full of confiscated gaming equipment, and she deferred prosecution pending further investigation. Why was that?"

"What are you suggesting?"

"I'm asking because I don't know."

"How well did you know Niles Buchanan?"

"I never met him before last night. I expect he'll tell you as much. If he hasn't already."

"Niles Buchanan died in surgery," she said solemnly.

An idea flickered through the weariness in Sinclair's eyes. "Is that why we're having this conversation? You're running low on witnesses?"

"David," she cautioned, "Niles Buchanan was a member of a motorcycle gang called the Outlaws. They are violent and irrational. There is some possibility they may blame you for—"

A telephone buzzed on the desk. Sunny suppressed a frown, picked up the receiver and pressed a lighted button. "Agent Tearoe." She listened carefully. "Yes, Sir." She cradled the phone gently, as if it were fragile china, and looked at Sinclair. "That was Arthur Wilkinson. Supervising Special Agent of the Miami Office. He's waiting for us."

"Can he release my property and let me go?"

"I'm afraid he doesn't understand how someone could be enticed into crime without being fundamentally corrupt. It will be easier if I can let him know you're ready to cooperate."

"What did you tell him?" Sinclair asked irritably. "Leave this twerp to me, Chief? He's a sucker for women? I can turn him out in nothing flat?"

Sunny collected a shoulder bag. Her smile made allowances for his fatigue, and the possibility of residual trauma. "David, you really are in serious trouble."

"Two weeks ago I was shot and left for dead. That's what I consider serious trouble."

"The Bureau can arrange protection."

"Protection from whom?"

"You'll have to tell us that, David."

"I can't. That's the whole problem. I don't know who shot me. Or why they did it."

"You must have some idea."

He shook his head in slow frustration. "Lying in the hospital waiting for them to try again, I realized how helpless I was. They could wait a week, a month, a year. They could step out of the shadows any time and finish the job. I'd never recognize them."

"Why did you go back to the casino last night?"

"To see if I could sucker them into showing themselves for another try while I was set for them."

"Then it did have something to do with the casino."

Sinclair compressed his lips.

"David, let me arrange protection. Once your assailants are caught and convicted, you'll be out of danger."

"If they're caught and convicted," Sinclair corrected. "If a bunch of overwrought police agents scare them to ground, I'm finished. Some enchanted evening I'll be shot dead in a dark parking lot, with no warning and no chance to defend myself."

Supervising Special Agent Arthur Wilkinson was a study in African-American dignity. He filled a high-backed leather chair behind an oversized desk, his freshly pressed gray suit tailored to the hard corpulence of a former linebacker. Sprinkles of gray salted tight curls of neatly trimmed hair. Portraits of the President and the Director hung one behind either shoulder, buttressing the gravity of his square classical features. He swept Sinclair with a dissatisfied glance.

"Agent Tearoe," he articulated with the precision of an elocution teacher, "would you please find Mr. Sinclair a presentable sport coat?"

"What I have on will get me home," Sinclair said.

Sunny measured him with a glance and left the office. Wilkinson opened a manila folder and read aloud in a disapproving rumble.

"Sinclair, David Edwin. Bachelor of Arts, University of Indiana. Commissioned Second Lieutenant, U.S. Army. Vietnam. Decorated for meritorious service. Returned to college on the G.I. Bill. Masters in Business Administration. Seven years with a national accounting firm. Controller, Atlantic City hotel/casino management firm. Discharged in a reorganization. Opened an illegal casino outside Miami."

Wilkinson closed the folder. His scowl demanded an explanation for Sinclair's fall from grace.

A wintry smile played on Sinclair's lips. "Could I get a copy of that? I had no idea I sounded so cool."

Wilkinson pushed a bulky manila envelope to the front of the desk. "Verify that everything inside is yours, and that all your possessions have been returned. Sign the receipt before you put anything in your pockets."

Pleasant surprise brightened Sinclair's features. He tore the envelope raggedly across one end and drew it along the desk. His wallet, wristwatch, key case and pen slid out amid wads of rumpled fifty-dollar bills. He scribbled a signature.

Wilkinson took the receipt. "There's over four thousand dollars there. Don't you think you had better count it?"

"I don't have a control number to count against. If you say it's four thousand, it's four thousand."

"That's a lot of cash to be carrying around. Especially stuffed in bits and pieces into every pocket you had. Were you trying to hide it?"

"I'll put it in my thrift account first thing Monday morning." Sinclair loaded personal items into his pockets and began organizing the currency into a manageable stack. "Excuse me. Tuesday morning. Monday is Labor Day, isn't it?"

Wilkinson stood up and put an electric razor on the desk. "You need a shave and a wash, Mr. Sinclair. Let's visit the men's room."

"Thanks just the same. I'll clean up when I get home."

"I don't remember releasing you."

Sinclair stopped squaring the stack of currency. "I don't recall being formally detained."

"That can be arranged."

"Look here, Mr. Wilkinson, I'm not a flight risk. I'll be glad to bring my attorney in any time during business hours."

"The Bureau is open for business twenty four hours a day."

Sinclair pocketed the currency. "I'd like to know what my status is, Mr. Wilkinson. For the record, please."

"There will be plenty of time for that later. Just now you have an appointment."

"With whom?"

"All in good time."

"How does this work?" Sinclair asked. "Do I call my attorney now? Or do we have some paperwork to do first? I've never been arrested before."

"An arrest could take all day, if I want it to," Wilkinson said significantly.

"What's my alternative?"

"This appointment is two hours, maximum."

"And after that?"

"You'll be free to go. If you still want to."

Sinclair found a hundred year old stranger in the men's room mirror. His eyes were bleak and harried behind dark pouches. Beard stubble sprouted like new weeds through dirt caked on his jaw. His hair belonged on the bride of Frankenstein.

Wilkinson's reflection hung in the glass, like an insistent conscience. "Does it bother you, Sinclair? Looking in mirrors?"

"Not since my fundamentally corrupt nature asserted itself."

Sinclair twisted both taps to full force. He bent under and let water run through his hair. He turned his head left and right to expose both sides of his face. When the water finally ran clean, he shut off the taps and fumbled for a paper towel.

Sunny smiled approval at Sinclair's fresh shave and took a powder blue sport coat off her arm. "I think this should fit," she said and held it open for him to try on.

"Thanks anyway. I'll go as I am." His suit coat hung as limp as pajamas, stained in the vague symmetry of a psychiatrist's Rohrschack Test.

"David, we'll be calling on an important man. You don't want to go dressed like that."

"I'd rather not go at all."

Blood rose in Wilkinson's face. "What I said about the arrest still goes."

"What you said about the arrest," Sinclair reminded him, "was that it wouldn't happen if I went with you. If you use the same threat to add conditions every time you see something you don't like, then I gain nothing by agreeing."

"I've had it with the smart mouth, Sinclair."

"I'm sure my attorney can keep a civil tongue in her head."

Sunny tapped her wristwatch. Wilkinson jerked his head to indicate the elevator lobby. They rode down to the garage in silence. Sunny got behind the wheel of a sedan. Wilkinson installed Sinclair in the rear and sat beside him.

Sunday morning stillness filled the streets of downtown Miami. Latin American bank buildings rose to heaven out of little swatches of manicured landscaping, glistening mausoleums prepared as if dead economies were dead Pharaohs, with immortal souls that must go on after they were buried under the rubble of fiery politics and foreign debt. Transients slept in chromium edged doorways and in the sheltered niches of exotic sculpture, with their possessions gathered around them in tattered knapsacks and plastic garbage bags.

Up on the Interstate eighteen wheelers rolled in ragged bunches, like tinned produce coming down a conveyor belt. They came on with swelling rattles of diesel exhaust and passed the sedan with buffeting gusts.

The only noise on Rickenbacker Causeway was the quiet hum of the tires. Biscayne Bay stretched away in every direction, lightly rippled and sparkling in the slanting sunlight. Wilkinson filled his lungs with a bracing charge of cool air.

"You know, Sinclair, one mistake doesn't have to be the end of the world. I had a football coach in college who told me you're only as good as the next thing you do."

"I had a Buddhist friend who told me the tree that shrieks loudest in the wind is the hollow one."

"You've got a real attitude there. Is that why your last company let you go?"

"Corporations don't give reasons. They just reorganize."

"And now you think that chip on your shoulder entitles you to do anything you please."

"There are things I'd rather be doing just now."

"If it were up to me, Sinclair, you wouldn't be getting this opportunity. You'd better make the most of it. While you can."

"If it involves my putting any faith in the Federal government, you're wasting everyone's time. Vietnam cured me of that."

"Not all Vietnam veterans are wandering through life feeling sorry for themselves. It's a few bad apples like you who give the country a sour taste."

"Half the country isn't old enough to remember Vietnam. The half that is couldn't care less about a face in the crowd that served there."

"They might all care, if they saw you making an effort."

"Like the man who was killed flying the Aztec?"

"What do you know about him?"

"You used him to boost your score. Get a round of applause. Maybe a leg up on promotion."

Wilkinson's voice dropped to an ominous rumble. "I won't dignify that crap with an argument. I'll just point out that his family could be in serious danger if certain elements got the idea he was cooperating with law enforcement, and hope you have the decency to protect them."

"This is a hell of a time to think about his family."

"That's a pretty cheap shot from a man who has never married, never made the commitment to raise children. Tell me, Sinclair, do you have a problem with commitment? Or are you just plain, old-fashioned selfish?"

"I've never felt sufficiently threatened by those questions to hide behind a marriage that didn't mean anything."

Hostile silence filled the sedan. Virginia Key came and the Seaquarium drifted past. The gates were closed. The monorail track hung like a loose thread on the breeze.

Key Biscayne brought golf fairways and picnic spots and wooded walking trails that gave way to walled-in estates shrouded in flowering shrubbery, where anything public seemed a brazen egalitarian intrusion. A speed bump slowed the sedan. The asphalt became narrow and curbless, like the path through some lush hedge row maze, worn smooth in a forgotten Druid ritual. Unseen blossoms left the still air heavy with their cloying sweetness. Occasionally there came a glimpse of stucco or roofing tile, bared as briefly and shyly as a southern belle's ankle. Sunny turned where sandstone gateposts framed a narrow breach in the shrubbery.

Sinclair saw no address or nameplate. "Since we seem to have arrived, would it hurt to tell me who we've come to see?"

"Congressman Earl Moncavage," Wilkinson said gravely. "I believe you are familiar with him."

"I owe him a little under eight million dollars."

"A building owned by a Delaware corporation registered in your name is mortgaged for seven million eight hundred twenty three thousand dollars to a bank in which his family is a major shareholder," Wilkinson corrected.

"I wasn't trying to crash his social set."

A sun-dappled macadam drive formed a curving shore for a lagoon of shaded emerald lawn. Mossy islands held the boles of two great oaks. Veiled and aloof behind their foliage stood an Italian renaissance mansion of buff colored sandstone. Chimney clusters rose above the tiles and warmed themselves in private patches of sun. Before the house spread a terrace where flowers bloomed as flowers only bloom in Florida. Steps fanned down from the porch to the terrace, and from the terrace down to the drive where Sunny brought the sedan to a stop.

Sinclair needed his cane to make the climb. The door was an eight-foot rectangle of oak under a fanlight of stained glass. Wilkinson made some respectful noise with a knocker shaped like a gargoyle.

"Earl Moncavage worked his way through Princeton. Waiting tables. His wife's family owned a small bank in Miami when they married. He personally built that bank into a statewide financial network."

"You make it sound like he married the charter and opened some branches."

"Does that give you some kind of cheap thrill?" Wilkinson asked. "Bringing everyone down to your level?"

"There are things I'd rather be doing," Sinclair repeated over the quiet snick of a lock.

CHAPTER 9

The door opened to reveal a woman in a freshly starched maid's uniform. Slim and supple as a rapier, she glanced at Wilkinson's credentials with Latin eyes accustomed to command. "Please come in," she instructed in an accent closer to Imperial Castile than any Caribbean barrio.

Stepping back with glacial hauteur she admitted them to a two-story hall. A formal mahogany staircase rose to a railed gallery overhead. At the rear sunlight streamed in through French doors and brought out subtle shadings in burnished parquetry at the edges of thick oriental carpet. She led them back and opened the doors then took them along a colonnade at the head of a tiled swimming pool sheltered from the ocean breeze by a low wall of the same buff colored sandstone used in the house.

"You may wait here," she announced, and left them standing on a tile mosaic edged in colorful perennials.

Dominating the mosaic was a pergola with a glass-topped table inside. Down five sandstone stairs lay a gently sloping white beach that stretched without end in both directions, smoothed by the foam-edged wash of a receding tide.

Two lines of shoe prints went away in the sand. One set was larger and longer of stride, more deeply and carelessly impressed, wandering a bit from the straight line of smaller, more precise marks. A man and a woman followed the shoe prints back. The man held himself to the woman's slower pace, fidgeting around at an exuberant jogger's trot, shadow boxing with the intensity of a fighter consumed by the roar of an imaginary crowd. He was naked but for blue athletic shorts with white stripes at the side, white athletic socks and blue running shoes with white jets. As he drew nearer, the overspecialized development of regular weight training became obvious under the softness of good living on his bare torso. He bounded up the stairs with a burst of energy, like an entertainer mounting a stage under a heavy round of applause, swept a beach towel from the back of a chair in the pergola and came out rubbing himself vigorously.

"Arthur!" he said enthusiastically, as if he had just that second noticed the three people waiting for him. "Good of you to come on such short notice."

"It was good of you to ask us, Congressman."

The two men shook hands warmly. "You've met Phyllis, of course."

Wilkinson smiled broadly and said, "Good morning, Mrs. Moncavage," to the woman who arrived puffing at the top of the stairs.

"Good morning, Arthur."

Sheathed neck to ankles in a designer sweat suit, she sidled into the pergola to retrieve a towel and patted perspiration from a prim face that was no longer at its best without make-up. Her smile dissolved like sand sculpture when her husband turned his enthusiasm on Sunny.

"Mrs. Tearoe, I will never understand how you manage to look absolutely radiant at seven in the morning."

"Congressman, that's pure flattery," Sunny scolded lightly as they shook hands.

Phyllis Moncavage stepped quickly to her husband's elbow. The transformation was profound. Side by side they were just another well-off middle-aged couple, a boy and girl away in school, twenty years' marital stress beginning to push through, like weeds cracking a concrete retaining wall.

With her position secure, she turned her attention to her company. Her eyes fell on Sinclair's disreputable clothing, and the beginnings of a fresh smile flickered out.

"Earl," she said uneasily, "I don't believe I know this man."

Moncavage's features took on the serious cast of a self-absorbed man in his managerial forties. He ran a disapproving gaze from the unruliness returning to Sinclair's drying hair down his stained suit to the caked mud that he hadn't been able to brush off his shoes.

"You are David Sinclair?"

Sinclair put his heels together and ducked his head like a Prussian military subordinate.

Phyllis Moncavage was stunned. "You can't be the man who bought Opal Lloyd's building?"

A meager smile lifted the corners of Sinclair's mouth. "Please excuse my appearance, Mrs. Moncavage. I did offer to present myself during business hours, but there seems to be some urgency about all this, whatever it is."

"What happened to you?" Her nose wrinkled at the residual aroma of the Everglades.

"It was sort of a scavenger hunt. It got a little messy, but I won some money and got to fly a fancy airplane."

"A scavenger hunt? Was it for charity?"

"I think it was supposed to help the fight against drugs."

Her voice fell to a confidential register. "You know, poor Opal's grandson has had a terrible time with drugs."

Moncavage took her hand and patted it to cut her off. "Would you be a love and ask Tonia if she'll serve breakfast now?"

"Of course." Her smile was reluctant and dutiful.

"And would you send that blue research cover out with her, dear?"

Phyllis Moncavage retreated along the colonnade.

Her husband stripped off a blue and white sweat band and ran the tips of manicured fingers through his styled hair, a politician making sure he looked right for an important appearance. He ushered everyone inside the pergola, gallantly installing Sunny in a chair. Wilkinson nodded curtly for Sinclair to seat himself so Sunny would flank him on one side. Wilkinson sat flanking him on the other. The arrangement left Sinclair squinting against the morning sun.

Moncavage sat unsmiling across the table. "Well, Sinclair," he said in a grave orator's rumble, "you got yourself into quite a mess last night, didn't you?"

Sinclair said nothing.

A door opened and closed in the house. The maid wheeled a wicker serving cart along the colonnade to the entrance of the pergola. She wiped the table and set silver and napkins, set out plates of ham omelet, toast and jelly, frosted glasses of grapefruit juice; all with the cold correct efficiency of slightly decadent continental hotels that didn't stoop to the tourist trade. She poured coffee and put a blue backed document at Moncavage's elbow. She went away silently and aloof, without waiting to be excused.

The door opened and closed before Moncavage found his voice again. "Tell me, Sinclair, how much do you know about the history of Cutler House?"

"I've never heard of it."

"The house you used as a casino was built by a man named Josiah Cutler, on a land grant to encourage white settlement in the Everglades following the Seminole Indian War."

The disinterested movement of Sinclair's shoulders neither acknowledged nor repudiated the casino. Rather than let his breakfast grow cold he began eating.

Moncavage consulted his research cover.

"Cutler arrived in Florida in 1839," he read aloud, "with one personal Negro and considerable wealth. He was, from the available accounts, a sociable man in spite of obvious infirmities, not at all the sort who would build a magnificent home in virgin swamp. Whispers about a guilty past were inevitable. Cutler, for his part, joked openly about the rumors, as if he welcomed such gossip to cover some darker and more specific truth. That truth surfaced when his Negro was severely injured in an accident. The man was Haitian, still under the influence of the Jacobin Catholicism practiced on the Island, and terrified of dying with his sins unconfessed.

"According to the testimony of the local doctor taken in coroner's inquest, and corroborated in its important points by historical researchers over the following century, Cutler had bought the Negro at auction when he was a young officer mustered out of naval service at the close of the War of 1812. Veterans found little promise in the nation they had served. The viable opportunities had gone to men who had stayed home and gained commercial experience, or apprenticed themselves in one of the politically powerful craft guilds. A series of failed enterprises carried Cutler gradually westward. By 1825 he reached the Mississippi River. At the end of his resources, he entered into an agreement to operate a keel boat for a syndicate of Natchez merchants.

"River commerce was perilous in those times. Vast, unsettled stretches were a haven for misfits, criminals and renegade Indians. The ponderous keel boats were easy prey for gangs that haunted the rocks and rapids. Cutler's boat was taken by a raiding party in 1829, below the notorious pirate lair at Cave-in Rock. After three days of torture, Cutler was tied to a horse and the animal driven off a cliff towering seventy feet above the river. It was a design, which, at the height of its cruelty, killed the mount on impact and left the rider strapped, still conscious, to hundreds of pounds of dead buoyancy. Cutler was swept downstream, dashed against one rock after another while he waited to drown. Eventually he came free and managed to struggle to the riverbank. With several bones badly broken, he seemed condemned to a lingering death. Fate, however, had not finished with him. His Negro had escaped during the raid and watched the pirate camp for a chance to help his master. He found Cutler and brought him to civilization. A few lines in the local newspaper were all Cutler received."

Moncavage jabbed a forkful of omelet at Sinclair for emphasis. "Cutler's employers repudiated their agreement with him. Impoverished and racked by pain, he devised a plan. Up river in St. Joseph, he negotiated command of a broken down keel boat. He brought aboard a quantity of eight gauge fowling pieces, and ordered key points sandbagged against rifle fire. Crewmen who became nervous at his precautions were replaced with the scrapings of the riverfront. Thus prepared, he set off for Natchez. At each port along the trip, Cutler mounted a heavy guard on the decrepit craft. He toured the markets, making discreet inquiries as to the price for prime furs, growing evasive whenever specific questions about his cargo came up. His was the crudest possible charade, but in a land ruled by rampant greed it worked brilliantly. He was attacked again below Cave-in Rock. He ordered his crew to hold their fire until the last possible moment. At close range, heavy fowling shot shredded the oncoming pirate canoes and decimated the raiders. The survivors were brained with tomahawks as they tried to climb aboard. Cutler beached the old keel boat and marched inland to the pirates' longhouse. The few loafers there were completely surprised. After a brief skirmish, Cutler and his crew found themselves in possession of the pirates' entire—"

A shadow fell across the research cover. Moncavage could not have been more startled if Josiah Cutler had come back from the dead. It was just the maid, with a fresh pot of coffee.

"Tonia," he said when she had refreshed cups, "there is a leather case in my study, a zipper case with a small combination lock and my initials. Would you bring it, please?"

She left without a word. Her icy, assured manner seemed better suited to lashing a vile-tempered thoroughbred through a steeplechase than to dispatching simple domestic duties.

"Cutler and his crew fell immediately to quarrelling," Moncavage read on. "Cutler insisted they take only the money and jewels, and flee on the fastest horses. The crew demanded he load the stores of liquor and furs and the valuable Negroes aboard the keel boat and pole to Natchez. The treasure was split at gunpoint. The crew reached Natchez and told their story with swaggering pride, fully expecting to be received as heroes. Cutler had undoubtedly known that many Natchez merchants made handsome livings trafficking with the pirates, buying stolen goods at ten cents on the dollar and selling at retail. Perhaps he also guessed that Territorial officials, after years of protesting they lacked the resources to combat piracy, would be loathe to admit that a band of drunkards led by a crippled pauper had made short work of the most feared gang on the River. Two of the crew were hung for murder and the remainder imprisoned for robbery. A warrant was issued for Cutler. The dying slave began to ramble as he told of their escape across the perilous Natchez Trace; of years when Cutler was hounded by greedy officials in half a dozen cities where he tried to settle. Then the doctor was left alone to wonder what vast wealth Cutler might finally have brought to the wilds of Florida, where a threadbare planter aristocracy would be ill-disposed to do the bidding of city politicians.

"Imagine the temptation," Moncavage digressed, "to a medical man with appetites cultivated by years of education, most of whose patients paid him with chickens and vegetables.

"The doctor enlisted two cavalier cronies, dissolute scions of influential local families who were constantly in need of money. They and a few pet ruffians would waylay Cutler near his house and leave him badly injured. The doctor would be summoned. He would have the run of the house long enough to locate the treasure. The scheme went awry at the outset. Cutler, habitually wary and well armed after years of persecution, scattered his attackers with pistol fire and left one cavalier dead in the road with a bullet in his brain.

"It was the resulting Coroner's inquest that opened the book on Cutler's past. Local residents either bade good riddance to the dead cavalier or attributed Cutler's exoneration to generous bribes. He married later that year, but lived quietly for only a short time. He arrived home one afternoon, pounding feebly on the door and crying for water. By the time his wife reached the porch, he was dead from four gunshot wounds. No one ever learned whether he had been shot by his enemies, and if so which enemies, or if he had simply fallen victim to robbery.

"Agriculturally, the plantation had never been self supporting, which made it a prime candidate for transfer to black ownership after the Civil War, to serve as evidence that Reconstruction was working. Thereafter it passed, usually by guile or by violence, from one owner to another, until a Haitian exile named Bastien Figaro came into title late in 1952. He operated it as a roadhouse and a juke joint; prostitution upstairs, dice on weekends and rumors of Voodoo. Eventually Figaro gained a foothold in lucrative inner city gambling, and was content to lease the old house to a succession of small operators. Currently it has been refitted as a casino by a politically powerful Miami syndicate, operated for them by a former Atlantic City gaming executive named David Sinclair."

Moncavage set the document aside.

"Josiah Cutler was like you, Sinclair, an embittered veteran who fell in with the wrong sort of men."

Sinclair set silver across his plate with an irritable click. "I've heard more about Vietnam in the last ten hours than in the previous ten years."

Moncavage's expression darkened with hints of terrible consequences. "This morning you are on the brink of a decision which may define the rest of your life."

Sinclair wiped his mouth and dropped the napkin in a disgusted wad on the table.

"What do you people want of me?"

CHAPTER 10

Footsteps with a light click of authority announced Tonia's return. She set a zipper case at Moncavage's elbow. He waited until she cleared the table and wheeled away the wicker serving cart before he worked the lock. The manila envelope he removed had Department of Defense markings. It was stamped *Top Secret* in bold red capitals.

"I had to call in a rather large favor to get this," he confided to the Federal agents.

He withdrew an eight by ten photograph and set it on the table. Presented in shadings of pink with traces of crimson, it looked more like a close-up of a shrimp cocktail than a military secret.

"Sinclair, have you ever seen one of these?"

"It looks like an infrared air photo."

"Do you recognize the location?"

"No."

"That happens to be the area around Cutler House. Look carefully in the rear."

Sinclair flipped the photograph and glanced at a combination date/time stamp on the back. "Is that when the exposure was made?" he asked, setting it face up again before anyone could focus on the numbers.

Moncavage let out an exasperated sigh. "No, no. Not the back of the photograph. The swamp behind the house."

"Did anyone tell you how to interpret these shadings?"

"The tones are made by variations in the ability to retain and radiate heat rather than light," Moncavage said, adding significantly, "which is why abandoned roadbed, for example, can still be seen long after it disappears from regular photographs."

"Do you see the hot spot?" Sinclair tapped a finger on the photograph. He was more insistent than specific. Moncavage peered at the profusion of detail without seeming to discern anything.

"What of it?"

"It's an FBI stakeout."

"How do you know?"

"That's the field where the Aztec landed. An experienced police supervisor like Wilkinson wouldn't commit the resources involved in last night's operation without watching his location beforehand."

Wilkinson emitted a skeptical growl and snatched the picture for a better look. His abrupt action confirmed what the resolution level of the photograph never could have shown. He checked the date/time stamp. It was two months old.

"All right, Sinclair, what's your game?"

"A lawyer named Bernard Cohn was murdered on that air strip. Probably in full view of your stakeout."

Moncavage stiffened. "Is that possible, Arthur?"

"The advance team did report seeing a vehicle," Wilkinson confirmed. "They thought it might have been a taxi, but their night vision equipment had limited range."

"They thought?" Moncavage asked. "Didn't they follow up?"

"They couldn't compromise the surveillance to investigate what may still turn out to be someone dumping garbage. The medical examiner has yet to determine the time of Cohn's death."

Restlessness brought Moncavage to his feet. He clasped his hands behind his back and stared out at the ocean.

"How much have you learned about this man Cohn?"

"According to the New York office, he was a parasite who scraped out a living representing drug pushers as victims of minority oppression."

Moncavage turned back abruptly. "But why was he killed? And why on that landing field?"

"We don't know, sir," Wilkinson admitted.

The Congressman stepped behind Sunny. He rested a hand on her shoulder. When she didn't flinch at the familiarity, he bent his bare chest down close to her so he could reach across the table. He turned the photograph until he had it oriented as he wanted.

"Look here, Sinclair." He traced a finger across the glossy surface. "This intermittent line runs straight from the back of the old house for almost a mile until it meets this secondary road, exactly perpendicular. That's hardly natural, wouldn't you agree?"

"I wouldn't know."

"Cutler house was raided several times during Prohibition. Newspaper articles mentioned a smugglers' road to the rear of the building. And a tunnel into the basement."

"Is the FBI planning another raid?"

Moncavage stood erect, giving Sunny's shoulder a squeeze before he released it. "We will ask the questions. You will answer them. Candidly and completely."

"Why didn't they go in last night, when there was a processing plant full of narcotics in the basement? Without that, the place is a tenth rate gambling joint. The equipment belongs in a museum. The volume barely covers the graft."

"The payoff envelopes," Moncavage snapped. "The proof of that graft. The casino and the cocaine are trivial. What matters is the evidence of corruption."

"You're not talking about crime," Sinclair said. "You're talking about politics."

Moncavage and Wilkinson glared at him. Sunny tried a conciliatory smile.

"I was in Philadelphia at the time, but apparently the first raid failed because you were able to get the money and the envelopes out undetected."

Sinclair's smile was a weary effort at innocence. "I'm just another retiree, living out my golden years in the Florida sunshine."

Wilkinson said, "You've already admitted knowledge of the casino and the narcotics."

"I was just repeating gossip."

Moncavage said, "This is not an official interview. In fact, this meeting never happened."

"Isn't it a little early for melodrama?"

"Would you rather take your chances with Dade County?" Moncavage asked. "They'll be looking for a scapegoat in the death of Captain Hewitt."

"What's your offer?"

"That," Wilkinson said, "depends on what you have to offer us."

"Not much," Sinclair said. "I didn't use the tunnel. It was blocked by an old Mercedes. The model foreign dignitaries used for State occasions in the fifties. Someone had prepared it for storage and left it there."

"How did you get the envelopes out?"

"I packed everything into an audit case and drove away."

Disbelief hardened Wilkinson's voice. "You were the primary target. Your license number had been circulated."

"The license number of my Chrysler?"

"Yes."

"Then you didn't know about the rent-a-dent Voyager I used whenever I had to haul anything?"

Wilkinson covered his surprise with an irritable scowl. "My agents had your picture."

"They were working in the dead of night in a parking lot full of moving headlights and pissed off gamblers who had no qualms about trying to run them down."

"Nonsense," Wilkinson declared.

Sinclair nodded agreement. "It didn't even seem reasonable to me when I was sweating through it. I just didn't know what else to do. I never expected a raid. I had no plan to cope with one. All I could do was try to control my panic and follow whatever thoughts came to me on the spur of the moment. It was a fluke. A brainless B-movie stunt that happened to work that one time. Harvey Ricks wouldn't try it in a million years."

Moncavage drummed his fingers on the table. "I hope your group will be better prepared tomorrow night, Arthur."

"We'll have to be. It's our last chance. The casino closes for remodeling after Labor Day."

The Congressman turned strict eyes on Sinclair. "Then all that remains is your part."

Sinclair let his gaze wander out over the endless freedom of the ocean. The white sails of a sloop billowed against distant clouds that lurked above the horizon like the foothills of an approaching storm.

"There is no such thing as petty crime," Moncavage lectured as he slid the photograph back into its incriminating envelope. "A night of seemingly harmless entertainment can be used to blackmail a government official for life. The first dollar of graft buys a police officer for the rest of his career. Every misdemeanor, every human frailty can be twisted to advantage by men like Judge Picaud."

Sinclair blinked and stared at the Congressman. "Who is Judge Picaud?"

"The Bureau is going to considerable risk and effort to seize Monday night's payoff envelopes for one purpose; to corroborate the testimony you will give in Federal court to break Picaud's strangle hold on Dade County."

"I've never heard of Picaud."

"Then you will testify against the underlings with whom you dealt and, when they are convicted, they will testify against him."

"If I wind up in court, the news media might wonder out loud how an alleged casino operator assumed an eight million dollar mortgage from a bank with a major shareholder in the U.S. Congress."

"Is that a threat?"

"It's an observation."

"A rather short-sighted one. Your assumption of the Lloyd mortgage predated your criminal activity. It was approved by bank officers independent of my control. I placed my family's stock in a blind trust immediately following my election."

"I'm not suggesting you're dishonest. I just don't see what you gain creating a public spectacle."

"You're not from the south, are you, Sinclair?"

"I grew up in Fort Wayne, Indiana. Sometimes I wonder why I left."

"You've never smelled a turpentine still, have you?"

"Not that I can remember."

"You wouldn't forget," Moncavage said. "I never have. My father worked the catch basins until his lungs were so bad all he could do was eke out a living as a night clerk in a twelve-room hotel. This was in a lumber town in the Georgia pines, where clerks weren't fit to spit on. He took every kind of abuse there was to take; a man so sick he had to hold the desk sometimes just to stand up. He'd come down to the little basement room where we lived and cough and cough until blood would come up. He made me promise never to tell. He was afraid it would cost him his pathetic job and his last ounce of pride. He died as hard as any man ever died to give me a start in life. I owe it to his memory to stand up and count for something."

Sinclair shifted uneasily, like a man who found himself trapped next to a mumbling mental defective on crowded public transportation. "There's a difference between counting for something and tilting at windmills. You know the media. Most of them graduated from the University of Mars. Give them two columns and a deadline and there's no telling what they'll say."

"Something other than concern over my public image is bothering you," Moncavage shot back. "What is it?"

"Three people died as a result of last night's fiasco. Have you thought what kind of body count you could wind up with if the casino raid gets out of hand?"

Sunny put a reassuring hand on Sinclair's forearm. "Lucinda Rivendahl won't be in any danger, David."

"Neither will the payoff envelopes. Ricks knows they're evidence. He'll prepare them just before pick-up and lock them in the strong room. The man inside will have orders to burn them at the first commotion."

"We can handle the situation," she assured him.

"How? By slipping an advance party upstairs to secure the strong room before the main raiding party moves in? They still have to get through a reinforced door before the man inside can flick a cigarette lighter."

Uncomfortable silence suggested Sinclair had guessed the actual raid plan.

Moncavage glanced at Wilkinson's wristwatch. "Well, it is Labor Day Weekend, Arthur, and I've an appearance schedule."

Moncavage and Wilkinson stood up and shook hands. Sunny stood and shook hands with Moncavage. Sinclair used his cane to reach his feet. Tonia appeared at the end of the colonnade, just on cue. She led the trio back into the house and along the two-story entry hall. There was a brief pause while she unfastened the door to let them out. A shadow moved where none should have moved, and prompted Sinclair to turn his head. Phyllis Moncavage stood watching them from the gallery above. She clutched the wooden railing for support. Her face was the taut prelude to a visit to the morgue.

The coolness of indoors left Sinclair shivering on the climb down to the car. "What's going on here, Mr. Wilkinson?" he asked when Sunny had the sedan rolling on the circular drive. "My security clearance was never higher than Secret, and that expired years ago. Two Federal officers watched Moncavage show me a Top Secret photograph and said nothing."

"Nothing you've heard this morning is to be repeated to anyone. Do you understand that, Sinclair?"

"I don't understand any of this. I particularly don't understand the nonsense about the tunnel. You knew it was there. You found it when you searched the house during the raid. You saw the Mercedes. You probably traced the title as a matter of routine, even if you weren't curious."

"I asked if you understood the confidential nature of this morning's meeting."

"Oh, for Christ's sake, Wilkinson, what have I got to gain blabbing your ridiculous secrets?"

"You've got a lot to gain by cooperating with us."

"Drop me at the first bus stop. I'll talk to my attorney and get back to you."

Stone faced silence was all Sinclair received. Sunny was only a few blocks from the FBI offices when Wilkinson finally instructed her to pull over at a transit kiosk.

"You're getting a break you don't deserve," he told Sinclair. "Don't make us come after you."

CHAPTER 11

Only shadows lurked in the lobby of the Lloyd Building. Sinclair took an elevator to the second floor, went quickly to a door with *Excello-Vend* stenciled on the marbled half glass over an exquisitely rendered antique jukebox; the legacy of a tissue-boned pensioner who had asked a few dollars and the chance to leave some precious memories. Sinclair fumbled with the key, racing both the clock and his own nerves. The office had gone stale during the two weeks he spent in the hospital. He raised a window. The second hand swivel chair squeaked under his weight. He put the telephone on speaker, pressed a speed dial number and unlocked file drawers while it rang.

A sleepy feminine voice mumbled, "Maureen Lefkowitz."

"Mo, this is David Sinclair."

The voice woke up. "All right, just stay calm, David. I'm on my way. Tell them no questions until I get there. And make sure the nurse has your medication chart up to date. Anything stronger than aspirin I can use to have the interview declared inadmissible. Give me your room number again."

"I left the hospital yesterday, Mo."

"Yesterday? Where have they got you?"

"I'm not in custody. That's what has me worried."

"You're worried because you're not in custody? David, that bullet wound isn't infected, is it?"

"This is new business, Mo. I got caught in a situation last night."

"Oh, God! And I swore I wasn't going to miss my son's Bar Mitzvah. All right, wait until I get my computer booted up."

Sinclair pulled file folders and paged through them for anything incriminating, working with harried concentration while he told his attorney what had happened since he left the hospital. She interrupted repeatedly with pointed questions.

"You were never seriously interrogated?" she asked skeptically when he finished.

"I'm also not under any visible surveillance," he supplied. "What's my exposure?"

"Briefly, life in prison, forfeiture of all fruits of crime, treble damages under RICO."

"Get real, Mo. Hewitt was going to kill me."

"You established the casino where the narcotics would be taken for processing," she reminded him. "Under the felony murder statute, anyone who willfully participates in a felony is culpable for any loss of life incident to that felony. The circumstances of death are immaterial."

"No one told me about any narcotics."

"I couldn't sell that to a jury if I gave away season tickets to the Dolphins. You may have been a patsy, but you looked like you were in charge. The prosecution will have witnesses to your authority. The Rivendahl bimbo—excuse the language—that flaky Reverend you used to launder the currency, Doctor Figaro who rented you the building. And God help both of us if the IRS ever ties you to that ridiculous vending company you used to smurf the slot machine coin."

Sinclair made a face at a folder of bank statements. "If I'm in such a predicament, why did the FBI turn me loose to shred evidence?"

"An educated guess, based on my six unproductive but highly instructive years working for Ruellene Kingman as a Deputy State Attorney, would be that the FBI is waiting for Dade County to turn the screws down for Hewitt so they can offer you a way out if you'll testify for them."

"Then why not turn me over to Dade County?"

"They probably haven't requested you. Captains and above serve at the pleasure of the Director, so we're talking major embarrassment here. The command structure will need time to develop an approach that projects just the right mix of politically astute professionalism and morale building zeal."

"What can the Feds do for me?"

"If the U.S. Attorney finds you severed your relationship with the conspiracy before the killings, the State Attorney will probably relieve you of culpability on murder."

"What's it going to cost me?"

"You will be required to plead guilty to at least one felony, but Federal prisons are safer."

"How long before I absolutely have to decide?"

"The next knock you hear may be Dade County with a fistful of warrants. Be polite. Try to smile."

"I'm all charm."

"Don't tell them anything," the woman insisted. "If they want more than your name, all you can remember is your right to have an attorney present during questioning."

"You're my first call," Sinclair promised. "Tell me about Earl Moncavage."

"He's the golden boy of Florida banking. Elected to Congress on a platform of enlightened capitalism. Destined—"

"Not that drivel," Sinclair interrupted. "I want to know what the girls say about him when they pass out the party favors in the powder room at Maximillian's."

"David, that's not—"

"Come on, Mo. I have to deal with this turkey. I don't think he's firing on all four cylinders."

And exasperated sigh came across the line. "He's a blow-dried moron. All the brains were on his wife's side of the family. Her daddy and granddaddy ran a small, snooty bank and skimmed the cream. Fat deposits, gilt-edged loans, not much overhead. Along came the Ivy League whiz kid and expanded his way onto the cover of Fortune magazine and into several hundred million in foreclosures. Another success story shot to shit."

"What does he have against a Judge named Picaud?"

"Politics. Picaud is the oldest of the old boys. His power base is the blue bloods and the rednecks who are trying not to notice Miami speaks Spanish now. Moncavage needs them, as well as the black and the ethnic vote, to promote himself to the Senate. Picaud doesn't want to share."

"Thanks, Mo. Keep your cell phone charged."

Sinclair hung up and hurried through the remaining files. A hasty search of the desk turned up a forgotten envelope marked *Personal—Crofton Lloyd* in evenly slanted architects' script. A memorandum of transmittal from the company Sinclair had retained to manage the building explained it had been found by accounting personnel during conversion of building records to their computer. Inside was a handwritten note to a Miami attorney, dated July 6, 1939.

> I refer to our conversation of last evening, and to your advice, which the last vestiges of my sanity compel me to reject. I can no longer continue unsupported in the belief that my wife loves me at all, let alone exclusively. You may, blessed as you are by the wisdom of emotional distance, dismiss this letter as the insecurity of middle age. But I must ask again that you provide me the name of a discreet and reliable private investigation firm.

Typewritten surveillance reports followed. One page had been crumpled then carefully smoothed and refolded.

> ...subject OPAL called at desk of Hotel CLAREMONT 2:00 PM and spoke with clerk PRICE. Subject OPAL entered room 816. Greeted by UNKNOWN male occupant. Subject OPAL departed hotel CLAREMONT 4:30 PM. Clerk PRICE declined to identify UNKNOWN male occupant room 816. Cited hotel policy. (NB: Subject OPAL tendered no funds therefore not guest of record. Suggest subpoena under Rules of Civil Proceedings.)

Sinclair stuffed everything he had found into a battered audit case. Traffic noise had begun to filter up from the street. He locked up and rode down to the lobby. His master key let him into Vernon Granger's office in the Parisian Theater. He culled correspondence and financial schedules from the files.

In the desk he found the folder Granger had shown him. He thumbed rapidly through a pile of random news accounts photocopied from microfiche. A 50th anniversary spread on the Lloyd Building contained the information that Crofton Lloyd had died of a heart attack on a train trip to Washington on August 7, 1939. His death had been a surprise. He had no history of heart trouble. The bottom article, dated August 9, 1952, also caught Sinclair's eye.

> HOTEL EMPLOYEE SLAIN
> Walter Thomas Price, night auditor of the Claremont Hotel, was fatally shot during an apparent robbery attempt. Mr. Price, an employee since the hotel was constructed in 1925, was shot several times at close range. Hotel management stressed that the safe containing guests' valuables was not opened. Police are seeking a slightly built Negro seen leaving the vicinity.

Sinclair locked up and left by the street door of the building. A small crowd had gathered in front of the shut-up theater. Past retirement age and dressed in clothing left over from quiet protestant lives, they were a Bible belt minority lost in a world of rapid Spanish and fervent Catholicism, groping for an answer to what had happened to their golden years. They were restless. The reader board said services should have begun five minutes ago.

Carrying a case crammed with incriminating documents, Sinclair did not linger.

CHAPTER 12

Cindy Rivendahl found her way home mid-morning, threading her tangerine BMW through the porte cochere. She took a white knuckled hand from the steering wheel and fumbled for the remote. A motorized garage door lifted. The car lunged ahead. She stopped it with a squeak of rubber, shut off the engine and climbed out.

Balancing was a chore, even in flat heeled shoes. On the way to the house she managed a studied nonchalance. It took serious concentration. She didn't notice the music until she opened the kitchen door. Keys fell from her fingers and rattled on the floor. The music drew her through a formal dining room, egging her on to a clumsy run. She caught the mahogany framing of an archway to keep from toppling over and stared into the living room.

Sinclair sat at the piano, immersed in his playing. With his unruly hair and filthy clothing, he might have been rehearsing a community theater production of *Dangerous Dan McGrew.*

Cindy said, "David?" then hiccuped.

He stopped in mid-phrase and turned on the bench. The beginning of a smile flickered out when he saw her. Her jeans were too tight to wrinkle, but her fashionable shirt showed the effects of a long night. The dregs of lipstick and make-up only emphasized the haggard cast of her features.

"Drunk?" he asked.

"No." She hiccupped again.

"Right."

She plowed purposefully across the room and stopped unsteadily in front of him. Her throat clamped tight, trying to hold down her stomach.

"You're supposed to be dead."

"I feel dead," he offered by way of apology.

"Captain Hewitt took you away to kill you," she insisted.

"How did you know that?"

"Harvey Ricks called me in his office and told me. Just like you'd been in a car wreck or something."

"Hewitt is dead," Sinclair said quietly.

Cindy hiccupped again, and giggled at herself.

He patted the bench. "Maybe you'd better sit down."

She shook her head, holding her breath to strangle her hiccups.

"It must've been some party," he said.

"It was your wake. All the people at the casino who used to work for you got together and held a wake."

"A little premature, but I appreciate the gesture."

"It wasn't a gesture." She hiccupped. "It was just an excuse to get drunk. We all sat around and said what a creep you were and how"—another hiccup, and she finished in a frustrated gasp—"how lucky we were to be rid of you."

"Excuse my arrogance."

Her eyes rebelled at his humility. "What happened last night?"

"Did you know they were going to use the casino to process narcotics?"

She smothered another hiccup. "Captain Hewitt?" she blurted. "I want to know."

"He went to pick up the drugs. The delivery turned out to be a Federal sting. There was some shooting."

A shiver shook her. "What happened to you?"

"The FBI cut me loose."

"How long have you been sitting there like that?"

"I just got home. I wanted to wind down."

"Couldn't you get up the stairs to change? Where's your fancy cane, anyway?"

"I have to start walking on my own sometime."

Cindy hiccupped and recovered her dignity. She gave him a few seconds of bored applause. "Are you ready to try the stairs now, Macho Man?"

He put a hand on the piano and stood up. "Maybe we'd better make it ladies first. I think the bromide and aspirin are in the upstairs bathroom."

A hot bath loosened the knots of tension in Sinclair's body and made room for fatigue. Red-traced eyes stared back at him from the mirror; he hadn't had two consecutive hours sleep since leaving the hospital. He ignored them to shave again and comb his hair. The door chimes startled him while he was dressing.

Cindy made unsteady noises going downstairs. Sinclair could make nothing of the muffled voices he heard. He zipped his slacks, pushed his feet into slippers and hurried out of the bathroom.

A powerful hand caught the back of his neck and built on his momentum to propel him along the hall. His legs were kicked out from under him. It was all he could do to throw up an arm to protect his face before he slammed down onto the carpet. Weight bore down on him. A gun muzzle made pressure at his neck.

"Police officers. Who else is in the house?"

A vein pulsed at Sinclair's temple. He breathed slowly and consciously, trying to absorb the adrenaline coursing through his system. His arms were pulled behind him and pinned together at the wrists by stiff plastic. Hands under either arm lifted him to his feet.

A gray haired man pushed a creased face into Sinclair's. "Who else is here?"

Sinclair forced a smile. "May I see some identification?"

A second officer put a gun to Sinclair's head. "Cop killer wants to do this the hard way," he said with a Latin inflection, savoring each word.

Cindy's voice came from below. "David, what's going on up there? Are you all right?"

She was silenced immediately, but her words established the presence of a witness to anything that happened.

The gray haired man took a badge case from inside a raid jacket. "Detective Sergeant Zebrisky, Dade County Police." He put his identification away and took out a printed form folded by thirds. "This is a Superior Court warrant authorizing a search of these premises." He tucked the warrant between two buttons of Sinclair's shirt.

The two policemen herded Sinclair roughly along the hall. The stairs were built in a tight spiral, and he had a difficult trip down on his sore leg. Through a narrow window he glimpsed a gray Buick turning into the drive.

Cindy lay face down on the entry tile with her hands fastened behind her. A rangy policewoman watched her, holding a shotgun at port arms. A stocky plainclothesman drifted in from the living room. He was an uncomfortable thirty, with longish side hair to compensate for a spreading bald spot on top.

"All clear," he told Zebrisky.

The door chimes chose that moment to ring, three musical notes that made a mockery of his police bass. Zebrisky opened the door.

Scott Birmingham, crisply turned out in a white polo shirt and lightweight slacks, looked as if he might have foregone a golf date to drop by. He identified himself as a member of the Criminal Division of the State Attorney's Office.

"Is one of you Detective Sergeant Zebrisky?"

"Right here, Mr. Birmingham."

Birmingham went straight into the living room, without another word. Zebrisky closed the door and followed him, cat-footed and curious. Nobody spoke in the entry. Birmingham's low-pitched voice carried, tense and angry.

"What's going on here? You're dressed up like you're raiding a crack house. You've got a pry axe and a steel ram out in your van. You've got people handcuffed. A woman on the floor."

"Procedure, Mr. Birmingham. This isn't a traffic warrant. A police officer has been murdered. We couldn't know who would be here. Or what their reactions would be."

"Well, you know now. Let's calm down. Everything you do and say here will be open to challenge before a court. I'd like to develop some evidence that won't be excluded on preliminary motions. And I'd like to do it in a way that won't have Sinclair's defense attorney painting swastikas all over my witnesses."

Zebrisky and Birmingham came back into the entry. Zebrisky gave orders to remove the handcuffs from Cindy and Sinclair. Cindy stood up, staring at the intruders with sick, helpless eyes. Sinclair put his mouth close to her ear.

"Let's get out of the way so they can do whatever they came to do," he said in a quiet voice that didn't quite escape Zebrisky's attention.

"Where do you think you're going, Mr. Sinclair?"

"We'll be in the kitchen if you need anything. I want to read my warrant."

"You stay with me, Mister. We have a field interview form to fill out. Then I'll have some questions for you."

"I'm sorry," Sinclair said. "My attorney won't permit me to answer questions without a subpoena."

Birmingham stepped close to Zebrisky, spoke confidentially. "All the court has granted is physical access and specific impound authority. If we attempt questioning without Mr. Sinclair's counsel present, anything we discover here could be tainted, inadmissible."

Sinclair bit the insides of his cheeks to keep from smiling. He and Cindy went into the kitchen.

Sinclair sat in a breakfast nook with a window open to the canal. A broad beamed power yacht idled past. Two school age children squabbled on the afterdeck. Random clouds drifted. Pressure had slacked from the air, warning that dormant summer was drawing to a stormy close. He set the warrant on the table and forced his tired eyes to focus, reading slowly, one line at a time.

Cindy heated water in an automatic brewer, made an exotic blend of coffee for herself and chocolate for Sinclair. Worry clouded her face when she sat across from him.

"David, what do they want? What's all this about?"

Sinclair teased her with a conspiratorial wink. "You're going to make a great shyster. Losing your nerve and interrogating the client in earshot of the opposition."

Anger flared to the verge of a scream in Cindy's cobalt eyes. She regained control by stages, finally screwing the lid down on her emotions with a look that admitted Sinclair was right by hating him for it. She scooted out of the breakfast nook and shuttled back and forth along the counter, dicing vegetables with an expertise born of years on various salad diets.

"Do you want anything to eat?"

"Thanks, I'd better wait. Listening to the Gestapo ransack my home won't do anything for my digestion."

"It's doing wonders for my head, too."

"Milk is the best thing to soak alcohol out of your system."

"We're out of nonfat. I already looked."

"Stop it, Cindy. You can't belt down Tequila Slammers until you glow in the dark then blame your weight on a glass of milk."

"Don't lecture me, David."

Zebrisky strode in. The gray Police Sergeant had taken off his raid jacket, exposing the dampness of nerves and exertion at his armpits.

"There's some locked furniture in that office," he said.

Sinclair accompanied him to the alcove, unlocked the credenza, the safe and the desk. He stood to leave.

Zebrisky blocked him. "The hard drive has been removed from your computer."

Sinclair kept his expression pleasant; said nothing.

"Those files are evidence."

"I'd have to discuss that with my attorney."

"You were using a cane to get around yesterday."

"Is there anything else you want unlocked?"

"I'll take the cane, Mr. Sinclair."

"According to the warrant, as far as I've read, you're looking for gambling records and related paraphernalia, controlled substances and firearms."

"If you've read that far, you know the warrant also authorizes personal searches of all individuals on the premises."

Sinclair and Cindy were taken to separate rooms upstairs.

CHAPTER 13

The police search dragged on well into the afternoon. Sinclair buried himself in a voluminous history of mathematics, where even uncertainty could be measured and all things returned eventually to normal because no other outcome was logically possible. He found little solace. The smile he forced when he bid good bye to Birmingham and the police did more to emphasize his sour mood than conceal it. He went back to the piano.

Cindy swayed across the room in time to the moody, downbeat *I Love An Angel* and sat shoulder to shoulder with him on the bench, her back to the piano. She hummed along with the final verse.

"When are you leaving Miami?" she asked before he could launch into anything else.

"I live here."

"The casino is gone. Why stick around?"

"The Lloyd Building is still standing."

"All the money came from the casino."

"Casino money kept the building out of bankruptcy until the management company could fill the vacancies."

"Screw the building. It's not worth dying for."

"The minute I put up a *For Sale* sign, I become a flight risk. If Dade County doesn't pick me up, the FBI will."

Worry infiltrated her eyes. "David, what really happened last night?"

"Did you know a lawyer named Bernard Cohn?"

"Who is he?"

"According to Captain Hewitt, Cohn was behind the takeover of the casino."

"I've never heard of him."

"He was murdered while I was in the hospital. His body had been left on the landing strip where Hewitt took me last night."

"Landing strip?"

"Where they were flying in the narcotics. The pilot was working for the FBI. I'm not sure who Hewitt was working for."

"Harvey Ricks."

"Ricks paid protection, just like I did. Hewitt answered to someone who ordered him to frame me for killing Cohn then kill me for resisting arrest."

"Who?" she choked out of a tight throat.

"Maybe a judge named Picaud?"

"What happened?"

His shoulders fidgeted in an imitation of a shrug. "Hewitt was shot. I was able to put the transport plane down at Opa Locka. The FBI caught up with me there."

"But they let you go," she said hopefully.

"After they took me to see Earl Moncavage."

"The Congressman?"

"Do you know him?"

She said, "He's a public figure, David," but the tension in her throat suggested something else. "Why did he want to see you?"

"He thinks I should sacrifice myself in some crusade against this Judge Picaud. It doesn't seem to bother him that people have already flushed out for nothing."

"He's something you'll never understand, David. A leader."

Sinclair made a face. "Between Vietnam and a business career, I've seen all the leaders I care to. A lot of pompous twits reacting frantically to events beyond their control while they pretended everything was going just about as they had planned."

"Didn't you think Earl Moncavage was charismatic?"

"All the lights are on," Sinclair agreed, "but I'm not sure there's anybody home."

The corners of her mouth turned down. "Are you going to tell me about all the cash I found when I turned your suit coat out to put it in the dry cleaning bag?"

"Harvey Ricks is no boss gambler," he said cheerfully.

"He isn't a black taxi driver either."

Confusion made Sinclair blink.

"You had a taxi driver license in the lining of your coat sleeve."

Sinclair snapped his fingers. "That scrap of paper Cohn was holding," he recalled, then frowned. "I wonder how the police missed it They must have searched the coat."

"I think they quit when they found the FBI receipt. That bitch spent forever asking me what you'd said about the time you spent with them, while I stood stark naked with the curtains wide open."

Sinclair lapsed into thought.

"David, my father used to close his feelings inside, but it wasn't hard to know when he was hurting." She stroked his cheek fondly with the tips of her fingers. Her smile promised a sympathetic ear.

"It hasn't anything to do with hurting, Cindy. When I was young, my feelings were used to manipulate me. Encouraging the child's interests to guide him into healthy behavior patterns, I think they called it. If I took an old radio apart in the garage loft, I'd better get straight A's so I could get into the best electrical engineering schools. And the best schools were looking for well-rounded students. Wasn't I tall enough to turn out for basketball? And what about girls? Other boys my age had girlfriends. Why didn't I like the Chester's daughter? She had such a nice personality. Was I afraid to ask her to the movies? It never stopped. The only way to minimize it was to shut everything inside. Once that kind of behavior pattern forms, it stays with you."

"That was just childhood, David. My parents named me Lucinda Noreen for my two grandmothers. My mother used to call me Little Lucy No whenever I wouldn't do something she wanted. Any time she thought I hadn't lived up to the family name, it meant a two-hour lecture. There were times I thought it would never end, but it's over now."

"If you think you shook that off the day you turned twenty one, you need to check the mirror."

A somber quiet settled over her.

He nudged her gently. "Talk about people locking their feelings away."

"Remember our first date?" she asked in a hollow voice.

Sinclair grinned foolishly. "Some date. I got to pick you up at your boyfriend's and drive you to your flying lesson. You were working on your multi-engine rating."

"I can still remember backing off to seventy five knots on short final, waiting for the instructor to chop an engine and thinking how easy it would be just to slam into the ground and put it all behind me."

The revelation startled him. "If I hadn't sat in the back seat watching you make those landings look easy, I don't know if I could have held myself together long enough to get that Aztec down last night."

Their eyes locked. Spontaneous confidences had come rarely in their time together. The magic had not yet diluted. Before either could speak, the door chimes rang their three musical notes. The last note had barely died when they started over again, and kept on ringing. Sinclair made an angry noise in his throat. He went out and opened the door.

Scott Birmingham slipped across the threshold with a nervous glance over his shoulder and sidestepped out of sight of anyone who might be watching from outside.

"Close the door, David."

Sinclair put his head out into the fragrant afternoon air. Nothing moved on the wedges of street visible through the hedge. Heat rose off the empty drive in waves that were almost liquid.

"Where's your car, Scott?"

"I parked down the block. Close the door, will you?"

Sinclair did so more from habit than from compliance. "If the police are watching the house, they've already seen you. And it's a little late to start worrying about the neighbors."

Cindy came out from the living room and leaned wearily against the archway. "Hello again, Scott."

He stepped close to her and his voice thickened with emotion. "Cindy, I'm sorry. Are you all right?"

"Oh, terrific. My head is splitting and David is in one of his piano playing sulks. Maybe you can talk some sense into him."

The attorney turned on Sinclair. "You're in serious trouble, David. Zebrisky wasn't asking about your cane just to make conversation."

Cindy jerked upright and swayed from the sudden tension in her body. "What about David's cane?"

Birmingham's eyes narrowed swiftly and shifted to Sinclair. A bleak smile told the lawyer he had said too much. "Maybe we'd better sit down and discuss this."

Sinclair put his hands in his pockets and rocked on his heels. "That'll be a nice change. Are you planning to be straight with me, too? Or would that be overdoing things?"

Birmingham stood close to Cindy and touched her elbow. "Let's go in and sit down and talk," he said thickly in her ear.

She stood her ground. "What about David's cane, Scott? I want to know. Now."

Birmingham spoke rapidly in a low, reluctant voice. "The cane was built around something called a barreled action. It was actually a shotgun."

Cindy's horrified eyes jumped to Sinclair's face. He gave a helpless shrug. The questions drained away and left her face bloodless. She turned her back on the two men, went into the living room and curled herself tight and withdrawn into a club chair.

Birmingham and Sinclair went in after her.

Sinclair made himself comfortable in another chair. "Help yourself to the liquor cabinet, Scott. I get the feeling the old silver tongue is going to need some serious lubrication."

Birmingham ignored the invitation, and the innuendo. "You had been released by the time the autopsy on Hewitt was finished, but someone remembered you carried a distinctive oriental cane. The idea of a cane gun came up. One of the Federal Strike Force people made some calls. Records establish that 240 barreled actions in .410 gauge were shipped from Westfield, Massachusetts to Singapore between 1934 and 1939. The police have identified the American manufacturer, as well as the jobber who made up the canes in the Orient."

"What I get from this conversation so far," Sinclair said peacefully, "is that some cane guns were made up in Singapore more than half a century ago."

"The State Attorney doesn't need the actual cane to put you on death row," Birmingham warned. "All she needs is the testimony of the man who sold it to you. He will testify. They all do when they're facing accessory to capital murder."

"The cane was a gift."

"All right, the man who gave it to you," Birmingham snapped. "His testimony will still convict you."

"Are séances admissible in court these days?"

"You're sure the man is dead?"

"Of natural causes," Sinclair assured him.

That only made the lawyer irritable. "It was damned lucky for you that I stopped into the office this morning and ran your name through the computer on a warrant check."

"What was lucky about that?"

"Don't you realize you came within an inch of blowing everything?" Birmingham demanded in a sudden fit of angry disbelief.

"Why don't you tell me about it?"

"Are you familiar with the felony murder statue, David?"

"Do you mean the law that gives you equal responsibility for Hewitt's death because you helped set up the casino?"

Birmingham regarded him with disdain.

"Come on, Scott. What gives? If the police knew I shot Hewitt, they should have me in an interrogation room right now."

Birmingham shook his head. "You know too much, David. Once you make an official statement involving high-level corruption, it can never be expunged from the record. Hewitt was an isolated bad apple, but the command structure would still look stupid for not catching him."

"They're not just going to let this go."

"If they can find enough independent evidence to put you on death row for aggravated first degree murder, they can offer a plea bargain. Second degree in return for life. Your confession will be a carefully negotiated document that scrupulously avoids any reference that could endanger senior police careers."

"And if they don't find their evidence?"

"You can forget about cutting a deal with the Feds. Dade County won't nolle prosse. They can't afford to have you on a witness stand giving a blow by blow of local corruption."

"That's not what I'm hearing from Maureen."

"I put it on the line coming out here this morning to run interference between you and the police. I'll have some explaining to do when Ruellene Kingman hears about it. Maybe I made a mistake."

"It was a mistake," Sinclair agreed, "but you were too worried they'd find something to connect you to the casino to stay away."

"How much cash can you raise, David?"

"You've had all the money you'll see from me. I'm not coming across just because you bop in and lay down a little improvisational theater."

"We'll need money to mount a legal defense," Birmingham insisted. "More than you could possibly have stashed away from the casino. We'll have to act fast to raise it."

Cindy unwound herself in the chair. "Do you have an idea, Scott?"

Birmingham held up a cautioning hand. "I still need to check a few details."

"How long will that take?"

"A couple of hours. This evening at the latest."

"You'll call?" she asked.

"The police are certain to put a tap on the phone here." A scowl dissolved into inspiration. "Crystal Springs. There won't be any eavesdroppers on the golf course. Give me an hour to arrange something with the Pro Shop. Then go to a pay phone and call them for the tee-off time."

"All right," Cindy said.

"David?" Birmingham asked.

"This must be one hell of an idea for you to blow a round of golf at the Crystal Palace."

"Yes or no?"

When Sinclair didn't answer, Cindy said, "He'll be there."

Birmingham nodded swiftly to seal the agreement. "Don't try to call me or get in touch with me."

"My pleasure," Sinclair said.

Birmingham touched Cindy's shoulder, said, "Don't worry, we'll make it work," and left with a smooth, stealthy quiet.

A flash of anger brought Cindy across the room. She stood over Sinclair with her feet spread and her hands thrust into her pockets. Her eyes were an accusing cobalt glare.

"Got all coked up on self pity and came out of the hospital ready to take on the world, didn't you? Well, you took it on, and look where it's got you."

"Where did you put that taxi driver license?"

"What the hell are you going to do with that?"

Sinclair stood up. She gave no ground. Their faces were inches apart.

"Look, Cindy," he said gently, "whether Scott likes it or not, we'll have to cut a deal. The more information we have to trade, the better we can do."

"So you're going to charge off on your own again."

"I don't know what else to do."

Cindy had curled herself back into the chair when he came downstairs again. He had changed into a summer weight suit of conservative cut and good material. He was studying a crumpled piece of card stock. Rather than an actual license, it was a form of photo identification prominently mounted by some taxi companies to reassure riders. The dampness of the Everglades had smeared the typewritten entries.

"Charles DesBrisay," Sinclair was able to make out. "His address is the New Lexington Hotel. That's in South Beach, isn't it?"

Cindy had withdrawn into sulky silence. Sinclair bent to kiss her good-bye. She turned her cheek to him. He went out to the garage and cranked his Chrysler sedan to life. He got the clutch down with an unexpected surge of pain and shifted to reverse. His leg lacked strength in the specific muscle areas he needed to maintain constant speed backing out of the drive. He set himself mentally, shifted to first and started down the street. His shift to second was barely passable.

He turned the car around, brought it back and put it away. He went inside, grinned sheepishly at Cindy and phoned for a taxi.

CHAPTER 14

Ocean Drive still held a few blocks of sun bleached art deco clinging to hundreds of millions of dollars of pristine shore front; the last fly-blown remnants of history on an island overrun by glitz, doddering along the brink of receivership while progress and preservation faced off in hushed courtrooms with stares as sharp and steely as fixed bayonets.

A glass door etched with a strutting flamingo let Sinclair into the New Lexington Hotel. Off the lobby was a radio room, little changed since the last stuttering run of the jazz bands had died up under the coved ceiling. A few elderly residents snoozed fitfully on quaint furniture while images flickered silently across a television screen.

The only African American in sight stood behind the desk; a placid man in his seventies. His three-piece suit came out every Sunday and went straight back into a closet, and he wore it just that carefully.

"Brother DesBrisay didn't come to services this morning," Sinclair informed him politely.

"That don't surprise me none," the man said in a faraway, asthmatic voice.

"It's Sunday," Sinclair said earnestly. "He promised he'd come."

"What church did you say you was with, Brother?"

"Do you know the Parisian Theater? Across the Bay?"

Some time went by while the clerk either thought about it or didn't. "There's services there, right enough, and Christian from all I hear," he finally said. "But not for a sinner like Brother DesBrisay."

"Where might I bring the Word to Brother DesBrisay?"

"His employer was in this morning. About a taxi that didn't find its way home. He tried Brother DesBrisay's door without rousing him."

"No door can close out the Word of the Lord," Sinclair said resolutely.

The clerk coughed apologetically. "The owner of this establishment is not a Christian."

Nearby elevator doors dragged open. Two younger African American men stepped out with baseball caps on backwards and shirts open to display symmetrical muscle development that came from walk-up gymnasiums rather than hard work. They sized up Sinclair as they sauntered past the desk on stealthy, splayed feet. The old clerk never looked at them, but they were out the door and gone before he spoke again.

"He is a priest of Guinee," the man said in a voice that worried about lurking spirits, "and does not look kindly upon those who do not believe as he does."

"Where the Lord walks, the dead sleep in eternal peace," Sinclair declared.

"You might try 631."

The elevator doors closed Sinclair in with a thud of old rubber. Remote machinery came ponderously to life. The car rose with the leaden slowness of lost hope, finally opening on six. The ghosts of old meals lingered in the corridor like visiting in-laws. Occasional television noises issued from behind a progression of dull brass room numbers. The door to 631 rattled at Sinclair's knock. No sound came from within. The knob squeaked in response to turning pressure. It would not yield. A sliver of light was visible at the mortise plate. Sinclair slipped a credit card into the gap.

The latch gave way with a tiny snap. He stepped quickly into a narrow foyer and closed the door. "Brother DesBrisay?" he called softly, and received no answer.

A kitchen table stood beneath a jalousie window. A few optimistic flies had wandered in through the tilted slats to buzz around the remains of a sandwich. A flat pint bottle lay on its side on the stained Formica. A chair was tipped backward on the floor. A bare black foot stuck out among the chromium legs.

"All right, Brother DesBrisay, time to sober up and repent. We'll never save your soul if you don't confess now."

Sinclair crossed a room that was half-parlor, half-kitchenette. The man lying on his back on the scaly linoleum was Charles DesBrisay, but he wasn't drunk. He lay as a spasm of sudden death had left him; a heavyset man dressed only in dingy boxer shorts. Post mortem lividity had come and gone from his skin. Blood had trickled from a small hole and dried on a battered ear. Sinclair glanced around nervously.

He seemed to be alone. Except for a new looking portable television, the furniture was early Goodwill Industries. A wrinkled shirt and trousers were thrown on a lumpy sofa. One cracked plaster wall held a faded baseball pennant. The other was thumb-tacked with recent football pictures and newspaper clippings.

A door let him into a narrow bedroom. Keys and assorted personal items littered the top of the bureau. In the clutter of the top drawer he found a shoe box crammed with memories; a picture of an elderly black man set against a backdrop of rowhouses that might have been anywhere from Harlem to Port Au Prince, pictures of a black family—a sturdy young husband, a slender pretty wife with children at the hem of her skirt, a small house, a bulbous Buick that looked to have been a few years old when the photo was taken. Folded inside an envelope were documents releasing Charles Des-

Brisay from the conditions and restrictions of parole, and a letter admonishing him that his status as a convicted felon prohibited him from, among other things, possessing firearms. Below that lay a worn gray Luger. It was empty. There were no shells in the shoebox. The only other item of interest was a residential mortgage given by Charles and Caroline DesBrisay, husband and wife, to secure a note payable to Bastien Figaro as mortgagee. Sinclair replaced the items in the shoebox, all but the pistol, and replaced the shoebox.

In the kitchenette he found a sink full of dirty dishes, a garbage pail full of empty liquor bottles. The old refrigerator held mostly frozen dinners and sandwich materials. He used the gun muzzle to probe in drawers. Television noise intruded briefly, as if someone had touched a volume switch—*Weather Service advises tropical storm Wanda Ann may be felt as far north as Dade County*—then it faded away. The floor trembled, as if warning of a coming blow. Sinclair froze.

A man had come into the apartment.

The newcomer lumbered across the room and sank to his knees beside the body of Charles DesBrisay, as if his two hundred forty muscular pounds had been brought down in a struggle with some ponderous weight. Powerful shoulders sagged to a limp mass inside a polyester blazer. Strong hands turned to clumsy paws as he reached out, shaking and lacking the last inch of nerve to touch the man on the floor.

Sinclair cleared his throat.

A broad young face came around in a series of spasmodic jerks. Blood had drained away and left black skin as pale as dirty cream. Teeth were a white glimmer between thick lips slacked apart. Chestnut eyes were full of disbelief and denial.

"He ain't dead, is he?" the youth asked in a shallow whisper.

Sinclair measured him with unsmiling eyes. "Who are you, young man?"

The youth came to his feet in a balanced linebacker's crouch. A collegiate patch covered the breast pocket of his blazer, making it an informal uniform that held him in check as effectively as a maternal lecture. He straightened up and fidgeted.

"This is my father, you know," he rumbled defensively.

"Did the hot weather and the bourbon get the best of you?"

"What you saying?"

"Did you come back to see if he might still be alive?"

"You think I killed my own father?"

"The door was locked when I got here," Sinclair said with a meaningful glance at the jalousie window. It was permanently fixed in its corroded aluminum casement. The glass slats pivoted a few inches to circulate air. There was no convenient ledge or fire escape outside. "The killer might've gotten in the way I did, but he needed a key to lock the door behind himself on the way out. Your father's key is on the bureau."

The flood of grief that had overwhelmed young DesBrisay receded, leaving an eloquent blend of hurt and hostility in his chestnut eyes. He had been deprived of much in life, but whoever had deprived him of his father had gone too far.

"You don't look like no police. What you come in my dad's room for?"

Sinclair tapped the empty pistol he happened to be holding against his trouser leg. He held the gun pointed at the floor, as if he were consciously restraining its threat.

The youth stared at it. "You going to shoot me?"

"I'd rather have a quiet talk with you."

"What you want, coming in my dad's place?"

"A man was killed in the Everglades two nights ago. A lawyer from New York. His name was Bernard Cohn. What did your father tell you about him?"

"My dad drove a taxi, you know. He wouldn't know no New York lawyer."

"A taxi was used to dump the body," Sinclair said. "Cohn had your father's identification in his hand."

"My dad didn't know no lawyer," DesBrisay insisted.

"What did your father tell you about Bastien Figaro?"

"Old Man Figaro?" Young DesBrisay stared in confusion. "He run the Wheel in Little Haiti. My dad wouldn't know him either, you know, except maybe his name."

"Your father knew him well enough to borrow money from him. There's a mortgage in the bureau to prove it. Cohn rented a casino building in the Everglades from Figaro. Cohn also used regular taxis to bring gamblers out from the Gold Coast."

The youth glared defiantly. "My dad didn't drive no night shift on no Gold Coast, you know."

"Turn that chair right side up and sit down like you were going to eat that sandwich," Sinclair instructed.

"Why should I?"

"It looks like your father was sitting there when he was killed. I'd like to know where the bullet came from."

The youth sidled around his father's body, keeping a wary eye on Sinclair. He lifted the chair gingerly to avoid touching the dead man with any part of it. He placed it carefully and sat down at the table.

"Face forward," Sinclair ordered.

He checked the position of the hole in Charles DesBrisay's ear. To have struck his son in the same position, the bullet would have had to come from the open jalousie window. The distance between the window wall and the youth's shoulder was less than a foot. Sinclair crouched and sighted past the youth's head. Across a service street stood one of the rare commercial buildings in South Miami Beach. Charles DesBrisay's view on the world had been dirty brick wall with metal ducts crawling down between narrow casement windows.

"From all the way over there?" the youth asked.

"A good .22 rifle can drive roofing nails at seventy five feet. There'd be some residual odor if a gun had been fired in here. The smell of nitro powder lasts for days."

"Who'd do something like that?"

"I'm going across for a look at those offices. You'd best call the police."

"The cops?"

"Your father has been murdered," Sinclair reminded him.

Young DesBrisay stood up. "The cops will think I done it, like you thought."

"They're going to think that whether you call or not. You'll look better if you call."

"I'm going with you," the youth declared.

"That's a bad move, son. You were right about my not being the police. I happen to be the prime suspect in the murder of a police captain."

The youth gaped. Sinclair neither looked a killer nor sounded a liar. It was too deep a puzzle for him.

"I'm going," he insisted. "Gun or no gun, you ain't big enough to stop me."

"Terrific." Sinclair sighed.

He tucked the empty automatic under his suit coat and went out. The two young men who had eyed him in the lobby were lounging by the elevator with the patient air of vultures. They saw young DesBrisay and lost interest in Sinclair.

"Hey, Henry!" one called in keening Caribbean singsong.

The other jitterbugged away from the wall. "Man, the TV was all over you last night. Most valuable player on defense. The pros gonna pick you on the first round, no shit."

There was some hand slapping and whooping gibberish. Sinclair pushed the elevator call button. The doors stuttered open. He stopped just inside the car, frowned at a sudden thought and held the door.

"Henry, we don't want to keep the alumni waiting."

The pair sent DesBrisay on his way with another round of hand slapping. The adulation boosted the youth's confidence.

"My father dropped me off at the team bus on Friday afternoon, you know," he told Sinclair as they started down. "That's the last I seen him alive. We went to Greensboro and practiced yesterday, you know, and played a night game and didn't get back until just this morning, you know. He was supposed to meet me at the bus from the airport, you know, only he didn't. I was with the team all that time, you know."

Sinclair wasn't listening.

"If you don't want me along," the youth asked, "how come you didn't leave me up there?"

"How do we get out of the hotel without being seen?"

DesBrisay stabbed a button. The car lurched to a stop and the doors bumped open. The youth led the way along an empty hall, moving at a rolling, purposeful gait to an unmarked door. He wedged himself into the door frame with the back of his shoulder against one side and the sole of a size fourteen shoe against the other and heaved with his considerable strength. The jamb sprung just enough to allow the door to swing open. He grinned, blowing.

"Ain't nothing stops me I put my mind on something, you know. That's what my coach tell me."

Sinclair gripped an iron railing and followed DesBrisay awkwardly down four turns of steep, ill-lit concrete stairs. At the bottom was a disused health club. Sunlight made chicken wire patterns in the dirty light-well glass up near the ceiling and filtered dimly down into a steam room lined with rotting cabinets. Sinclair and the youth went through another room with a huge dry sitzbath in the shape of a flower petal sunk into a floor of old tiles. There were discarded cigarette butts, an aftertaste of marijuana smoke. More stairs took them up to a heavy door secured by shiny deadbolts top and bottom. The door opened out into the service street behind the hotel.

Sinclair went down half a block and crossed to the rear of the office building with the big youth rolling silently in his wake. Unreinforced opaque glass had been used to replace two chicken wire panes in a service door. Sinclair picked up a stray piece of broken concrete. He looked up and down the empty service street. People went past on the sidewalks at either end, lost in their own concerns. Sinclair put the concrete through a pane of glass. He reached in and fumbled the door open.

DesBrisay followed him into a dim maintenance passage. "We be busted if we get caught, you know."

"We'll also be tried and convicted," Sinclair assured him.

The passage took them into a narrow lobby under twin copper vaults gone green from age and salt air. An elevator lifted them to a hot, empty upper hall. Sinclair led the way to a door at one end.

"Your turn," he told DesBrisay.

The youth used his strength again. The door pivoted into an office crammed with desks, calculators and tables stacked high with bingo cards. One wall held a detailed street map carefully marked off into sectors; individual locations denoted by colored pins.

"This wouldn't be Figaro's?" Sinclair asked.

"Old man Figaro be in Little Haiti. He run the Numbers Wheel, you know. He don't do no little old lady bingo. I told you already."

"Has anyone told Figaro?"

DesBrisay peered out a window. "That's my dad's room over there. You can see right inside. You can see his pennant."

Sinclair went to the other window. A faint burn track scarred the sash. He cast about but didn't catch the glint of a cartridge casing under any furniture.

"Do you know where Figaro would be today?"

"We'll go," DesBrisay said. "The both of us."

"Not a good idea."

"I ain't going to do nothing to him, you know. I just want to ask him straight to his face did he shoot my dad."

"Figaro is a boss gambler; a man who makes his living playing the house percentage. Your father's murder wasn't a percentage play. It was very risky. If he'd moved an inch at the critical moment, the gunman wouldn't have had a second shot. If Figaro was responsible, then there's something going on that neither you nor I understand."

Young DesBrisay was two hundred forty pounds of hard muscled resolve.

"Look him up in the phone book," Sinclair suggested. "It'll be a lot safer."

"He won't talk to me on no phone, you know."

"I don't know that he'll talk to me in person."

"Let's you and me go find out."

Cynical resignation played on Sinclair's lips. "The Scarecrow and the Tin Woodman…off to see the Wizard of Odds. You wouldn't have a car with you?"

CHAPTER 15

Young DesBrisay led the way to an old white Camaro. Duct-taped upholstery burned Sinclair's legs through his trousers. The youth fired a reluctant engine and turned onto Ocean Drive. A sedan with Dade County license plates sat at the curb. The man inside watched the New Lexington Hotel. Sinclair grinned privately and used the headrest for cover as DesBrisay drove past with his scavenger pipes grumbling.

"My dad drove a taxi, you know. A lousy, smelly taxi. Wasn't no reason for nobody to kill him."

"The taxi is missing," Sinclair said.

"Who gives a shit?"

"For a New Yorker like Cohn, taxis are second nature. He'd hop in glad of a ride and never suspect he was being driven someplace where he could be quietly murdered."

"Nobody had to kill my dad to get a taxi, you know. They could have stole one easy."

"No car thief did the kind of shooting that killed your father," Sinclair said. "What kind of trouble was he in?"

"He be in prison once," the youth said defensively. "The rest was just jive talk, you know."

"Some truth finds its way into every lie."

"In all that jive about him walking with the Black Baron?"

"What about it?"

"That was just something he made up to be bragging on when he be drinking."

"Tell me about it."

"You know who the Black Baron supposed to be?"

"A Voodoo spirit who lives in cemeteries and traffics in the souls of the dead."

"He don't really exist, you know."

"Neither does Bugs Bunny. That hasn't stopped him from becoming Warner's most jealously guarded property. How recently was your father involved in Voodoo?"

"He never was," DesBrisay insisted.

"Someone went to a lot of trouble to kill him."

The youth fell silent. The Camaro's exhaust was a brooding rumble across the Causeway. They drifted into a maze of neglected streets where storefront signs spoke Haitian Creole. Faded graffiti mirrored fifty years of Island history. The oldest paint wished death on the Tonton Macoute. Later slogans demanded a similar fate for the Attaches. The freshest were an indecipherable polyglot of factionalism that had made its way to America with the most recent wave of boat people.

A motorcycle policeman had traffic stopped at an intersection. A hearse and two old limousines drew slowly past, leading a procession of lighted cars. The procession originated from a mortuary in the next block, two stories of tan stucco built to fill a triangular lot created when an arterial cut through the congested neighborhood.

Young DesBrisay eyed the mortuary like a child alone in the dark listening to a monster breathing in his closet. Sinclair had to tap on the side glass to get the youth's attention.

"Is that where we're going?"

"Old man Figaro ought to be there of a Sunday."

Young DesBrisay guided the Camaro across the intersection and stopped where the mortuary's faded green awning came out to the walk, killing the exhaust noise quickly. Sinclair got out and went in under the awning. The youth came on silent feet and stood behind him. The door was locked; all signs of the recent service gone. He pressed a button. A small speaker behind a brass grille emitted a solemn voice.

"I regret we are closed. Today is reserved for the worship of the Lord."

"My name is David Sinclair."

The solemn voice came back, full of quiet pleasure. "Ah, Mr. Sinclair. Please wait one moment."

DesBrisay's chestnut eyes grew suspicious. "He knows you."

"He knows my name," Sinclair corrected.

A lock snicked and the door opened a careful foot. A solemn face peered out. Black hair was slicked back as smooth and shiny as tile at the sides of an otherwise bald head. Sound white teeth glistened in the crescent of a satisfied smile.

"Good afternoon, Mr. Sinclair. And Henry DesBrisay. This is a pleasant surprise. Please accept my congratulations on a magnificent game last evening."

The youth moved his big frame uncomfortably. "You Loofer, ain't you? The one they call Preacher?"

The solemn man smiled very slightly, like a celebrity trying to live down a juvenile nickname. He drew the door back to admit them into the hush and subdued light of an entry. Heavy drapery softened a gothic archway to the dim chapel. Sunlight put a glow in a stained glass consecration high up in the far wall behind the pulpit and gave everything an air of piety. Preacher closed the door reverently.

"In view of your recent activities, Mr. Sinclair, I'm afraid a personal search will be mandatory before we see the Doctor."

Sinclair spread his arms. Preacher's light touch lifted the empty automatic from his belt. Nothing changed in his expression.

"This way, please, Gentlemen."

Preacher inserted a card into a wall slot. A pocket door slid soundlessly to admit them to a paneled elevator deep enough to accommodate a coffin. The elevator was hydraulic and lacked any of the sense of movement of gearless traction machinery. After a time the door opened on an upper hall. Noiseless carpeting took them past closed doors with small mysterious sounds like the scampering of rats on the other side. The hallway ended at a door. Preacher knocked lightly and respectfully then opened it without being bidden.

The room was deep and dim. Soft individual lights shone up from the bases of framed nudes on the paneled walls, collectors' pieces selected for vulnerability and naive prurience. Muted strains from the caustic saxophone of Earl Bostic flowed from an unseen sound system. Windowless and machine chilled, it was a place of retreat and sanctuary.

Behind a desk, dwarfed and protected by its vastness and fragile to look at, a slightly built African American sat with flawless composure in a high backed leather chair, preserved so carefully that he seemed to have no particular age, except that he was somewhere past sixty. The black flannel of his suit coat swallowed the brilliance of a bankers lamp as if it never existed. He wore no accessories, in a part of Miami where a man's standing was the gold and gemstones he sported.

He unhooked rimless reading spectacles from his delicate ears and looked at the newcomers with small pink eyes. They were the penetrating eyes of a voyeur. Eyes that could caress and possess without ever touching. Eyes that devoured by proxy.

"Do sit down, Gentlemen," he said in words as dry and ethereal as the cigarette smoke he exhaled behind them.

"Thank you, Doctor Figaro," Sinclair said. "It's nice to finally meet you."

Figaro watched Sinclair settle into a chromium and leather chair facing the desk, taking in the awkwardness of Sinclair's leg and catching his barely perceptible reaction to the minute click of the door latch.

Sinclair forgave the close scrutiny with a cheerful smile. "I telephoned a couple of times when you were my landlord, about the title to an old Mercedes I found in the tunnel under the house."

"And were you able to establish ownership?"

"I got as far as the trust division of a New York Bank in the Florida Motor Vehicle records. The bank stonewalled me."

"That is a shame." The sympathy in Figaro's voice was as thin as cellophane, and just as transparent.

Preacher placed the Luger on the desk in front of the slight black. "Mr. Sinclair brought this, Doctor," he reported and withdrew to station himself by the door.

Figaro lifted the pistol. His fingers were small and well cared for, manicured extensions of his voyeur's eyes, and he caressed the smooth old metal with the thinly disguised pleasure of unexpected gain.

"Please do sit down, Henry," he purred distractedly.

Only one chair was available. It was the twin of the chair Sinclair occupied, designed for ease and comfort. DesBrisay sat as erect as its architecture would permit. He didn't say a word.

Figaro put the pistol away in a drawer. "My name is Bastien Figaro, Henry. We have never met, but I do know of your achievements. You are a source of great pride to your community. And, I am sure, to your father and mother."

"I guess you don't know my father was killed." It wasn't quite a question, nor exactly an accusation.

Figaro stopped all movement, like a man stunned. It was perfect. He was made of stone. A tendril of smoke wafted from the tip of his cigarette.

"No," he said solemnly. "I am sorry, Henry. I did know your father, some years ago. If there is anything at all I can do, please tell me."

"Mr. Sinclair said there's some gamblers that rent a place in the Everglades from you, you know."

Sadness settled over the fragile man like dusk over a street of dissipated neon, leaving a pallid glow of knowledge. "I have been terribly afraid that something like this might happen."

A sharp light of wonder winked on in Sinclair's eyes. "Something like what, Doctor?"

"Henry mentioned the death of his father in connection with Harvey Ricks. The conclusion is obvious, is it not?"

"He mentioned the casino," Sinclair corrected. "The casino is, or was, owned by a New York lawyer named Bernard Cohn."

"You made a point of saying *was owned* by this man Cohn,"

Figaro remarked nicely.

"Cohn's throat was cut two nights ago. A Dade County Police Captain seemed pretty sure a black man had done the job. A taxi was used to deposit Cohn's body on a landing strip in the Everglades. A chauffeur's identification card belonging to Henry's father was found in Cohn's hand."

"Found by the police?" Figaro was curious to know.

"I expect you'd know if it was. In fact, Doctor, stop me if I'm boring you with things you know better than I do."

"Perhaps there has been another power struggle, with Mr. Cohn meeting the fate you very nearly met."

"That wouldn't explain a rifleman shooting the boy's father from an office building across the street from his hotel. Nor why you recognized a pistol I found in his room."

Figaro removed his cigarette and snubbed it out in a copper ashtray built into the desk. He snubbed it out carefully, working it all the way around the rim. A lever dropped the butt out of sight. It was not a signal in the sense that it sent a specific message. It simply communicated a change in attitude, and that only to someone experienced in reading his moods.

Preacher took a miniature automatic pistol from his pocket, a hammerless .25 Beretta, prized for its compactness and its ability to snuff out a life without any great fuss of flash and sound. He pointed it at Sinclair's head. There was the barest glint of a square cut fingernail as he caressed the trigger.

Music died away. An air conditioning duct brought a vague chant from another world, and with it a hollow, rhythmic sound like Voodoo drums.

The sound system re-cued. A woman's vibrant contralto began to drift, low and haunting. Figaro smiled at young DesBrisay. He spoke in the serene voice of a hypnotist putting a subject under.

"Henry, you are Haitian, a direct descendant of the rebel slaves who won their freedom two centuries ago. Your father's father was forced to flee the Island in the terrible years of mulatto rule, before the black majority came to power. Your father accepted that legacy proudly."

DesBrisay came to his feet. "My father worked for you," he realized. "You're the Voodoo man he always warned me about."

"Your father came to me with many difficulties," Figaro droned on. "There is a saying on the Island that the enemies of Voodoo in times of plenty are often its friends in times of trial."

DesBrisay moved to the desk like a moth drawn to fire. "You made him be a Tonton Macoute."

"Your father was a patriot, Henry, in a hostile land where patriotism was a lonely calling."

"Why would those gamblers kill him?"

"A man named Ricks has been cheating me of rent. He knows I will take measures against him. Perhaps he was afraid your father would be involved."

"Was he?" the youth wanted to know.

Figaro smiled sadly and shook his head. "Your father and I have not spoken in many years."

"These measures, you know, what you going to do to this Ricks?"

"I shall collect the amount due me, plus punitive damages."

"He killed my father," DesBrisay protested. "All you going to do is take money away from him?"

"When men kill for money, depriving them of money is the most effective way to punish them."

"How much money?"

"The bank would be at least half a million dollars these days, wouldn't you think, Mr. Sinclair? Perhaps you can guess what the play will be. I couldn't begin to estimate it."

"It doesn't matter," Sinclair said. "The casino is closing for remodeling after tomorrow night."

"That much is true, Henry," Figaro was quick to concede. "The project is scheduled for midnight tomorrow. As tragic as your father's death was, it is simply not feasible to postpone."

"How does this project work?" DesBrisay wanted to know.

The haunting contralto died away. The driving beat of *Pachuco Bop* grew from nothing and filled the room. Figaro gave it a few seconds to work up everyone's pulse rate, and then spoke with an electric trill.

"The casino is built on a natural mound, which rises out of the swamp. Between the base of the embankment behind the building and a gravel road a mile distant, a wagon track once ran through the swamp. It is overgrown now, but still passable. The house is close to the edge of the embankment. There are no outside lights. Anyone climbing up can reach the rear door without being seen."

Figaro lit another cigarette and exhaled smoke in a long streamer. It broke and curled over DesBrisay's face. The youth's broad nostrils twitched at its harsh texture. He blinked traces of water from his chestnut eyes.

Figaro smiled benignly at his discomfort. "Have you ever breathed tear gas, Henry?"

"I smelled it, you know. Just walking on the street, you know, after the riots."

"Tear gas diffuses quickly in open air. In a crowded casino, it would take very little to create infinite panic. One gas grenade in the kitchen, where Ricks' men take their breaks, and one in each gaming room will be sufficient. Men wearing gas masks can slip upstairs without interference. A fourth gas grenade will subdue the single man inside the strong room. Then it is simply a matter of packing the money and leaving by the same route."

"I can handle that," DesBrisay said.

Sinclair spoke up immediately. "Going out the same way you went in is a major no-no. Ricks' men will be waiting in the tall grass with assault rifles."

DesBrisay smiled grimly. "That'll be their hard luck, you know."

"That kind of revenge isn't like beating the cross-state football team," Sinclair cautioned. "For me it was standing in a driving monsoon rain, staring at a bunch of dead North Vietnamese soldiers and feeling as empty as a scarecrow's pocket. I had enough artillery and air support to win that fight. You won't win yours. Ricks is too well prepared to be taken by a simple-minded hold up plan."

The big youth had no experience to match against Sinclair's, and no patience with the mental exercise of argument. He faced Figaro smartly, as if that shut out everything else.

"I been on the street, you know. I can handle anything from a .357 on up to full automatic. I ain't boozing and I ain't blowing. I'm in the best shape of my life."

Figaro smiled tolerantly. "I must admit, Henry, that I have admired your leadership on the football field. But what assurance would I have that you wouldn't deviate from the plan to seek justice for your father?"

"I got to do it your way. I got no guns and no gas, you know, and I don't know nothing about no house in no Everglades."

Figaro hesitated on the brink of an affirmative nod. "Henry, if your father's body is discovered, I'm afraid the police may suspect you."

"They won't find me, you know."

"All the same, it might be best if I arranged to bring his remains here. I promise you he will receive the best of care."

"Better than some lousy morgue," DesBrisay decided.

"There is an abandoned health club in the basement of the hotel where your father lived," Figaro said.

"I been there, you know."

"You will meet the two other men involved in the project there at ten tonight. I will give you specific instructions then."

"I see you at ten tonight, Doctor Figaro."

DesBrisay made a clenched fist salute. It probably meant something to him. Figaro just smiled.

Preacher put the miniature automatic in his pocket and opened the door. The big youth carried his hulking frame lightly across the room. A middle-aged man in shirtsleeves waited to escort him out. Preacher closed the door and put the gun on Sinclair again.

The music died away. The silence it left behind was as deep and cold as a grave. Sinclair who broke it.

"I don't understand," he told Figaro.

"Don't understand what, Mr. Sinclair?"

"Why you want to raid the casino. Harvey Ricks has to move the money along eight miles of lonely roads just to get it out of the Everglades. That's the time to jump him, when he's got one underpaid crazy leading him in a scout car and a couple of coked up shooters in a chase car half a mile back. The way you're telling macho boy to do it, the whole thing will fall apart in a shooting match as soon as they cook off the first gas grenade."

Figaro crushed out the remains of his cigarette with delicate care. He addressed Preacher without bothering to look at him.

"Mr. Sinclair is beginning to annoy me. See to it, please. And have the car brought around."

"Yes, Doctor."

CHAPTER 16

Preacher stopped Sinclair in the hallway to give two middle aged men room to maneuver a metal coffin cart out of the elevator. Airline bags chalked with codes were heaped on the cart. A Kalashnikov assault rifle teetered precariously atop the load as the men wheeled it along.

One of them opened a door, revealing a large room where more men sat around a long table covered with ledger sheets and stacks of bills and coins. The chanting Sinclair had heard was the counting of money; the Voodoo drums the rhythms of printing calculators echoing in the air ducts.

"The numbers wheel in Little Haiti must be worth millions," Sinclair said. "Figaro can't possibly be concerned over a few nickels from a broken down house in the Everglades."

Preacher motioned him into the elevator.

"What was the plan?" Sinclair asked. "Was the DesBrisay boy supposed to find his father's body and call the police? Was Figaro going to bail him out when he became a suspect and give him a chance to get even?"

The door slid shut. The elevator became a silent cocoon, suspended in time and space. Preacher pushed a button.

"Why bother?" Sinclair asked. "The kid can barely tie his shoelaces. He'll be useless against Ricks."

Nothing changed in Preacher's solemn smile. The door opened on a basement garage. A handsome boy in a leather jacket was dusting a maroon Packard limousine, a carefully preserved relic of the early fifties.

A snap of Preacher's fingers brought the boy's head up. "He wants the car."

The boy slid in under the wheel and fished keys from above the visor. The old straight eight engine ran with no sound, and only a wisp of exhaust. A motorized door segmented up in iron tracks, letting in a dazzling wedge of torpid afternoon. The door came back down when the Packard was gone and the garage was as it had been, cool and silent, not quite empty. Fluorescent tubes made highlights in the fresh lacquer of a formal sedan.

"The Mercedes from the tunnel," Sinclair realized. "Figaro got a nice paint job."

Preacher escorted him across the garage and put his card into a slot. An iron door slid open to admit them to a stark, windowless trapezoid. The short wall was brick, with an iron door like the fire door of a bakery oven. The only furnishing was a stainless steel table that shimmered beneath a fluorescent fixture. What was left of a man lay on his back on the table.

The man had been Vernon Granger. He was naked and bloodless. The soles of his feet were scorched. White bone broke the skin of one leg. Cigarette burns covered his genitals. Contusions massed below broken ribs. His face was unscarred, except for the eye sockets which were black from whatever had burned his eyes out. Too tough to die from the torture, Granger had been shot in the ear with a small caliber gun.

Sinclair turned gray. "Was it necessary? Or did you just get a thrill out of it?"

Preacher closed the door, sealing them into the crematorium. "The Reverend Granger stopped by last night. I'm afraid he was quite deep in his cups. He made a number of veiled references, and some rather outrageous demands."

"What did he know that I don't?" Sinclair asked in a voice unstable with the fervency of thawing numbness.

"That would depend on what you know, Mr. Sinclair."

"I know you won't get away with burning both of us. You're in a regulated industry. Vernon and I together are almost four hundred pounds. That will show up in your gas consumption."

"All verification procedures are relative to business volume. Four hundred pounds is within our range of precision."

The words hit Sinclair like a strong gust of wind. He swayed and caught the edge of the table for support. His grip was nerveless and palsied. He lost his hold and began to fold down. Preacher stepped behind Sinclair and thrust his forearms under his armpits before Sinclair could fall.

It was the habitual reaction of a man accustomed to coping with fainting spells. It left his gun under Sinclair's right arm, pointed harmlessly at the wall. Sinclair reached across his chest with his left hand and seized Preacher's right wrist. He pushed up hard with his good leg, driving his right elbow up and back into Preacher's jaw. The impact jolted both men. The pistol came loose and rattled on the concrete floor. Preacher's wrist came loose from Sinclair's grip. Two stumbling backward steps put Sinclair behind the stunned man. He looped his left arm around Preacher's neck, put his left hand into the crook of his right elbow to make a locked rear strangle hold. The hold was something half-remembered from a hand to hand combat manual, simple and unbreakable. Sinclair clamped it tight with the strength of adrenaline. Preacher clawed at Sinclair's forearm, trying to pull it loose enough to tuck his jaw inside. When that failed he tried to back into Sinclair to get leverage for a hip throw. Sinclair shuffled his feet, backing around in a circle, shifting this way and that, so the man could never quite gain his balance. Preacher stamped at Sinclair's moving feet.

For all its desperation, the struggle had the comic overtones of a syncopated dance to an unheard orchestra; Rudolph Valentino locked in a silent tango with Helen Domingues in *The Four Horsemen of the Apocalypse.*

Preacher was too powerfully developed through the neck to be manually strangled by a man of Sinclair's slim build and limited endurance, but sustained pressure on the man's carotid arteries began to take its toll. He lost coordination. Presently he could no longer move or support himself. His slack weight carried Sinclair to the floor with him. Stress had locked Sinclair's arms painfully, and he had to use his own weight to twist them free of Preacher's neck. He fumbled the little automatic off the concrete floor and gripped the steel table to gain his feet.

The struggle had left Granger lying askew. Sightless eye sockets seemed to grope for contact with life, an open mouth to scream silently for vengeance.

"I'd kill him, Vernon," Sinclair managed to gasp out, "but it wouldn't help. It just wouldn't help." He stooped, fumbled in the pockets of Preacher's coat and stood up with the magnetic security card.

The garage was empty, echoing the irregular footfalls that took him across to the elevator. The door opened to admit him to an empty car. His finger lingered a millimeter from the first floor button and the promise of escape when he hesitated. He cursed his foolhardiness with a half-hearted, "Oh, shit," and stabbed the second floor button.

His wingtips made no noise on the thick hallway carpet. The muffled rhythms of the counting room came from another solar system. Figaro's office was dim, deserted. He closed himself in and sat behind the desk.

The upper right drawer was fitted out as an arsenal. A variety of pistols occupied individual, felt-lined slots. The Luger from Charles DesBrisay's room lay across a lacquered box. The lid lifted to reveal a variety of ammunition. Sinclair put Preacher's automatic in the drawer, loaded the Luger and set it close at hand while he continued his search.

The lower drawer was fireproof; a metal-lined bin stuffed with file folders. One folder tab held the license number of the Mercedes in the garage. The topmost correspondence was on bank letterhead.

> I am in receipt of an inquiry from Federal officials regarding the status of an automobile owned by this bank and found by law enforcement officers during a gambling raid.
> According to our records, the vehicle was entrusted to you in support of your former efforts to enhance the bank's relationship with the then current Haitian regime. Since you are no longer an agent of the bank, I must insist that you surrender the vehicle immediately. Otherwise, I shall be compelled to order repossession.

The letter was signed by the bank's general counsel.

In a folder tabbed *Personal* Sinclair found a letter from an obscure college reminding Figaro of the honorary doctorate they had bestowed, and suggesting a modest increase in his generous annual donation to offset inflation. He also found portfolios containing mortgages, tax statements and evidences of title to real estate. The documents were uniformly current, though few of the names were Figaro's, and none of the others were identified as legal nominees. Sinclair found a deed in lieu of foreclosure for the New Lexington Hotel in one portfolio and in another a purchaser's assignment of contract for the office building across the service street. On an envelope he scribbled a rough outline of the contents of each portfolio, then tucked the Luger under his coat and went out.

The hallway was empty. The counting room door opened while he waited for the elevator. The two men who had seen him with

Preacher wheeled out an empty coffin cart. The Kalashnikov rattled as they pushed along to the elevator.

"Kind of fractures the rules, you being here alone like this," one told Sinclair in a deep, soft bass. "Maybe you could tell us some about it."

The elevator chose that moment to open. Sinclair got on first and stood to one side for them to bring the cart on. He pushed the button marked *G* and the door closed.

"It's about a car," he said. "I came to pick up a car."

"It's the alone part," the man said. "Maybe you could tell us some about that."

"That would kind of fracture the rules, too."

They stared at each other. There was no sense of movement except the uneasy passing of time. The elevator door drifted open on an empty garage. The crematorium door was shut tight. Nobody was pounding on the other side.

A horn honked impatiently.

"Too mother fucking many rules," the man decided.

He and his partner pushed out. The motorized door opened long enough to admit a white Oldsmobile coupe. The two men began unloading bags from the trunk.

Sinclair crossed the garage, trying not to favor his injured leg. The Mercedes was not locked. He folded himself in and found a set of keys above the visor. The engine caught and ran with a faint burble. Sinclair pushed the Luger between the seat cushions where it was easily accessible. He could reach only the front window controls to clear a limited field of fire. The two men finished unloading. The door started up in its tracks. Sinclair took a final, forlorn look at the crematorium door.

"Okay, Vernon," he said, "let's see if I can get out of this trap and put some damage control in place before anyone else gets hurt."

Mercifully, the sedan was an automatic. Sinclair put it in gear and rolled toward the door. Outnumbered and outgunned, all he could do was cover his thin bluff with a poker face and an unwavering stare.

CHAPTER 17

Sinclair followed the Oldsmobile out of the dim garage, squinting against the brilliant afternoon sun. No one yelled after him. No one shot at him. His rear view mirror gave him a glimpse of the garage door segmenting down as he turned onto the street. Only when he was safely established in arterial traffic did he take out a handkerchief and wipe the sweat from his face. He drove downtown and put the old Mercedes in the Lloyd Building garage. Up in his office he phoned for a taxi then pressed out another number and drummed his fingers.

"Maureen Lefkowitz," came a harried voice with the noise of children in the background.

"David Sinclair, Mo."

"Are you arrested yet? Or still just worried? Or is it none of my business, being I am only your attorney?"

"I had an experience."

"Oh, God. Give me a minute." The background noise vanished. The click of a keyboard told him she was readying a computer. "Tell me no one is dead this time."

Speaking slowly and carefully so he wouldn't overwhelm the dictation software, Sinclair told her about the taxi driver's identification he had found in Bernie Cohn's dead hand when Hewitt had taken him to the landing strip in the Everglades. He told about going to the address on the identification and finding Charles DesBrisay's body, about meeting DesBrisay's son, about their trip to the undertaking parlor and Bastien Figaro's plan to rob the casino. He omitted the Luger that now lay on his desk, telling her nothing of finding it in DesBrisay's room, or of Figaro's interest in it. His hand trembled when he finished by telling her of finding Vernon Granger's body.

"How did you meet Granger in the first place?" she asked.

"Vernon was my platoon sergeant in Vietnam."

"Old war buddies who stayed in touch all these years?"

"I hadn't seen him in more than twenty years. I just happened to notice his name and picture in a small newspaper ad for church services when Cindy brought me down to Miami to meet Scott."

"After she seduced you in Atlantic City?"

Sinclair made a face at the telephone. "You've been watching soap operas on your clients' nickel."

"You don't have to be coy, David. My mother explained the birds and the bees to me."

"You'd better have another talk with Mom. Cindy brought me down on approval. She wasn't about to close the deal until the merchandise had passed inspection."

"Who did the inspecting?"

"Scott."

"Nobody else?"

"What would be the point of using Scott as a cutout if the principals were going to deal with me directly?"

"David, did you really not ask who they were?"

"I asked out of curiosity, but I didn't press the issue."

"Why not?"

"I've been looking at organization charts all my life. Neat little pyramids of names to make the stuffed shirts feel safe and important. It doesn't matter who's on top. The people on the bottom have to live by their wits."

"Don't try to sound cynical, David. You're a straight arrow who was knocked a little off target. You could walk into any up-tight Presbyterian church in the country and feel right at home."

"Let's stick to my legal situation," he said sourly.

"All right. Tell me how Granger got mixed up in this."

"I looked him up and told him I was opening a casino and I'd need a way to launder the soft count."

"Speak English," she ordered.

"Soft count is folding money. Most outlaw operations push it through some kind of religious front, where it has limited IRS scrutiny. The slot coins are called hard count. Vending machine companies are the standard conduit there."

"What was your deal with Granger?"

"I became a deacon in the church and sole signatory on the bank account. I kept the books. Vernon got a salary as minister and the Parisian Theater to conduct services."

"Any formal paperwork?"

"Bank signature cards. Rental agreement for the Theater. Vernon gave me a certificate to make it official that I was a high hipster in the salvation industry."

Silence for a minute, then, "All right, these are the facts as we know them. The Rivendahl broad recruits you. Scott gives you a franchise to run a bootleg casino. He provides police protection and a bankrupt building for a business front. You recruit Granger as a money laundry. Eight months later, you're ambushed and shot. Someone named Harvey Ricks shows up and takes over the casino. You go out there to ask him who shot you and your police protection takes you out into the swamp to finish the job. Except this particular piece of swamp happens to be a landing strip with a dead lawyer named Cohn lying on it and the FBI staked out in the weeds. A planeload of narcotics shows up. Hewitt gets killed. You get caught. The FBI takes you to Earl Moncavage who wants your testimony to get Judge Picaud out of the way of his ambitions. You stall him, find two more bodies and stumble onto Bastien Figaro's plan to rob the casino. Anything else?"

"DesBrisay's taxi was probably used to take Cohn to the swamp."

"You'd better hope nobody ever proves that."

"Why not?"

"You withheld the information from the police, which makes you an accessory after the fact in two more murders."

Sinclair let out an exasperated sigh. "You're forgetting about the ambushed and shot part. Legal charges won't matter if I don't live to face them, which I won't unless I find out who wants me dead."

"David, I could have used that threat to get you into the witness protection program when the charges were just gambling and bribery. Will you just stay home and let me manage this situation? After all, I am your attorney."

"Speaking of lawyers, did you check out Cohn?"

"Small time, small crime."

"Harvey Ricks?"

"No such person. Or if there is, he's was never born, died, licensed, sued or arrested in New York State. No motor vehicles, no real property, no nothing."

"What do you know about Figaro?"

"Well, he used to be the house Nigger in charge of Haitian gambling, big connections in the white power structure, but no more."

"What happened?"

"Civil rights happened, David. Where have you been all your life? Who needs a house Nigger when you've got some darkie yelling at you across the City Council table? Black power comes in, brown noses go out. Equality for Japs and Jews and Jigs. A Spic can run the town. A frumpy Kike broad can even set up a law practice. That's considered progress in some circles. Right up there with indoor plumbing."

"Who were his connections?" Sinclair asked.

Her voice fidgeted. "My information is second hand, you understand. The crafty, steely-eyed baldies telling a female upstart how it was in the bad old days so she won't know all they ever did was warmed a chair."

"Okay, here's something tangible. Figaro has collected some real estate over the years, a good part of it in shadow names." Sinclair fished the envelope from his pocket and read from his scrawl.

"What am I supposed to do with this, David?"

"Check on it. Get anything you can."

"What are you looking for?"

"Figaro is in this up to his eyeballs. He owns the casino building. He was involved in Cohn's murder. He had Vernon killed. If we can figure out how it all fits together, maybe we can trade him to the U S Attorney."

"I'll look into it, but don't count on anything. Figaro operates by remote control. He's a tough target, even for the Feds."

"So who do we tell about his plan to rob the casino?"

"Don't even think about it. You can't report the plan without telling the police where you got the information, which will open the whole can of worms."

"Isn't that pretty irresponsible? Or do I just not understand the law."

"David, it's not like there's any risk to life or limb. The FBI is raiding the casino tomorrow night. The whole area will be crawling with Federal agents. Speaking of which, have you heard from the FBI? Or the police?"

"Dade County showed up with a search warrant."

"When?"

"This morning. They stayed more than four hours."

"Harassment," she decided. "If they really wanted evidence they'd still be there pulling the walls apart."

"Scott Birmingham stuck his face in and cut off any questioning."

"He didn't do you any favors, David. If he panics, he could send all of you to prison."

"I think he's close."

"David, have you any idea why Scott and the Rivendahl bimbo picked on you? Between them they probably know enough real crooks to fill a good sized jail."

"I haven't a clue, but I do have a taxi waiting."

Sinclair thanked the woman and hung up. He met the taxi in front of the building and called at the twenty-four hour pickup window of an express company. A bulky package had been waiting several days.

Cindy was waiting when he got home. Her smile was cool and barely tolerant. The anger in her cobalt eyes was building fast toward critical mass.

"Just who the Goddamn hell is Sunny Tearoe?"

"Did she call?"

"If she looks anything like she sounds, you're in way over your head."

He looked Cindy up and down, said, "maybe the FBI is fighting fire with fire," then made his way into the office alcove and pressed out a number on the telephone. "Special Agent Tearoe, please…Yes, would you please tell her David Sinclair returned her call?" He spelled his name and hung up.

Cindy perched herself on the corner of the desk. "Scott won't like that." The tempo of her words was quick, irritable.

"Scott isn't my attorney. Maureen thinks a deal with the Feds may be the best option."

"I'll never understand why you hired that twit. She's as shrill as a cat fight in a pillow case."

"She doesn't have any obligation to the power structure."

"Of course she doesn't. She's a camp follower at every protest in existence. She probably got herself knocked up at an anti-Vietnam rally."

"She's too young for that," Sinclair said, and his voice became grave. "You know, we're in a lot more trouble than Scott can bail us out of."

She dismissed the idea with a toss of her head.

"When the going gets narrow, he'll try to sell us out to save himself."

"Scott made you. He was the one who gave you the casino deal."

"Why me?" Sinclair asked.

Her shoulders moved aimlessly. "Why not you?"

"One suit is as good as another? Was that all there was to it?"

"How would I know?"

"Scott was working full time in Miami. You were the one in Atlantic City. You had to make the selection."

She considered him with a meager smile. "Maybe I liked you better than the others."

He shook his head. "If it had been your choice, you'd've gone for the big, strong, ambitious type. I get the feeling you were told to find a very special patsy."

Cindy stood impulsively and took his hands in hers. "If I went away with you, would you leave Miami?"

"Wherever we went," Sinclair said solemnly, "all we'd find is ourselves."

She dropped his hands. "You'd better get some sleep. Scott got us a pretty early tee off time."

CHAPTER 18

Cindy's BMW snarled muted defiance between the lines of tall eucalyptus trees screening the private access road to Crystal Springs Golf and Country Club. She had to brake for a family crossing the parking lot; a distinguished father, a mother serene in the knowledge that she was on display in surroundings suited to her station, an athletic youth of twenty squiring a honey haired young woman, a petite girl of sixteen self consciously waiting her turn at life. Cindy jazzed her engine and whipped the car into an empty stall, beaming smugly over the glares she got.

"What was that about?" Sinclair asked.

"Your parents never dragged you to any stupid holiday breakfasts at the club." Her voice rose to a mocking falsetto. "But Lucy, love, he's been accepted to medical school. Don't you think he's handsome? And his mother was saying just the other day he's not dating anyone seriously right now."

"Let's find Scott. It's time he saw how cranky you can get on three hours sleep."

Sinclair climbed out of the car in plus four knickerbockers, argyle knee socks, an argyle sweater vest over a white shirt and a snap-brim cap. Cindy kept a little distance going across the parking lot, less than thrilled by his choice of attire. He looked as much a relic of the nineteen twenties as the clubhouse, two stories of white stucco roofed over with red tiles and pierced by lancet windows. Double doors let them into an entry as wide as a boulevard. Sinclair scanned sociable little cliques of people in semi-formal summer outfits.

A tall, corpulent man appeared. His tentative smile was a thin veneer over forty some years of habitual strictness. A manager's proprietary eyes peered inquisitively through rimless spectacles.

"Are you a member, Sir?" he inquired in an obsequious tenor.

"My name is David Sinclair. I'm to meet Scott Birmingham."

The tentative smile brightened. "Ah, yes, Mr. Sinclair. Mr. Birmingham asked that you meet him on the first tee. Do you know the Club?"

"We'll find it."

He turned to go and found a woman directly in his path. She was past eighty. Drawn erect, she was a foot shorter than he. She might have weighed ninety pounds. Feisty brown eyes gave her the bristly look of a cornered terrier.

"Do you know who I am, Mr. Sinclair?"

He smiled tolerantly. "No, ma'am."

"I am Opal Lloyd."

His smile vanished. "Life in the fast lane has taken its toll, Mrs. Lloyd. There's an old portrait of you gathering dust in one of the building storerooms, if you'd like to remember what you looked like when you looked like something."

"Do you think you can put me off with insults?"

"The insult was purely for my own enjoyment."

"Is it not enough that you stole my grandson's building? And you not even a member of this community!"

"That's a fine thing to say to the man who saved you from an embarrassing mortgage default."

"The building belongs to Lewis," the woman insisted. "His grandfather built it."

"The building was developed by his grandmother's husband. It wouldn't surprise me if the blood claims got a little fuzzy after that."

Hatred fumed like acid in Opal's eyes. Her mouth twitched angrily, but no sound came out.

Disgust prevented Sinclair from enjoying any triumph. "It's too bad I can't challenge the legal foundation of your former ownership without clouding my own title."

The manager squeezed his corpulence between them and began spouting low-pitched nervous words at Sinclair. "Here, here, this won't do. Kindly remember you are a guest in this club."

"I'll be delighted to, if you can persuade the members to do the same."

The manager turned a solicitous expression on Opal. "Perhaps you might be wise to consult your attorneys in this matter, Mrs. Lloyd."

She unleashed a string of invective that rocked him back on his heels. Cindy took Sinclair's arm and eased him around the pair and out the front door. They crossed to her BMW.

"Well, that was an eye opener," she said while he lifted golf bags out of the trunk. "I didn't realize you were touchy enough about that building to pick on a defenseless old lady."

"I think that defenseless old lady murdered her husband," Sinclair said, and left Cindy poised on the brink of an incredulous laugh.

An asphalt path took them around the building. Scott Birmingham stood alone on the first tee, swinging two clubs as one with his feet tight together to set his balance and rhythm. He stopped when he saw Cindy.

"I was beginning to think I'd lost my charm. I saw your car come up the drive several minutes ago."

"Opal Lloyd waylaid us," Cindy told him cheerfully. "David thinks she's going to murder him to get the building back."

"It was her husband she murdered," Sinclair corrected.

Birmingham frowned. "Didn't Crofton Lloyd die of a heart attack?"

"On a train trip north, conveniently out of Miami, where it wouldn't be likely to come out that he'd just spent a month paying private detectives to keep tabs on his wife. Or that he had enough evidence for a divorce."

"David, a heart attack is a heart attack. There had to be an examining physician to sign the death certificate."

"I read somewhere that Nazis and Communists used to knock each other off with hydrocyanic acid in the thirties. One squirt from a perfume atomizer would have been lethal, and looked exactly like a coronary."

Cindy patted Sinclair's forearm. "David's just paranoid about his precious building."

Birmingham fell somber. "I'm afraid you will have to give up the building, David. Opal Lloyd has made a lot of noise in the right places. The word has come down."

"Come down from whom?"

"Don't ask questions," Birmingham snapped and strode out onto the tee.

His careful address suggested he had chosen the golf course not for its isolation but as the venue where he could best create the illusion of mastery. He hit a low, rising shot that went two hundred sixty yards to set up an easy approach. Cindy's swing spoke eloquently of a country club upbringing. Sinclair's tee shot faded off the fairway. His second shot was a hundred thirty yards over trees to a green he couldn't see. He hit a risky seven iron that looked for a moment like it might clear. It clipped a twig high up and dropped into a bunker placed with sinister prescience.

Birmingham put his shot on the green and walked with Sinclair, speaking confidentially. "David, I learned that Ruellene Kingman has requested Grand Jury time. We're all going to be indicted for a long list of felonies. You, me, Cindy, everyone connected with the casino."

"Exactly what is included in this list of felonies?"

"You ought to know that better than anyone."

"I just ran a gambling trap," Sinclair said. "I never knew what other schemes you people had hatched."

"You had plenty of chances to ask questions."

"A minute ago I wasn't supposed to ask questions."

Sinclair took a wedge down into the bunker and put his ball on the green in a spray of sand. Birmingham watched him rake away his shoe prints.

"It's all fallout from that FBI raid on the casino. The U.S. Attorney referred your case to Ruellene Kingman, and turned over the confiscated gaming equipment to the Dade County Police. They must've had the equipment under surveillance when Hewitt turned it back to you."

"I thought at the time that charade of yours went a little too smoothly," Sinclair recalled.

"It's a little late for post-mortem. If we're going to defend ourselves against the charges that will come out of this, we'll need money. More than any of us have."

"That observation is about as useful as my post mortem."

"We both know where to get it," Birmingham said.

"Hang on to your chairs, people. Here it comes."

"There won't be less than a quarter of a million cash in the casino strong room tonight."

"Spectrographic analysis says there is gold in the Asteroid Belt, too. Maybe we could talk NASA into a mining venture."

"Ricks will hold at least that much in reserve to bank the Labor Day drop," Birmingham insisted.

"Forget it, Scott. Drop and hold are things accountants and actuaries understand. You don't know any more about them than I do about Habeas Corpus."

Sinclair squared the head of his putter behind the ball, stroked it methodically. Both men watched it roll forty feet to break within six inches of the cup. Sinclair was more surprised than Birmingham.

The threesome scattered off the next tee. Birmingham and Cindy walked together, a little apart from Sinclair, and talked in low, tense voices. They fell silent when they reached the green. Number three was a short par three, and they had to wait for the green to clear. Sinclair touched his leg tenderly and sat down on the bench to rest.

Cindy sat close beside him. "We can do it, David."

"Scott is talking about outright robbery."

"Do you have a better idea?"

"I might, if I knew what we were mixed up in."

Cindy broke eye contact. The elevated green cleared and she went to hit off. They walked up together with Birmingham doing the talking.

"You and I will hike in by an old road that leads through the swamp to the embankment behind the casino," he told Sinclair. "The tunnel is clear. That old car is gone. There is nothing but plywood closing up the basement end. Ricks trucked all the processing equipment away the morning after the delivery, so there won't be anyone in the basement. The service stairs are off limits to the casino crew. Ricks is afraid someone will snatch a cash box off the dumbwaiter. We can reach the attic without being seen. The ceiling above the second floor is old lath and plaster. We can drop straight through it into the strong room. We simply tape up the man inside, pack the money and walk down the main stairs and out the front door. I'm well known in the casino. We won't be challenged. Cindy will have a car waiting in the parking area."

They reached the green and Cindy putted out. Birmingham followed suit. Sinclair missed the short putt his tee shot had left him.

"What time is all this supposed to happen?" he asked as they walked off the green.

"A little past midnight. Just before the payoff envelopes are picked up. We'll leave some money on the tables then, but the activity downstairs will cover us."

"Has it occurred to you that other people might have the same idea? Tonight is the last chance for anyone who ever got sweaty palms thinking about the cash in that casino."

Anger blazed in Cindy's eyes. "Quit stalling, David." She strode onto the tee to hit off.

Sinclair played a sloppy fourth hole. He hit into the trees off the tee, and then put his recovery shot well short in the opposite rough. A fat eight iron flew badly and left him disgusted enough to three putt from the apron. They had to wait again on the next tee. Birmingham and Cindy sat one on either side of Sinclair on the bench.

Birmingham asked, "Do you have any logical objections to the plan, David?"

"The strong room and Ricks' office are wired together for two way sound. I put the system in myself and I watched it work the other night. If the circuit is switched against us, Ricks will hear everything."

Cindy shook her head. "Harvey Ricks didn't spend five minutes in his office last night. He's busy organizing things so he can get all the gambling equipment out as soon as the place closes. He's paranoid about a police raid on the last night."

"What makes you think he won't get one?"

Birmingham said, "Dade County already has enough to take to the Grand Jury."

"Dade County isn't the only law enforcement agency with jurisdiction."

"The FBI has had its fling."

Before Sinclair could decide how much he wanted to say, Birmingham and Cindy stood up and went out to hit. All three of them kept their shots in the fairway.

"Were either of you aware that the man in the strong room has an assault rifle?" Sinclair asked as they trudged off together.

"We'll have a .22 along," Birmingham said.

Cindy uttered a quick, adamant, "No! No guns. Either one of you."

"Only if the man resists," Birmingham said soothingly.

"No guns," she repeated.

Birmingham's glance at Sinclair was a wordless call for help.

"Shooting people isn't like shooting golf," Sinclair said. "Not everyone has it in them. No one knows for sure if they do until they're forced to try."

"David, just because I wasn't in the military during some war doesn't mean I lack resolve."

"It hasn't anything to do with strength or weakness, Scott. It's just a fact of human nature."

Birmingham was angry enough to hook his second shot over the rough onto the next fairway. He rejoined Sinclair and Cindy on the green, smiling and conciliatory.

"All right, we're all agreed, then," he said, and lined up his putt.

Cindy let out a sigh of relief. Sinclair said nothing.

Birmingham gave Sinclair instructions to pick him up at his mother's condominium at ten. "Steal a car from the airport parking lot, where it won't be missed for a while."

"How do I go about that?" Sinclair asked.

Birmingham stared helplessly. "Well, David, I can't do everything myself."

Sinclair was breathing raggedly when they quit after nine holes. A film of perspiration glistened on his face. His leg troubled him more than he could conceal.

CHAPTER 19

Expensive vehicles filled the parking lot and overflowed down the margins of the access road. Well-dressed families trooped toward the clubhouse. Women kept up smiling conversations, soothed fidgeting children and threw warning glances at husbands and older boys whenever they showed signs of chafing under quiet desperation.

"The holiday parade," Cindy said as she eased the BMW past them. "I remember how much I hated it, and how secure I felt then, all at the same time."

"Sometimes memories are a warning about what you're up to when you're doing the remembering," Sinclair said.

"How is your leg, David?"

"Is that what this morning was about? Nine holes of golf to see if I could stand the trip through the swamp tonight?"

"Can you?"

"I don't know. I was too timid when I first got out of the hospital, then I pushed myself too hard yesterday. I don't have a good feel yet for how much I can tolerate."

Cindy wound through a seedy residential area that flanked the exclusive club. She turned along a palm-lined boulevard and followed the gentle curve of the ocean with a heedless velocity that suggested uneasy thoughts and nagging questions.

"What was it like in Vietnam, David? I mean, what was it like to kill someone?"

"The fighting happened at night. There was no enemy in the sense of distinct people. Just parachute flares and gun flashes. And a constant numb feeling I'd never see the sun shine again."

"What did you get out of it?"

"Something I needed in the worst way. The kind of confidence that comes from doing something I thought was right when there wasn't any visible progress and a lot of people my age were saying very insistently it was wrong."

"You never had any doubts? No anger or nightmares?"

"Not all veterans are shrink bait."

"Feeling disoriented because you saw all those awful things doesn't make you crazy, David. It might just make you normal."

"You're talking about news media sound bites. The real thing had a lot of quiet time to sort out the thousand yard stare and the survivor guilt and all the rest of it."

"Were you scared? You must have been scared."

"I grew up scared," Sinclair recalled fondly. "College was the first time I'd been away from home for more than a family vacation. I was commissioned into the Army straight out of ROTC and woke up with a rifle platoon looking to me for orders."

"What did they think of you?"

"Combat infantry units are like leper colonies. No one wants to be there, no one else wants anything to do with you and there's no escape. You become companions in misery. It just doesn't seem important to pass judgment on each other."

"Is that what you think I'm doing?" she asked. "Passing judgment on you?"

"I think you're frightened about tonight. You're looking for someone to share your nerves with. Watch your driving."

Cindy left rubber on the road to avoid rear-ending a line of vehicles clogging an off ramp. Children peered and pointed and giggled in a minivan ahead. From behind issued the rumble of motorcycle engines. Sinclair's head snapped around.

Two gaudy choppers filed past on the margin, leaving dust and noise in their wake. Bearded men in faded denim lounged against chromed backrests and regarded the world through reflective sunglasses. They idled down the ramp, gunned through a stoplight at the bottom and rumbled off into downtown Miami. Cars began to stack up behind the tangerine BMW.

"What a mess," Cindy said. "Everyone in Florida must be going someplace today."

"Last rites of summer," Sinclair said. "People desperate for one final fling, whether they enjoy it or not. You're looking at the Labor Day drop Scott was talking about. It's totally unpredictable. If play is heavy enough, it could freeze every dollar in the house on the tables. Scott's quarter of a million could turn into two cents faster than Cinderella's prom night turned into Halloween."

"If you think it's such a crummy idea, why are you going along?" The light changed and she began to inch forward with the traffic. "You're not doing it for the money. You never asked Scott how much you'd get."

"Scott didn't mention any split either," Sinclair remembered. "And he's the one harping on the subject of money. Has he told you what he has in mind for a getaway car?"

"I'll drive his Buick out."

"Scott's car is pretty well known at the casino. If anything goes wrong inside, Ricks is liable to connect you with us before you can get clear of the parking lot."

"I can handle Harvey Ricks."

Sinclair sighed hopelessly and stared out the windshield. The Lloyd Building was visible in a niche in the skyline, against a backdrop of gathering clouds. Falls of sunlight illuminated faded blue and gold in the window spandrels. He admired the sight with the uneasy pride of a teenager worried about keeping gas in his first old car.

Labor Day flooded the city with traffic. Crosswalks filled and emptied like the diversion channels of an irrigation system. Cars leaked in and out of side streets and garages. Jaywalkers dribbled here and there.

Cindy made her way through the flow and stopped in front of the building. "Do you want me to wait?"

"Thanks, but I've got some work to catch up on. Why don't you get some sleep? I'll be home by four."

Cindy caught his sleeve. "You really did have to shoot Captain Hewitt, didn't you, David?" she asked in a choked, timid voice. "He was going to kill you, wasn't he?"

"Someone may be killed tonight," Sinclair said gravely. "It may be necessary, or someone may just panic. If it happens, it'll be with all three of us as long as we live."

Cindy's hand fell away. She shifted to first gear and checked traffic. Sinclair got out and shut the door. He watched the BMW out of sight, and then hailed a taxi.

The Garden Court of the elegantly restored Belle Biscayne Hotel was crowded when Sinclair arrived for lunch. He opened a zipper case on a marble tabletop and took out the manila folder he had removed from Granger's desk.

"Okay, Vernon," he said, "is this what got you killed? Or something you guessed from this? Or am I wasting my time?"

Sorting through the articles he found considerable copy on Opal Lloyd. A prominent family and a rebellious life prior to her 1934 marriage to Crofton Lloyd had made her a darling of local society columnists. She was featured in the widely reported marriage of her son and only child following his graduation from Yale, again at the birth and christening of her grandson, Lewis, and at the death of the boy's parents in the crash of a chartered plane. Other people seemed to exist largely as an excuse to put her in the newspapers.

Other articles traced the decline of the Lloyd Building, chronicled Lewis Lloyd's drug problems and reported sporadic vice raids on Cutler House. A 1952 story reported the appointment of Llewelyn Picaud to the judgeship he still held. A sketchy biography stated Picaud had graduated from Yale Law School, was a prominent attorney and had served in the American Military Government of occupied Germany. A flicker of movement brought Sinclair back to the present.

An attractive hostess made her way among tables with Harvey Ricks close on her heels. His pinstriped charcoal suit imposed a grim formality. Starch gave his white shirt the shine of funeral satin. The crimson in his tie was the shade of freshly drawn blood. Cadaverous and impatient, he looked like death paying a hurried business call. He helped himself to the chair across from Sinclair and waved away the menu the hostess tried to put in front of him.

"Roast beef sandwich and milk," he told the woman in a curt rasp. "No coffee and no liquor. That's five minutes anyplace."

Her smile could have iced a cocktail. She took Sinclair's order for a club sandwich and left.

He zipped Granger's articles away in his case. "It's nice to see you again, Harvey. I've been hoping we could finish our talk."

"I had a punk in your back pocket all morning, looking for a situation where we could get a few things straight." Ricks swept his eyes across little islands of lush indoor greenery to satisfy himself that clusters of marble topped tables held nothing more than families eating and talking under a sun kept comfortably in its place by an expanse of tinted skylight. "Someplace you wouldn't try to settle the score for Saturday night."

"How did you get mixed up in that circus?" Sinclair asked. "What's the real reason you took over a casino you know nothing about running?"

"I needed the processing equipment."

"You'll have to educate me. I'm too square to know what makes a chemistry set worth the risk you took coming here."

"Any inner city nitwit can schlepp crystal. The real Benjamins are in packaging the powder for the up-market shoppers. The Ivy League shysters and the Wall Street wonders; the turkeys with the fat paychecks who bend your ear about how they can reconcile a productive lifestyle with recreational pharmaceuticals."

"It could be a short venture," Sinclair said dubiously, "if one of them bends an ear in the criminal justice system."

"They can't afford to prosecute. When one of the in-crowd gets caught doing a line, they got to sweep it under the carpet to keep the leadership image polished up. The junkie goes in for the cure and that's it. If a dealer laid a notarized confession on them, they'd shred it."

"Is that the voice of experience?"

"I know the dealers. The runners and the back room gophers and the broads in steno. I been keeping them in high class grass for years. But I need precision cutting and custom packaging to break into the white powder market. That takes capital. More than I could put together terrorizing a basement full of refugees bagging sinsemilla in Fun City."

"Who did you connect with in New York to wind up doing your processing under a casino in the Everglades?"

"A shyster named Cohn was shopping the proposition. It was an obvious screw job. The locals could take over as soon as they learned the processing routine. That was fine by me. All they knew about the business was they saw some wasted freak cooking up a crack pipe on *Good Morning America.* I wanted all the distance I could get from that shit. I figured to do one run to make sure I had the process nailed, then pack the equipment and do unto them before they could do unto me."

"What are you hanging around for? After last night, the FBI has you taped."

"The college boys don't know it yet, but they got squat. And tonight's casino skim will give me a little more working capital."

"How much did Figaro pay you for the Mercedes you pulled out of the tunnel?" Sinclair asked.

"Figaro?"

"I saw it in the garage of his funeral home. Unless there are two with the same license number."

Unpleasant thoughts crept into Ricks' eyes. "Three days now I ain't been able to get hold of the guy doing the repaint."

"The legal owners are also trying to repossess it."

"Fuck them. That iron could bring forty large from the right collector."

A trim young waitress arrived with their lunch. Ricks began eating immediately. Sinclair analyzed his thick, dripping sandwich for the least messy point of attack.

"The car isn't an isolated problem, Harvey. It's tied in with the casino and a lot of other things you don't seem to understand any better than I do."

"The local masterminds are the ones who don't understand the casino. They still think a quarter slot is only good for fifty frogs a week. I did a little tinkering the first night I was there. Figured I'd get a look behind the smoking mirrors. See how the big operator from Atlantic City got over. You had every bell set to clear three hundred per."

"Shut down the casino and clean it out this afternoon," Sinclair advised. "That gaming equipment is evidence against both of us. It's not worth one more night's take to give the FBI a crack at it."

"You worried about the law? Or what might happen if I get another chance with Cindy?"

Sinclair stopped the sandwich halfway to his mouth and stared at Ricks' acne-scarred face. "You want to make time with Cindy?"

"You think it's funny? Me and Cindy? That give you a hoot?"

"I'll think it over," Sinclair promised, "when I've heard it from her." He took a bite of his sandwich.

"All the time you were in that hospital, nobody could get close to her. Not even a smooth hunkie like Scott Birmingham. But you're out now, and not doing so hot. Maybe she'll take a second look at the field."

"Maybe she isn't looking for Mr. Right. Not all the girls are these days."

"She didn't stick around the casino for the tips," Ricks insisted. "She could have walked any time."

"Have you talked to her about it?"

"I thought I had a start on it Saturday night, breaking the news to her you were dead. You screwed that up for me, turning up alive."

"You must have sounded her out a little."

Ricks studied Sinclair shrewdly, getting an idea. "Maybe you're getting some on the side? Maybe you're afraid she found out?"

"It's been so long since I've had any I didn't know they'd moved it."

"Fuck you," Ricks said with more resignation than animosity.

"What did the two of you talk about?"

"I didn't have time to schmooze. I had a load coming in."

"Okay, let's talk about that. Whoever set this up must have solid distribution if they're planning to put twenty million dollars a year through the casino basement."

"Those dipshits got a wild hair up their ass. I told Cohn the South Bronx was sewed up. I told him the gang bangers were shining him on for a rip job. All he'd get was a skinful of nine millimeter hardball. Think he listened? Think anybody listened? Typical management. Hire an expert then tell him how to do his job. I just agreed with whatever they said. What did I care? I was history as soon as I set them up in business."

"Who exactly?" Sinclair asked.

"Besides Cohn?"

Ricks drained his glass of milk in a swift gurgle. His eyes were sharp, probing. "I stayed out of the office night before last so Cohn could talk to some judge," he offered in a tantalizing rasp.

"Picaud?"

"Is he the one that's in a sweat to get you clipped?"

"Where did you hear that?"

"What do you take me for?" Ricks demanded. "Some kind of street fighter? All gun and no brains?"

"I don't think you're the loose cannon you pretend to be."

"I let that drop about the slot machine skim so you'd know that I know. I had a hell of a time smurfing two weeks worth of coin back into the economy. You did it for eight months. That means organization. A front company. Bank accounts. A paper trail. If some concerned citizen tips the law how much is involved, they'll trace it eventually. Deal or no deal, you'll walk away with nothing in your pocket but a snotty handkerchief. You feed me to the sharks, I'll make sure they eat you, too."

Ricks dropped a twenty-dollar bill on the table and stood up. He strode out with shifting eyes, like a man fearful of remaining too long in one place.

Sinclair finished his sandwich and signaled for his check.

The hostess brought it. "What's your friend's problem?"

"Drug dealer's paranoia?" Sinclair wondered out loud.

"He looked the part."

"That's what worries me. Nothing is ever what it seems to be."

The woman stared wordlessly.

Sinclair grinned. "Don't try to figure it out. It's all done with smoking mirrors." He paid her, went out to the telephone bank in the lobby and pressed out a number.

"Federal Bureau of Investigation," came a crisp male voice.

"Special Agent Tearoe, please. David Sinclair calling."

A brief pause, then her cool, clipped Radcliffe voice, slightly short of breath. "David, where are you?"

"This minute? I'm at the Belle Biscayne."

"Can you wait for me? I need to talk to you."

"Am I going to be arrested?"

"No," she assured him instantly. "I promise you won't. Can you meet me in the lobby?"

Sinclair agreed in a voice made uneasy by the woman's urgent tone. He sank into the depths of a thickly upholstered armchair in an out-of-the-way corner to wait. Elevators opened and closed. People and conversation drifted.

He grew as wary and watchful as Harvey Ricks.

CHAPTER 20

Sunny Tearoe stepped off an elevator and scanned the lobby. A cocktail dress suggested urgent business had cut short a social engagement. She saw Sinclair rise unsteadily and she came quickly to put a precautionary hand on his sleeve.

"David, hello. How do you feel?"

"Morose, paranoid, distraught. About what you'd expect from a disillusioned veteran brooding over his lost innocence."

A buoyant laugh took the edge off her concern. "At least you feel well enough for golf."

"Just don't ask my score."

"Are you staying at the hotel?"

"I only stopped for lunch."

"My treat."

"I've eaten. Thanks."

"The lounge is more private, anyway." She took his arm and they went down three carpeted stairs and under a bit of decorative neon. "How is your leg?"

"Is that a nice way of asking where my cane got off to?"

"The Dade County Police are very upset about Captain Hewitt," she said in a soft, serious voice that wondered about his experience with them.

Sinclair held a chair for her at a small table tucked away in an intimate corner; in appearance a quiet man stepping out of character in a hopeless attempt to impress an extroverted beauty. A waitress moved in fast, smelling a big tip. Her smile faded when Sinclair asked for a Coke and Sunny wanted diet.

Sinclair sat across from Sunny. "I feel a little like I remember feeling when Cindy gave me the big rush in Atlantic City. That's probably my imagination."

"She gave you the big rush?"

"Atlantic City was full of ticking biological clocks. Any executive with a heartbeat was a tin duck in a shooting gallery. Cindy had a lot of accumulated resistance to overcome and not much time to do it. Sometimes I flatter myself that it wasn't all business."

"Cindy is Lucinda Rivendahl. I've been calling her Lucy, haven't I?"

The waitress arrived and set out two glasses. Sinclair gave her five dollars from the pocket of his sweater vest before Sunny could open her purse.

"This is actually compliments of Harvey Ricks."

"You've spoken to Harvey Ricks?"

"He caught up with me at lunch. We sparred for a few minutes while he hoovered down a sandwich."

Her smile flickered and vanished. "David, tonight's operation is much bigger and more important than you could possibly know. I hope you haven't compromised it?"

"Ricks seems to think he can operate under your noses."

"What did he say? Specifically?"

"He wasn't specific."

"Please, David, this is critical. Did he give any clue to the location of the cocaine he processed Saturday night?"

Sinclair stared at her. "Wilkinson lost a whole planeload of cocaine?"

She shifted uncomfortably. "It was a difficult operation. We couldn't plant transponders because the bales would be broken open at the casino for cutting and repackaging."

"There is only one road out of the casino," Sinclair reminded her.

"A van came out just before dawn. A surveillance team followed it all the way to Queens, in New York. It was locked in a garage, still loaded. Last night a team went in to wire the vehicle and check the evidence. The crates inside contained slot machines."

"Do you think you'll have any better luck taking the payoff envelopes away from Ricks tonight?"

"Harvey Ricks has to win every battle, David. We have to win only one to take him out of circulation."

"Any estimate of casualties?"

"There won't be any trouble," Sunny said. "As long as you haven't warned anyone."

"There may be trouble," Sinclair said, "but it isn't my doing. You people can still prevent it, if you move quickly."

"What do you mean, David?"

"How much do you know about Bastien Figaro?"

"The owner of the casino building?"

"I expect you know he's more than that. If you don't, he's worth investigating on his own. More to the point, he's sending a gang to raid the casino strong room tonight."

"How do you know that?"

"One of the gang is a boy named Henry DesBrisay. He plays on one of the local college football teams. Wilkinson seems to talk that language. Maybe he can head the kid off."

"Arthur was called to Washington yesterday. His plane isn't due until seven thirty this evening. Do you know where we can find Henry DesBrisay?"

Sinclair repeated from memory the street address on the elder DesBrisay's mortgage. "His mother may be there. Or somebody who remembers her. Before you talk to your people, though, there is something else you should know."

"Yes, David?"

"Scott Birmingham has cooked up his own scheme. He and Cindy and I are also supposed to raid the casino tonight."

There was impending laughter behind the disbelief in Sunny's eyes. "You can't be serious."

"Scott is," Sinclair said, and the laughter and disbelief went away.

"David, I have to call in. Will you wait for me here?"—she pushed her chair back and paused to say more urgently—"wait for me."

She was gone the better part of twenty minutes. She came back smiling as tentatively as a novice ballerina who knew she had just blown an audition and sat down with a conscious effort at grace.

"The duty agent was able to connect me with Arthur in Washington."

"Uh-huh?" Sinclair said expectantly.

She ran a forefinger around the rim of her glass. "Scott Birmingham is a sworn officer of the County. The Bureau isn't in a position to interfere with his activities unless he violates Federal law."

Sinclair shrugged to lighten his disappointment. "It's really nothing to worry about. He's allowed us only an hour to make it through a mile of swamp in the dead of night. If we don't get lost, we should arrive about the time you people are loading the gaming equipment onto your trucks."

"David, do you think it's wise to go into the Everglades alone with Scott Birmingham? You're not a hundred percent, physically. And you are a potential witness against him."

"He's liable to come up with something even nuttier if I don't humor him."

"Are you afraid Cindy might be hurt if you don't go along with his plan?"

"She'll be waiting for us in the parking lot. She won't have done anything. Wilkinson won't learn anything hassling her. She just digs in her heels when things don't go her way."

"Arthur isn't the callous bureaucrat you think, David. He is carrying a tremendous load of guilt about the pilot. His career may be in trouble as well. A summons to Washington is quite unusual."

Sinclair said nothing.

"Arthur asked me to interview the DesBrisay boy's mother," Sunny said. "Will you come with me to see her?"

"There's a Grand Jury going to be asked to indict me for murder."

"I really would appreciate your help, David."

Franklin Park lay in the depths of Coconut Grove; close packed bungalows built generations ago on the quarter tips of colored waiters and porters and bellhops; a place of quiet streets where hedges grew faster than penny-wise respectability and creeping arthritis allowed them to be trimmed. A solitary girl in a cotton print dress rode a tricycle along the fissured sidewalk. She stopped and watched with big brown eyes as Sunny and Sinclair got out of a shiny blue Acura coupe. Sunny smiled at her. She turned the tricycle and pedaled away furiously.

"White visitors must be a curiosity here," Sunny said fondly.

"The few they get are probably trouble," Sinclair said.

"Perhaps we'll be in time to prevent trouble."

The house looked as it had in the background of Charles DesBrisay's photographs. The lawn was brown from the intensity of summer and the demands of a mature oak, but the flowers fighting for life under the windows had been tended. A concrete walk buckled by gnarled roots led to a screened porch. Gathering storm clouds made the enclosure dim. Wind had sprung up, picking bits of dry dirt out of the fine wire mesh. Sunny used a small black knocker.

The door opened and a woman in a full front apron looked out at them. Her skin was the color of coffee heavily diluted with cream. She had been beautiful once, before the gray and the brittleness had come to her hair. The dignity that had been part of that beauty remained like the bone structure under decades of worry on her face.

"Yes?" she inquired.

"Mrs. Caroline DesBrisay?" Sunny asked.

"Yes."

"Mrs. DesBrisay, my name is Sonia Tearoe. I'm with the Federal Bureau of Investigation."

The woman inspected Sunny's identification warily. "I'm afraid my husband doesn't live here anymore. He hasn't for many years now. Not since before he was sent to prison."

Sinclair looked into the woman's eyes and spoke with sudden, quiet anger. "You know we haven't come about your husband, don't you, Mrs. DesBrisay?"

A shiver rippled through Caroline DesBrisay, as if she had been stung by a lash. Sunny spoke up quickly and contritely.

"The gentleman with me is Mr. Sinclair. May we come in?"

The woman stepped back, drawing the door inward. Her manner could not have been more gracious if Sunny and Sinclair had been standing on the veranda of a mansion, with an acre of emerald lawn at their backs.

A shallow living room spread the width of the bungalow. The furniture was slip-covered in faded floral patterns. An upright piano dominated one wall. Sheet music ranged neatly across the rack. The walls were crowded with portraits of children at various stages of growth, mingled with faded shadings of black people dressed as no people had dressed for a century. There were more photographs on a small mantle, flanking a wooden crucifix with rosary beads coiled at its feet. Freshets of gladiolus stood in delicate vases. It was all spotless, waiting for the next visit from a dutiful son or daughter.

Caroline DesBrisay closed the door and swept the room with a compulsive glance, to be sure nothing was out of place. "Please sit down. May I offer you some lemonade?"

"That's very kind of you, Mrs. DesBrisay."

Sunny seated herself on a sofa. Sinclair sat a decorous eighteen inches away from her. Caroline DesBrisay left the room. Sunny moved close to Sinclair.

"Please let me handle this, David," she whispered. "I'll cue you in when I need support."

"She's mulatto aristocracy," Sinclair warned under his breath. "We were invited in because courtesy demanded it. If you want anything else, you'll have to use your wits to get it."

Sunny's lips parted in surprise. She composed herself at the sound of footsteps.

Caroline DesBrisay had shed her apron. She wore a paisley dress that was as close to good color for her as she could manage at a sidewalk sale. She served lemonade in tall glasses and perched regally on an aging chair.

"Have you come to tell me Henry is in trouble?" she asked.

Sunny smiled quick reassurance. "We hope to keep your son from getting into trouble, Mrs. DesBrisay, if you will help us."

Unquiet memories haunted the woman's voice. "Henry is the youngest of my children. He was only five when his father went to prison. He lived for the day he could have a father of his own, like the other little boys."

Sinclair tasted his lemonade. "Did Henry know what your husband was convicted of, Mrs. DesBrisay?"

The woman sat wringing her thin hands on her lap, not deigning to betray shame in her face. "I never found the courage to tell Henry his father was in prison for murdering his grandfather. I never knew what terrible influence that might have on him. I always dreaded the time his father would be released."

"Was it a family argument?" Sinclair asked. "Or was there more to it than that?"

"I'm sorry—?"

"Was your father active in Haitian politics, Mrs. DesBrisay?"

"At one time he was a highly respected legislator," the woman said with sad, quiet pride.

"Your husband was a police agent, wasn't he?" Sinclair asked. "He was an agent of the Tonton Macoute. He killed your father on orders from Bastien Figaro. Figaro ordered your father killed because he was an enemy of the regime, and your husband killed him because he was in debt to Figaro. For this house, and probably for a lot of other things families need that an out of work former baseball player wasn't able to provide."

Caroline DesBrisay acknowledged with the barest inclination of her head. Sunny covered her surprise under a pleasant, professional smile.

"Do you know where your son is now, Mrs. DesBrisay?"

"He played a football game in Greensboro this weekend. Mr. Sinclair, you may have seen him on television."

Sinclair shook his head reproachfully. "What did he say when he called you, Mrs. DesBrisay?"

"I beg your pardon?"

"He would have called," Sinclair insisted. "You've trained him in habits like that from birth. He would have called and told you not to worry. You knew from that call that he was going to do something he shouldn't. You are trying to shield him and hoping nothing really serious will come of it all."

The woman's expression was a calm, maternal indulgence. "Did you never do anything you shouldn't when you were a young man of twenty two, Mr. Sinclair?"

"I was a rifle platoon leader in Vietnam when I was twenty two. I was very nearly killed more times than I like to remember."

"Henry isn't in the Army, Mr. Sinclair."

"Bastien Figaro has tricked your son into participating in an armed robbery tonight," Sinclair told the woman.

"Henry wouldn't do such a thing. He doesn't know Doctor Figaro, anyway."

"I believe Henry knows a good deal more than either you or Figaro think he knows. I believe he's going to try to settle a couple of scores tonight. He's had a lifetime of idiot football coaches pumping him full of confidence, and now he thinks he can get the best of Figaro. You know he can't. If Mrs. Tearoe can't find him and stop him, Figaro will kill him."

Caroline DesBrisay stood. It was a reflex action and, when she was on her feet, she had no idea what she should do. Sunny stood quickly and took one of the woman's thin brown hands in both of hers.

"Please, Mrs. DesBrisay, we really are trying to help Henry. I know it must be terribly difficult for you, but please do try to trust us."

The woman withdrew her hand from Sunny's. "I am sorry," she said serenely. "I really don't know where Henry is. I'm afraid I won't be able to help you."

Sinclair stood and addressed her with a hard patience that offered no quarter to any illusions she might harbor. "Mrs. DesBrisay, my mother raised me the way you raised Henry. I know the thinking that goes on between you as well as I know my own. Hell, it is my own. When I was young, I confided in my mother. She used every confidence to try to manipulate me to measure up to some grand expectations she had, living on faith in the face of all reality that her dreams would come to pass. They never did. What happened was that I told her less and less to protect what little independence I had. We don't talk anymore, except in formal, meaningless ways. The way you and Henry talk now. He told you enough to signal that he was in trouble, because he wanted help, but not enough for you to do anything on your own because he was afraid you would smother him. I want you to think about what might happen to him if you don't face up to reality. When you've thought about it long enough, call Mrs. Tearoe. She can help."

Sunny smiled hopefully and put her business card in the woman's hand. "Please call any time, Mrs. DesBrisay. The office can put you through to me immediately."

Caroline DesBrisay saw them out and closed the door softly. The wind made rustling noises in a nearby screen of holly. Sunny stopped Sinclair on the porch.

"I don't know when I've seen anything so tactless," she said angrily. "That poor woman was nearly out of her mind with worry."

"What do you want to do?" Sinclair shot back. "Kill her son to spare her feelings?"

Sunny turned on her heel and stepped off the porch. Her flimsy summer outfit flattened on one side of her body and whipped away from the other like loose sails in a hurricane.

They walked to the car without speaking.

Sunny used a driveway to turn around and set off along the winding streets. "David, you were very blunt about telling Mrs. DesBrisay to be realistic about her situation. How realistic are you being about yours?"

"I'd like to have my attorney involved in that discussion."

She turned onto a boulevard. "I hope you know what you are doing."

CHAPTER 21

Gathering overcast shut off the last gossamer falls of sunlight. Fat drops of rain splattered against the windshield. Rising wind churned Biscayne Bay into a sea of white caps. Tall palms flanking the boulevard flexed and shivered. A piece of vegetation scooted across the asphalt and startled Sunny back from her thoughts.

"David, I have to stop for a change of clothes. I hope you don't mind."

"You can drop me at the next bus stop."

"No, listen, you went out of your way to help me. The least I can do is drive you home. It won't take me ten minutes."

It took that long to reach the first cluster of shorefront high rise apartments. Sunny braked down an asphalt ramp and used a magnetic security card to roll up the steel entry grille of a concrete parking labyrinth. An elevator lifted them noiselessly to a chromium-accented hallway.

Sunny let them into an apartment and excused herself to step into a powder blue bedroom, leaving him staring at a matrix of glass shelving full of fussy feminine knick knacks. An eight by ten wedding portrait stood alone on one shelf, framed in heavy white bond. The groom was handsome and square-jawed, with the general look of a man accustomed to winning. Sunny was radiant and demure for the occasion.

"Phil is really a sweet guy," she said, coming out with a hanger of clothing in cleaner's bag. "He just thinks if he doesn't look aggressive, people will take advantage of him. A little like you, David. I think you're basically a decent guy who got in over his head."

She took the clothing into a bathroom. The door didn't quite close behind her. A mirror hung beyond the sliver opening. Sinclair could see her reflection as she began to undress. He went to a window and stared out moodily. Model automobiles, perfect in every detail, made shifting patterns on the darkening street far below.

"I remember my first night ambush patrol," he said. "We worked our way through pitch black jungle for three hours and set up along a trail. Rain was coming down in sheets. All I could do was lie there and wait, miserable and scared, thinking about things that could go wrong if a North Vietnamese unit actually showed up. Nobody would be able to hear orders over the gunfire. Muzzle flashes would leave us all night blind. If anyone forgot the evacuation sequence or got turned around, we could easily be separated. I might have to decide whether to abandon people or risk the rest of the platoon searching a jungle crawling with enemy troops. That was the last time I ever felt like I was in over my head."

"David, do you have time for a cup of coffee?"

Sunny had replaced the cocktail outfit with an oriental lounging robe. The robe was silk, and clung wherever there was movement. She led him into the kitchen and turned on the flash heater of a counter top brewer.

"You're not at all what you seem to be, are you, David?"

"What do I seem to be?"

"You're not the troubled veteran your FBI file suggests. You're not a cold-blooded gambler. You're certainly not the hardened killer the County Police would like to believe."

"That pretty well exhausts the clichés," Sinclair said. "And I gave up coffee ten years ago."

She made chocolate instead, led him down two carpeted steps to a sunken living room, put the mugs on a glass-topped chromium table and sat on a sofa. Sinclair sat down and she scooted close to him. Rain fell steadily out on the balcony. Harder rain made a dark, turbulent front advancing across Biscayne Bay. Sunny shivered and put a shoulder against Sinclair.

"Tonight's weather is going to be horrid," she said. A minute passed in silence. Then another. "You aren't really going with Scott Birmingham, are you?" she finally asked.

Sinclair put an arm behind her on the back of the sofa. "Scott is like you in some ways. He wants to believe he has people persuaded to his way of thinking. Pandering to his fantasies is one way to handle him."

"Was the casino your fantasy, David…a sort of romantic adventure?"

"Running a gambling trap is about as romantic as a nosebleed. When the help isn't bitching, the losers are whining. Protection is expensive, the equipment is cranky and cash control is a nightmare."

"Was it the money?"

"At this point, I couldn't begin to estimate how much I made. Which is a hell of an admission for a four-eyed bookkeeper."

"I'm just trying to understand, David."

"Twenty years of hard work had just ended in a twenty minute meeting. Management said they were downsizing and put a severance agreement in front of me. It was a real body blow. The casino was an opportunity to get back on my feet."

"Opportunity is a big word, David. Weren't there other channels you could have taken?" Her voice was a caressing lilt riding a subtle drift of gardenia.

"Does your husband ever come home in the middle of these coffee and confession sessions?"

"Phil is batching in Pittsburgh while I'm on special assignment in Miami. He's managed to come down for a couple of weekends, but new law practices need a lot of babying."

"And at noon he plays handball at the athletic club when he could have met you for lunch?"

Sunny's eyes were steady under his scrutiny, but her cheeks flushed. "That's rather personal, don't you think, David?"

"To an outside observer, you could have done better than Phil, and I could have done better than what I'm doing. But outside observers don't matter. All that counts is what the people involved think and feel."

Their eyes locked, poised between tentative stirring and faltering inhibition. Sinclair kissed her lips, a fleeting, experimental touch. She did not respond, nor did she draw back. He kissed her again, more warmly. She tried to withdraw. His arms were around her. She parted her lips to protest. Before she could find words, Sinclair kissed her hotly and deeply. Her hands went to his face, but stopped short of pushing him away. He released the silken belt from her waist. His hand moved inside the robe. The cocktail dress wasn't the only thing she had taken off.

Rain came in wind driven torrents, eddying on the windows of the Acura and threatening to overwhelm the wipers. Sunny drove fast on deserted streets surfaced by an inch of pockmarked water. Brooding silence burst like a dam, and words gushed from her.

"David, I was desperate to have your help. Desperate for a way to reach you. I was thinking on the spur of the moment and not thinking very well, and I hope you won't take that personally."

"I was at least half the mistake," he confessed.

"Sexual manipulation is not my game. I don't know why I thought I could beat Cindy at it."

"Cindy isn't some police stereotype."

Sunny opened her mouth to say something emphatic, but closed it without speaking. She brought the Acura to a stop where the driveway pierced the sodden, wind-lashed hedge in front of Sinclair's home.

"I don't want to see either of you at the casino tonight."

Sinclair collected his case and made a dash for the house. When he reached the shelter of the porch, he looked back. The Acura was already gone.

Cindy was waiting in the entry. The velvet lyric of Ivory Joe Hunter's *Since I Met You Baby* drifted from the depths of the house and mingled with the fragrance of her Jasmine. Fashionable slacks and a clinging pullover in complimentary shades of blue set off her cobalt eyes. She took his wet hands in hers and kissed him warmly.

"Whose car was that?"

"Sunny Tearoe's," he said, quickly adding, "The FBI agent assigned to my case." He took half a step back, in case the damp smell of his woolen golf wear hadn't completely smothered the residue of Gardenia, and gave her an admiring look. "Is that a new outfit? It's a great combination on you."

"Thanks." Cindy flushed under her tan. "What did she want?"

"To get me back on the straight and narrow."

"Is that what you want?" She dropped his hands and searched his eyes.

"There is no more straight and narrow. The days of forty years and a pension are gone. You live by your wits now, or not at all."

Warmth returned to her smile. "Why don't you get changed? I'll start dinner."

Sinclair inspected his clothing with guilty obsession before he put it in the laundry hamper. He showered with volumes of scented lather to cover any trace of his sins. Cindy was fussing over the Jenn-aire when he came downstairs. A bottle of champagne stood on the counter. He raided a cupboard and found traces of tarnish on the silver ice bucket.

"It looks like we owe ourselves a couple of back installments of the good life," he remarked idly.

"We can make a payment tonight."

Had Cindy been looking at him, she would have seen panic. He polished and filled the ice bucket and carried it into the dining room. Fluted wall sconces spread a soft glow over white linen and elaborate service.

Cindy shuttled hot dishes from the kitchen. "Look how dark it is. It isn't even five o-clock yet."

Wind rattled the windows and put a white chop on the broad canal. Rain came in angry waves, clawing at the house.

"Another summer going out with a vengeance," Sinclair said. "Time to climb back into reality."

"Is that all we are, David? Slaves to the calendar?"

"Calendars measure time, and when time runs out, there isn't anything else. The older you get, the more aware of that you become. And the more you're willing to risk to make something of what you've got left."

He lit a pair of serpentine candles. They sat across from each other. Sinclair raised his glass in a wordless toast.

Cindy's reply was a soft, sincere, "True love." Reflected candlelight flickered like remorse in the curve of her glass when she drank. "It's been a good eight months, David. I think we've both grown a lot."

"That sounds too much like goodbye."

"Have you thought seriously about what you're going to do after tonight?" she asked.

"I'd like to improve my standing with you. Even if I have to keep my mouth shut and let you study."

Cindy put her silver down and spoke softly and rapidly. "David, I don't want you to doubt my feelings for you. I didn't know how strong they'd gotten myself. The time you were in the hospital and I didn't know if you'd be all right was the worst I ever spent. Can we just leave it at that?"

"I've always taken our relationship for the potential I saw in it. The future is a lot more important to me than the past."

Her eyes were a frantic plea. "David, can we just let it drop? Can we, please? At least for the couple of hours we have together tonight?"

They finished dinner with pleasant small talk. The chimes of an art deco clock announced it was five-thirty. A motor yacht straggled up the canal with the deck canvas in place and lights in the cabin ports. That was all the only life outside. The rest of the world was distant and small.

Sinclair blew out the candles. Tiny curls of smoke rose in the subdued glow of the sconces. Hand in hand he and Cindy went upstairs.

They began as tentatively as strangers, kissing lightly and touching experimentally, full of banter. Sinclair heated suddenly and unexpectedly, kissing her neck and mouth, exploring her freely, without heed to her struggles. She resisted only briefly. Then she was content to move his hands where she wanted them. Finally she just held him, caressing the back of his neck and cooing into his ear until her throat contracted in a spasm of shuddering gasps.

It was not quite seven when Cindy came back into the bedroom zipped into knee boots and buttoned into a black raincoat with puffy, pleated shoulders. She sat on the side of the bed.

"Will you be all right tonight, David?"

"If anything goes wrong, you look out for yourself," he said with slow, serious emphasis. "Don't worry about anything or anyone else."

She touched his cheek and kissed him a quick goodbye. "Be safe tonight, David."

She got as far as the door before she turned and rushed back. "David, it didn't work and it can't work, but you are the guy I knew I'd never find."

She kissed him again and went out.

Her footsteps were quick noises on the staircase. Rain beat hard against the house. Presently the garage door opener whirred, and then her BMW snarled softly away.

"Sucker," he told himself passionately. He set an alarm clock on the nightstand and turned out the light.

The strident, tinny bell woke him at eight thirty. Rising with the tortured slowness of sore muscles, he took another shower and put on military fatigue trousers. He went downstairs, loaded the dishwasher and put a compact disc on the stereo. The banshee scream of bagpipes swelled through the house with the relentless cadence of an army advancing out of the cold mists of dawn, as hard as highland steel and as demanding as the code of the old clans.

On the carpet in his office Sinclair laid out heavy socks, hiking boots, an oversized woolen shirt, a dark blue stocking cap, black gloves, a lensatic compass and two field medical dressings. The package he had claimed the previous day contained an armored vest and a field jacket packed with a set of Kevlar plates. Printed instructions directed him to slide the plates into pockets inside the jacket to make a bullet resistant outer garment. When that was done, he telephoned for a taxi. He laced the boots, tucking the fatigue trousers deep, and put on the armored vest. From the safe he retrieved the Luger he had taken from Figaro's desk. He pushed the streamlined pistol nose down into the armhole of the vest and buttoned the shirt over that. He used an extra bootlace to tie the compass around his neck, and tucked it inside the shirt. The reinforced lines of the jacket camouflaged the bulk beneath. The outfit left him looking like a character from *Mad* magazine; a thin, serious face grafted over a muscle bound body.

Bagpipes were swelling to a chilling crescendo when the taxi honked in the drive. He turned off the stereo, buttoned the medical dressings, a padded spectacles case, money clip and a spare bootlace into various pockets, put on the hat and gloves, turned off the lights and went out.

He carried neither personal items nor identification.

CHAPTER 22

Wind-driven rain machine-gunned the boulevard and overwhelmed the storm drains. Sinclair herded the old Mercedes to the curb. A condominium tower rose into the night and disappeared in a swirl of low-hanging black clouds. He fought the drenching gale to a glass door and yelled his name and destination into an intercom.

A geriatric heavyweight in a double-breasted lavender uniform came gingerly in thick-soled shoes to admit him. Indirect light and sourceless creaking gave the lobby the atmosphere of a carnival scare. Wind howled in the elevator shaft. The rising car shuddered on its rails. The upper hall held filigreed doors set into flocked pastel walls. Sinclair pressed a lighted pearl button and waited.

A woman opened the door to the limit of its chain. She peered out with dictatorial blue eyes set in a face etched by decades of determination.

"Are you David Sinclair?"

"Yes, Mrs. Birmingham. Is Scott here?"

She released the chain and stepped out into the foyer. "Has my son spoken to you about what you are doing to poor Opal Lloyd?" she asked in a razor-edged voice that would not be audible inside the unit.

"Is Scott here, Mrs. Birmingham?"

Scott Birmingham spoke from beyond the door; the quick, edgy tone of a mind busy elsewhere. "Let him in, Mother, will you please? I'll be out in just a minute."

The woman did as she was asked, placing herself protectively between Sinclair and the noise of children playing somewhere in the unit.

"You know, Scott was very fortunate," she confided importantly. "He was able to begin his law career as a clerk to a judge. Only the top attorneys from the best families are chosen."

A sudden thought creased Sinclair's forehead. "Especially with a jurist of Judge Picaud's standing."

"It might interest you to know that Judge Picaud and Opal were once very close. There was a lot of talk about them before she met and married Crofton Lloyd."

"Yes, Ma'am, that interests me greatly." Sinclair waited for her to elaborate.

Hesitation gripped the woman. It wasn't clear whether she had exhausted her knowledge of the subject, or simply realized that even second-hand information would date her. After a moment's confusion, triumph filled her face.

"Perhaps you should just think about that."

"Yes, Ma'am. I've already started."

Scott Birmingham came into the entry wearing a sport coat over an open collar dress shirt. He was *Vogue* magazine's idea of how the properly domesticated, upwardly mobile husband would dress himself.

"I may be quite late, Nicki," he was telling a slim, attractive woman. "It really would be better if you and the kids stayed over with mother. This storm looks pretty bad."

Birmingham's mother spoke up immediately. "Oh, yes, Nicki. It's much too nasty out for you to drive. You and the children are always welcome." She emphasized the word 'children'.

Nicki Birmingham smiled graciously. She and her husband kissed good-bye. As a show of mutual affection it was nicely timed and executed. He pulled a capacious lawyer's case out of a closet, kissed his mother's cheek and nodded crisply to Sinclair.

They took the elevator down and the doorman let them out into the storm. Birmingham held the lapels of his sport coat together and trailed Sinclair out to the Mercedes. Sinclair got behind the wheel. He took a minute to wipe his glasses before he reached across and unlocked the passenger door. Birmingham closed himself in while Sinclair started the engine. He set his case on the floor between his feet and squirmed without getting comfortable.

"You stole this from the airport parking lot?" he asked skeptically.

"Don't be ridiculous."

Sinclair pulled out onto the boulevard. Headlights came at them out of the rain. Droplets of water glistened on Birmingham's face like cold dew on an iron statue.

"Didn't you hear what I told you this morning?"

"I'm a bookkeeper, not a car thief. I have to take them where I can get them."

"Where did you get this?"

"I stole it from Bastien Figaro. As I understand, Harvey Ricks hauled it out of the tunnel under the casino without benefit of title and Figaro filched it from him." Passing lights made Sinclair's eyes sparkle with malice. "If you want a stolen car, they don't come much more stolen than this."

"Goddamnit, David, what's wrong with you? We don't want to connect Figaro with tonight's business."

"Why not?"

"Forget it," Birmingham snapped. "The schedule is too tight to do anything about it now."

"You had that schedule pretty well fixed in your mind this morning," Sinclair recalled. "Exactly how long have you been planning this little venture?"

"What's the difference?"

"You left Cindy with the impression that raiding the casino was necessary because I shot Hewitt."

"Cindy really got under your skin, didn't she, David?"

"I don't like you putting her in a narrow place just so you can short change the local power structure."

"Me, short change them?" Birmingham's laugh was brief and sarcastic. "You don't know the first Goddamn thing about it."

Sinclair accelerated up a ramp and merged onto the East-West Expressway. "Your mother was telling me something about Judge Picaud and Opal Lloyd. Is that where you got that nonsense about my having to turn the building back to her grandson?"

Birmingham opened the case and dragged out a waterproof hiking boot. He shook one foot out of a stylish loafer and began to wrestle the boot on.

"I was maybe six years old when my mother first started spoon feeding me her ludicrous version of growing up and being a man. She hasn't let up since. All the advantages I had. All my potential. How my family were all expecting great things of me. How she and my father had worked all their lives to give me the chance to prove myself to the influential men in Miami. How they just knew I would be a wonderful success."

"Why fight it?" Sinclair asked. "You'd have gotten your turn at the top. It's practically automatic."

"Remember last spring when I took Nicki to Micronesia? I thought it would be a chance for us to find something that had slipped away. Sort of a second chance to fall in love. To her it was the big chance to get me alone and work on me. I don't think she missed anything. Did I really think I was living up to my career potential? The girl she sponsored into her sorority had just bought a new house. Couldn't I work to improve my relationship with the kids? Other fathers spent more time at home. When was I going to shoulder my share of the family responsibilities so she would be able to have a career of her own? Why didn't we get away together more often? What had happened to our lovemaking? Why wasn't I spontaneous, like I was in school? Didn't I want to discuss it with her? Weren't we partners in life? She loved me and wanted to help me. Two stone solid weeks of it. Ten thousand miles from home, watching my marriage dissolve in front of my eyes. The funny thing is, I don't think Nicki has a clue it's over."

"You're not the first man who has found himself in an impossible domestic situation," Sinclair said. "Why not just walk away from it?"

"Walk away to what? Nicki would cream me in a dissolution. House, alimony, sliding scale child support. I wouldn't see daylight for ten years."

"The court wouldn't know about your graft from the casino. Or any of the other little things you've probably got going under the table."

Birmingham finished lacing the second boot. "I get just enough to keep up appearances. When I ask for more, I get a lot of crap about how great things will be if I'm just patient. Then for the next week, nothing I do is good enough."

"So why suck Cindy and me in? Why not just use your clout at the casino to grab the money and run?"

Birmingham ignored the question. He fished a holster from his case and withdrew a .22 Browning automatic. A long barrel suited it more to sport shooting than concealment. Birmingham needed two tries to work out the magazine. Sinclair watched him fumble with slender, shiny cartridges.

"Have you ever shot that thing? Even for target practice?"

"It's a small room, David. And Harvey Ricks' gun is a .22. He'll get official credit for any shooting."

"Ricks' automatic is a Colt. The rifling, firing pin and extractor will all have different signature marks."

"This isn't *Your FBI In Peace And War*. Dade County homicide is swamped. If any ballistic evidence doesn't fit, it doesn't get written up. The important thing is to get the case disposition signed off."

Birmingham pushed the magazine home, snapped a round into the chamber and slid the pistol into the holster. He fitted the holster onto his belt under the sport coat, dragged a camouflage parka from the case and wrestled his way into it.

Sinclair turned off the expressway and the Everglades swallowed them. Meeting another car became a notable event. Oncoming lights began as a shimmer in fields of sawgrass hunkered down in the wind, spreading a gradually widening aura then exploding into a flash of high beams against the rain soaked windshield. Red taillights receded into pinpricks in the mirror, and the darkness grew deeper and emptier.

A slit appeared in the vegetation ahead and widened to an irregular gap as they drew near. Sinclair used the brakes. Tires slithered in a sharp turn. Wind harried vegetation hemmed in the secondary road on both sides, groping in the headlight beams like the tentacles of something alive and hungry.

"Watch for a *No Trespassing* sign," Birmingham instructed. "Red reflective letters on a white background."

"When did you put that up?"

"Harvey Ricks marked the old road. He used it to move the processed goods out of the basement Saturday night."

"Then he knows the road is passable."

Birmingham checked his wristwatch. "Eleven o'clock. We'll have to push to keep the schedule. How is your leg, David?"

"I've been on it since six this morning."

"Well, you'll just have to keep up." Birmingham fished a flashlight out of his case. A brief test projected an intense red circle on the dashboard. "What kind of gun are you carrying."

"I'll have a .22, as soon as you wise up and give me the pistol."

"I know what I'm doing, David. Remember, this whole idea was mine."

"It'll be the first thing out of my mouth if Harvey Ricks shows me the business end of an assault rifle."

A glint of reflected red appeared against a white rectangle in the periphery of the headlight beams and grew into block capitals. Sinclair brought the car to a stop under the sign. He killed the lights and motor. Darkness and the storm closed in around them, full of sudden nightmares.

CHAPTER 23

Birmingham pushed out into the gale, dragging his case behind him. Sinclair palmed the keys out of the ignition, tucked them swiftly above the visor. He folded his glasses away into their padded case, buttoned that into a shirt pocket and got out. Somewhere in the blackness of the swamp a tree limb fell in a prolonged series of rustling crashes. Sinclair caught Birmingham by the arm as he came around the car.

"Are you sure you can find your way?" he yelled into the lawyer's ear.

"Come on!"

Birmingham pulled free and plunged ahead. There was sound footing going down a brief slope then they were splashing ankle deep with mud sucking at their boots. Birmingham swept the red beam of the flash in a high arc. He caught the colorless glint red light would make on a red reflector.

"This way!" he yelled, and went down almost immediately in a rustle of undergrowth. Cursing savagely, he struggled to his feet.

Sinclair grabbed the hood of the lawyer's parka. "You can't fight a swamp! You've got to pick your way carefully!"

"I'm all right," Birmingham insisted. "I'll be all right."

He got the flashlight turned right way around and located the marker again. Using his case to break trail, he pushed ahead more cautiously. When they stood beneath the reflector, Birmingham swung his light until he located the glint of the next marker then set off, repeating the process again and again. Sinclair was content to follow, letting Birmingham tire himself making way and finding footing for both of them. They followed the reflections deeper into the swamp, like boys chasing a will-o-the-wisp.

Sinclair squinted at his compass periodically. The unvarying position of the luminous needle showed the trail of reflectors was taking them in a straight line. The ground underfoot was slimy and treacherous, but water was never more than knee deep. Vegetation grew thick, often reaching above their heads. Wait-a-minute vines snatched at their legs. Thorns clawed at the exposed skin of their faces. Strenuous minutes passed. Sinclair's breathing became labored, his steps mechanical.

Sinclair counted each pace, forming numbers from one to one hundred on his lips, starting over at one while he made another knot in the spare bootlace he carried. He counted eight knots in the lace when the first glimmer of light shone high up in the trees far ahead. The glimmer vanished as soon as it appeared.

"Headlights!" Birmingham yelled over his shoulder. "That's the casino parking lot." His voice held more relief than triumph.

"That light was half a mile off," Sinclair yelled back.

Birmingham read his wristwatch in the red beam of his flash. "Eleven thirty. We can still make it in time."

He pushed ahead, and Sinclair resumed his pace count. There were eleven knots in the bootlace when the distant slam of a car door came on the high wind that blew against their backs. Birmingham stopped short, and Sinclair bumped him from behind.

"What was that?" the lawyer gasped.

"Someone found the Mercedes."

"Dade County doesn't patrol that road. I'd know if they did."

"Like you knew they were investigating us?"

"It's not Harvey Ricks, either. He's moved the processing plant. His mules wouldn't be on the road tonight."

"It's the FBI, Scott. Tonight is their last chance to raid the casino before Ricks remodels and their intelligence has to start over from zero."

"We'll have to move fast."

Sinclair grabbed a handful of the lawyer's parka. "Forget it, Scott. The FBI will close in from all sides. The money won't help us in Federal prison. Our best bet is to lie low out here until the raid is over."

The wind brought a voice; three syllables of profane filth in the keening bass peculiar to the Caribbean.

"That was no Federal Agent," Birmingham said.

"Tonight is also the last chance for anyone with the same plans you have."

"We're half an hour ahead of whoever it is. We can do the job and get out before they reach the casino."

"If they're quicker than you think, you and Cindy and I could be caught in the middle of a shooting match. Ricks' people won't sit still if a stick-up gang puts in an appearance."

"If we don't get there first, Cindy will still be in the parking lot when they show."

Wind and rain lashed the surrounding growth, as insistent and undeniable as the truth of Birmingham's words. Sinclair released his parka.

Birmingham turned and attacked the brush with renewed fury. Sinclair had to abandon his pace count to keep up. Without warning, the sky blazed in a flash of sheet lightning. For an instant the old house made a stark outline looming on the heights ahead of them. In another few minutes they were leaning against the base of a steep embankment, fighting for breath. As soon as Birmingham could move, he tugged at Sinclair's arm. The lawyer's words were lost in the wind, leaving only the frenzied tone of his voice. Sinclair pried himself away from the embankment.

Leaves dangled on broken stems in the red beam of Birmingham's flashlight, marking a path beaten through the thorny undergrowth. The path took them into the eerie stillness of the tunnel. Spindly plants grew out of the dirt floor. Tendrils of foliage grew up ghastly in the red light and rank air. Rodents scurried on whispering feet. Sinclair found a support pillar to grasp.

Birmingham probed ahead. "Damnit, David, come on! We don't have time to dawdle."

The upward slope of the floor made the going difficult. Sinclair struggled from pillar to pillar. New supports had been pushed in beside rotting ones. Red light flooded across a vacant rectangle of ground where the Mercedes had stood. The shaft ended abruptly at a plywood wall that smelled as fresh as a lumber yard. Birmingham pushed his flashlight at Sinclair.

"Hold this. Give me some light to work by."

The lawyer opened his case and pulled out a foot-long ripping chisel. He jammed the blade between abutting sheets of plywood and put his strength against it. The wood bowed and splintered, but the nails held fast. Birmingham relented, breathing hard.

"At the rate we're going," Sinclair observed, "we'll still be in the strong room when the gang behind us gets here. We'd better just get Cindy out and forget this silly robbery."

"You don't seriously think she'd leave without the money?" Birmingham jammed the blade of the ripping chisel into the small opening he had made. "Put your back against something so you can get some leg pressure to help me."

Sinclair braced his back against a support pillar. He put his good leg up and set the sole of his boot against the chisel. Birmingham counted and they heaved together. Nails let go with tortured screams. Plywood gave way with a splintering crack. The chisel slipped and the wood returned broken to leave a gap of inches.

The following silence was as fragile as thousand year old china. It cracked to dust at the sound of a male voice from somewhere outside the tunnel entrance.

"No wind ever made a noise like that. I don't care how spooky it is out here."

"Better get Wilkinson on the UHF," a second man said. "Tell him we have one group inside."

"Me call him, huh? Thanks a lot."

"Well, Christ, it's not our fault. This storm has visibility down to ten feet. If we can't see them, we can't stop them."

Sinclair killed the light. "That really is the FBI, Scott. The party is over."

"It's over when I say it's over. Remember who has the gun."

"You're in a trap, Scott."

"So is Cindy."

Sinclair wormed past the broken plywood into the dirt-floored basement under the old house. Moving headlights splashed through a slit of filthy window up near the ceiling, crawling among a forest of support pillars and casting long shadows over sturdily built tables set in the crowded geometric flow of an assembly line. Patterns of bolt holes in the table tops showed where machinery had been fastened. The lights reached the base of a plank stairway, and then swept away. A steady hum of voices filled the following darkness. Supporting joists overhead creaked under the weight of milling feet. Sinclair rose cautiously. His breathing had stabilized. He opened his armored jacket enough to fish out his glasses.

Birmingham pushed his case through from the tunnel. A nail caught his parka as he crawled after it. The noise of rubber backed cloth tearing seemed to go on forever.

"Damn!" he whispered violently as he got to his feet. "Where's that light?"

"We've already attracted enough attention. I can find my way in the dark, if you can't."

"All right. Come on."

Birmingham felt his way through the blackness to the plank stairs. Ancient wood groaned at his first step. He hesitated briefly then continued upward, placing his feet experimentally at the supported edge of each tread before he committed his full weight. Sinclair followed with the silence that only habitually unobtrusive men can manage, using a makeshift railing for support. They came to a landing where the harsh aftertaste of marijuana smoke lingered. Light and voices leaked around a door that had warped in its frame. The conversation had the careless brutality of coarse men keyed up and killing time, the bored, edgy slang of casual poker.

Birmingham led the way along the narrow service passage between the inner and outer walls of the old house. Streamers of cold wind penetrated the warped siding and brought a musical hum from the taut cables of the dumbwaiter. The tense, quiet atmosphere of the dice room on the other side of the lath and plaster demise permeated the claustrophobic space, as if the games were being played a foot away in the dimness.

They climbed to the second floor. Neither light nor sound came from the other side of the hall door. Birmingham took the flash from Sinclair and snapped on the red beam. Another narrow passage took them to yet another flight of stairs. A door lay horizontally in the ceiling. Birmingham pivoted the door into the attic above. The rafters overhead were steep where the stairs ended, barely high enough for Birmingham to climb up and stand.

"Step on the joists," he warned quietly. "This old plaster will barely support its own weight."

Sinclair came up painfully on his sore leg and found a precarious balance in the darkness. Waves of rain passed in drumbeats across the roof. Wind forced its way through the ventilator baffles, like the wailing of distant mourners. Sinclair shivered.

An electric blue spark singed the air, a sharp prelude to the hum of a small motor/generator unit. Light shot up through two slots in the ceiling, shimmering on the cables that moved there.

"Dumbwaiter drive," Birmingham whispered. "That should keep the man in the strongroom busy for a few minutes."

He moved from joist to joist with the dexterity of an ape. Stopping astride the humming motor/generator with his feet spread between two joists, he stood to full height. He pocketed the flashlight and found enough room to lift the case above his head. His whole body went into the motion that hurled it straight downward.

The case went through the old plaster with no more noise than a Graham cracker breaking. It hit something solid below, and brought a startled burst of adenoidal profanity. Light gushed up into the attic with the brilliance of a nuclear flash. Birmingham dragged the automatic out of his clothing and dropped feet first into a rising mushroom cloud of white dust.

Sinclair moved to a crouch on the joist beside the hole. He could make out a coin counting machine with canvas bags dangling over the edge of a heavy table. Stacks of currency had been scattered by the impact of Birmingham's case. The case itself lay a foot from the deep gouge it had made. Birmingham's boots had left tracks of damp mud. Plaster dust was beginning to settle on everything.

Sinclair worked the Luger out of the armhole of his bullet resistant vest and zipped his armored jacket to the neck. He vaulted sideways and let himself drop to the table. Taking the impact on his good leg, he caught the coin counting machine with his free hand to secure his balance. From his crouch on the table he dropped immediately to a standing position on the floor, with his back to the nearest wall.

Birmingham and the man named Mal stood one on either side of the open dumbwaiter access. They faced Sinclair across the table. Birmingham pointed his pistol at Sinclair's chest.

"Stand very still, David. Put your gun on the table."

CHAPTER 24

The room had once been part of a suite. Pocket doors had been permanently secured with iron straps and the windows boarded shut to make a claustrophobic space barely large enough for the table that separated Sinclair from Birmingham and Mal. The assault rifle Mal had carried into Ricks' office two nights previous was nowhere in sight. A single chair faced a laptop computer open on the table. The rumpled suit coat draped over the back could not have concealed more than a handgun. Sinclair held his Luger at his side, pointed at the floor, and cleared his throat of plaster dust.

"There are Federal Agents in the crowd downstairs, Scott. Any gunshots, even a .22, will bring them up here fast."

Birmingham glanced at the securely bolted hall access door. "I'll have time to climb out the ceiling with the money. Disappear into the crowd. Wait my chance to leave."

"No, Scott. I made sure the FBI knew we were coming. Do you really suppose it was an accident they let us pass their perimeter?"

"I told you to put your gun on the table, David."

Sinclair addressed a plastic intercom box. "Harvey, this is David Sinclair. The FBI is not your only problem. Bastien Figaro has sent a gang to raid the casino. They are no more than ten minutes behind Scott and me. You need to do two things, and you need to do them quickly. First, tell your man in here to start packing the money to travel. Second, wake those goons in the kitchen and tell them to get ready for trouble."

A small click preceded the rasp of Ricks' voice. "Birmingham, Figaro's gang, true or false?"

"David doesn't know who was out there any more than I do."

Ricks was not impressed. "Pack the computer first, Mal. Then start with the big bills and work your way down."

Mal fidgeted and glanced at the intercom, as if Ricks could see him through it. "Things are getting out of hand, Harvey. I think it's time for me to eighty-six myself out of this play. I'll just get my coat and mingle with the crowd downstairs."

"Pack the cash," Ricks ordered. "Do it in two minutes."

Mal snatched Birmingham's case and dumped the contents. He closed the laptop, put it inside and pushed currency in after it. Birmingham kept his automatic pointed at Sinclair's chest while he groped his shoes and the ripping chisel off the floor. He set them on the table and held out his free hand.

"All right, David, give me the gun."

"It's over, Scott. Get a clue, will you?"

Ricks' voice came again, cool and derisive. "Sinclair ain't here for conversation, Hunkie. He's your job. Do it."

Birmingham's eyes grew desperate, his breathing shallow. Beads of sweat appeared on his face and began to run, leaving tracks in the white dust that had settled there. His jaw tightened and his hand clenched. The report of his .22 was sharp rather than loud. The impact of the bullet against Sinclair's chest armor was audible. It had no more effect than a pebble. Birmingham's face went stupid with disbelief.

Sinclair snapped the Luger up level. An ear-punishing crack reverberated off the walls. There was a tug on the sleeve of Birmingham's parka. His gun slithered from his fingers and landed on a cushion of money. Sinclair retrieved it.

The intercom came to life. "What's going on in there, Mal? That was no .22"

"Nine millimeter, if it matters. Sinclair is holding both guns. Pretty boy is taking a standing eight count."

Birmingham touched his arm. The fingers of his glove came away red and slippery with blood. "I'll kill you for this, David," he said in the tight, passionate timbre of a high school tough; a startling contrast to his normally polished speech.

"You were going to do that anyway," Sinclair pointed out. "What was the plan, Scott? Were Mal and I supposed to be found looking like we killed each other?"

Mal shot a venomous glance at the lawyer while he transferred fistfuls of currency from the cash box.

Sinclair stowed the Luger in the armpit of his hardened vest. "Our entrance was a little too convenient, you know. The reflectors, the right tool, the empty passage. Just enough effort to leave me scratched and dirty, so there wouldn't be any question how I got in when I turned up dead."

Birmingham worked a handkerchief out of his pocket to try to stanch the flow of blood from his arm.

Sinclair reached across the table and nudged him with the muzzle of the .22. "Who wants me dead, Scott? It isn't Ricks. He had to be in on the game, of course, but he doesn't care whether I live or die. Who is pulling the strings?"

Birmingham repeated his threat.

"Not just now, Scott. Slip the bolts on that door. And remember, Ricks can cover the hallway from his office."

Exertion reduced Mal's voice to an adenoidal wheeze. "You getting an earful of this, Harvey?"

The intercom was silent.

"You there, Harvey?"

The only answer was a gunshot from downstairs. The noise of gambling fell to nothing. A muffled burst of machine pistol fire set off a frightened chatter on the floor below. The case was not quite full, but Mal closed it anyway, leaving currency scattered on the table and the floor.

"Harvey don't trust the punks downstairs with automatic weapons," he warned.

"Get moving," Sinclair told Birmingham.

The lawyer slid two bolts. The door sprung inward an inch. Birmingham stepped back quickly to the dumbwaiter. A curl of smoke drifted from the open shaft.

Sinclair jerked his head at Mal. "Out. You first."

Mal clutched the heavy case across his chest as if it were armor plate. He hooked a foot around the door and pulled it open with his face averted, like a nervous janitor checking a gas smell.

"It's me Harvey. Don't get trigger happy, huh?"

Two quick shots downstairs were drowned by another machine pistol burst. Screams echoed through the corridors of the old house.

"Hadn't oughtta be me." Mal's moist olive eyes twitched to indicate Birmingham.

"Shut the door," the lawyer said. "We can get out through the ceiling."

"And get mouse-trapped on the service stairs," Sinclair snarled. "Get going, Mal. Before we have more to worry about than Harvey Ricks."

Mal stepped reluctantly into the doorway and stopped with his back tight against the jamb. When no one shot him, he edged carefully out along the wall until he disappeared from sight. Sinclair jerked his head at Birmingham. The lawyer slid out behind Mal.

Sinclair extinguished the light in the strong room so he would not be silhouetted then slipped out. The only light in the hallway crept up the staircase, bringing with it fidgeting shadows of the panic below. The sounds of terror reverberated in the dim passage. The floor shuddered underfoot. Doors vibrated in their frames. A brilliant flash appeared beneath one door then another, advancing toward the three men.

"Spotlight!" Mal's exclamation was barely discernible over the pandemonium. "Somebody's sweeping the house from outside."

Sound amplification equipment emitted a riveting squeal, followed by an emphatically moderate voice. "This is the FBI. Please remain calm. Move at a normal pace. Do not push. Exit the building by the front door. Be prepared to identify yourself to Federal officers."

Sinclair reached past Birmingham and prodded Mal with the gun muzzle. "Take the first door with a window to the veranda. It'll be a short drop from there."

Rusted hinges squeaked lightly behind Sinclair, like fingernails on glass; a prelude to Sunny Tearoe's tense voice.

"Federal Officer. Don't move."

Mal stopped short. Birmingham's head jerked around.

Sinclair said, "Good news," and discarded Birmingham's pistol into the center of the hall. He strangled a cough. An irritant trace of tear gas mingled with the pungent smoke of wet wood burning.

At the far end of the hall the door to Ricks' office swung open. Cindy Rivendahl stepped out. Her elongated shadow amplified the nervous tension in her movements. Before she was fully clear of the doorway, Ricks eased out into view behind her, where he could not be shot readily by anyone unwilling to endanger her. A clean-cut African American man stepped out behind Ricks. Even without his blunt automatic he would have looked like a Federal Agent. He took a UHF handset away from his ear.

"Sunny! Arthur says we've got a fire down in the dice room, and another in the kitchen."

He moved past Ricks and Cindy and peered over the banister to assess the situation. A machine pistol thundered briefly on the stairs immediately below him. His armored vest absorbed a quick succession of impacts. He slammed back against the wall and sat down stunned.

Ricks yanked Cindy back into the cover of his office.

Sunny crouched sideways into a doorway, putting herself between the balcony and the strong room. "Lie down, you three. Stay on the floor until I tell you to get up."

Mal scrambled down and positioned the case to protect his head. Birmingham dropped flat beside Mal, close to the case. Sinclair flattened within reach of Birmingham's pistol. The trembling floor was unnaturally warm.

The gunman came up quickly. His black rubber face had bulging glass eyes and a snout like some huge insect. He held a black assault weapon at stomach level.

Sunny managed to yell, "Federal Officer!" before a thickening concentration of smoke and gas forced a spasm of coughing on her.

The machine pistol thundered again. Sunny's return shots blended too well to be distinguished. Their effect couldn't be missed. The black head jerked back. The gunman fell bonelessly.

A canister arced up from the staircase and landed on the balcony. It rolled idly, burning first with the blinding intensity of Thermite, and then spewing dense gray smoke.

Sinclair reached Birmingham's automatic from the carpet while he could still see it. "Cindy! Tear gas! Get out!"

Pencil-thin shafts of light cut through the thickening atmosphere, originating where bullets had gouged holes in the walls. The shafts played like baby spotlights on the figure of a second man who materialized at the top of the stairs, fuzzy and hulking, like some monstrosity from an out-of-focus creature movie. Sunny fired, without noticeable effect. A shotgun responded with a brutal cough. There was nothing more from Sunny.

Sinclair shot from the floor, more than once. He aimed at hip level, below any armor the gunman might be wearing. The figure stumbled backward, hit the banister. Rotting wood gave way and he was gone.

Sinclair's eyes began to water. He came to his knees, racked by coughing. There was coughing and movement around him. He groped blindly along the wall and sprawled through an oven door. A blast of heat swept back the choking gas.

The room was something from a medieval portrait of Hades. Fire had pierced the floor in two places, casting wavering shadows on the wainscoting and sweeping the cries of the damned up from below on currents of super-heated air. Flames licked up one corner. Damask blackened, then curled away from the walls and disintegrated.

Sinclair was lying across Sunny Tearoe. He got to his hands and knees and dragged her along the hot floor. She struggled feebly in response to the temperature, without coordination or effect. Sinclair collided with a wall. He released Sunny and groped until his glove slipped on glass. He caught the sill of the window and pulled himself up. Fire ran up the exterior wall of the house and turned the night outside into a wavering curtain of flame. Sinclair sagged back down, soaked in sweat.

"We'll have to jump," he gasped through a parched throat. "We'll never find our way through the gas in the hall."

"Strong room." Sunny coughed. "The envelopes..."

"No graft tonight. Ricks expected Scott to stick him up. Leave me for dead to take the blame. He knew he wouldn't have to make any payoffs."

"The computer disk...records..."

"Gone."

Sunny slumped back. Part of the floor broke away in the nearest corner. Fire and smoke boiled up and curled beneath the ceiling. Pools of flame formed on the carpet and spread outward in all directions, merging into one another like oil slicks. The floor became unsteady, as though the whole surface might give way any second and plunge them down into an inferno.

Sinclair drew his good leg under him. With one shoulder under Sunny's rib cage he pushed up, leaning against the wall to avoid the need to balance himself. The limp woman jackknifed clumsily over his shoulder. His leg wavered under him. He rolled forward, using the shoulder he had set against the wall as a pivot, and launched Sunny like a novice tossing a highland camber. She went through the window with a crash of wood and glass.

The momentum from her release left Sinclair helplessly overbalanced. He grabbed blindly for support and caught only air.

CHAPTER 25

A fit of coughing roused Sinclair.

He lay with one cheek buried in a sodden clump of pulpy grass. Wind driven rain pelted the other side of his face. Before he could rise a figure appeared from the swirling smoke, knelt and put a small gun to his temple.

"Not just yet, if you please, Mr. Sinclair," came a solemn, familiar voice.

"Hello, P-preacher. I should've g-guessed Figaro wouldn't s-send those punks out h-here alone."

Preacher worked Birmingham's pistol loose from Sinclair's fingers and stood. "You may get up now. Very carefully, if you please."

Sinclair came awkwardly to a sitting position. His glasses hung crookedly after his fall. They were filmed over with water. He took them off and squinted to focus the surrounding blur. The tubular shape of a dark raincoat towered over him. He struggled to an uncertain balance on stiff legs. Fire raged and crackled up the side of the building not twenty feet away. The heat was intense, but he could not stop shivering. He glanced around.

"I th-threw a w-woman out ahead of m-me. D-Did you see where she l-landed?"

"Misdirection won't work a second time, Mr. Sinclair."

"I'd like to m-make sure she's all r-right."

"Stand perfectly still. I must check you for weapons."

Preacher put his own miniature automatic away in his raincoat pocket and held Birmingham's .22. Two layers of stiff armor frustrated his attempt to pat down Sinclair. The blare of automobile horns from the front of the house was an insistent reminder that Federal agents could stumble onto them at any moment.

"We will go around to the parking area," Preacher decided.

Rough ground and tangles of sopping grass made walking difficult. Flame smothered in thick smoke and tear gas poured out of windows and kept them away from the building. Shifting headlights threw long, mobile shadows into the weed-grown side yard; dancing omens of the bedlam in front.

"You will observe," Preacher said, concealing Birmingham's long-barreled automatic in the folds of his raincoat, "that there is sufficient noise and confusion to allow me to shoot you and simply walk on without attracting the slightest attention."

Sinclair wiped his glasses as best he could and put them on. Preacher was right. Gamblers who had come in taxis had no way to leave. They had coagulated into an aimless mass in front of the house, milling about in the wind and rain; so many that they must have been packed into the casino under pressure. Men and women with FBI in yellow reflective letters on the backs of blue raid jackets tried to cajole them away from the burning building. It was an exercise in frustration. Receding panic left the gamblers bloated with frenzy. Men shouted angry demands. Women shrilled obscenities.

Behind the mob, headlights moved fitfully in the parking area. Blue police strobes marked a checkpoint at the single exit road. Federal agents probed inside each departing car with high intensity flashlights before they let it pass. The back up was impatient and turning ugly. Bumpers clicked. Horns blared. Preacher touched the muzzle of his automatic against the base of Sinclair's spine.

"Where is the Mercedes you stole from Doctor Figaro?"

"The M-Mercedes belongs to a New York b-bank."

"Where is it?"

"Tell me why it m-matters and I'll tell you where I put it."

"The bank provided it to bring dignitaries of the First Republic to Miami for conferences. Dignitaries who had come by yacht to the Keys to avoid the annoyance of Customs. The car is the Doctor's only remaining corroboration of the bank's involvement. Where is it?"

"The FBI has it by now."

"You are lying."

"No, I r-ratted out Figaro's plan. The Feds were laying for his gang. I p-parked the Mercedes on their route in."

"The Doctor will not be happy."

"That'll m-make two of us," Sinclair said.

His attention focused on the parking area. Frozen in the hopeless jam was Scott Birmingham's Buick. Two silhouettes inside had no inkling of the dark figure who edged along the rear fender toward the driver's door. The figure's movements had the jittery stealth of impending violence. Sinclair ignored the threat from Preacher and pushed ahead into the crowd.

A woman materialized in his path. Whatever outer garment she had worn was gone. Naked except for panty hose, she stood lopsided in one high heeled shoe. Rain had soaked her hair into dark tangles that looked like writhing snakes in the moving lights.

"What's the matter with you?" she screamed over and over into his face, as if he were personally responsible for whatever had happened to her.

Sinclair put a hand between her breasts and pushed hard. She sat down on the gravel, stunned.

Something profound had happened during the moment he had been distracted. The dark figure beside Birmingham's Buick lost muscle tension and melted down among the cars like a shadow. Night held the memory of a tiny sound, like the strike of a match.

Out at the edge of the parking area light shimmered in the window of a large sedan as it rolled up.

Sinclair lost control of his direction. He was a prisoner of the crowd, at the mercy of tempers frayed to a thread. Outraged gamblers lashed back savagely at the slightest jostling. Sinclair was shouldered, elbowed, punched, kicked. He kept an arm high to protect his glasses and used his armor to absorb as much of the punishment as possible, trying to slip the blows he couldn't deflect. His momentum finally carried him out of the mob into the shifting mass of cars. Before he could get his bearings Preacher was behind him with a gun at the base of his spine.

"That was foolish," Preacher chided. "We mustn't keep the doctor waiting."

The large car at the edge of the parking area stood the old Packard limousine from the garage of Figaro's funeral home. Preacher stepped ahead and opened a rear door.

"None of them came out the back, Doctor. The house was fully involved when I came across Mr. Sinclair. I thought you might wish to speak with him."

Figaro's dry purr drifted disembodied from the dark interior of the car. "Do get in, Mr. Sinclair."

Before Sinclair could move, Preacher pressed the muzzle of the .22 against the lower part of his abdomen. "I had no chance to search him adequately, Doctor. He is heavily armored."

"We haven't time to deal with that now. We shall simply have to be most careful. I do hope you won't mind sitting on the floor, Mr. Sinclair."

The rear of the limousine had a generous expanse of foot well to accommodate the jump seats that were folded into the front seatback. Sinclair sat there and drew his knees up under his chin. Preacher closed the door. The stale memory of harsh tobacco smoke asserted itself.

Preacher closed himself in front, behind the wheel. "We are quite exposed here, Doctor."

The massive FBI presence only yards away troubled the slight man not in the least. "There is a gray Buick sedan," he said serenely. "Scott Birmingham is the passenger. A woman is driving. Mr. Birmingham appeared to be injured when he came out of the building. Perhaps Mr. Sinclair can enlighten us."

"H-he has a b-bullet hole in his arm."

"A hurt animal makes for its lair," Figaro observed. "Would you be interested, Mr. Sinclair, in seeing where Scott Birmingham runs to?"

"It's n-not Scott I-I'm interested in."

The Packard inched forward. The rear window was bathed in a hell red glow. Fire billowed out of every penetration in the old house. Flames licked under the soffits and curled up around the eaves. Finally, pent up gasses blew through the roof and scattered burning shingles like ash from a volcano.

Sinclair's shivering abated in the warm car. "What did you lace the grenades with? Tear gas doesn't burn hot enough to cook off that kind of inferno."

Figaro put the glow of a lighter to the end of a cigarette. A silencer equipped .22 rested on his knee, the muzzle inches from the back of Sinclair's head. Figaro's index finger was a delicate presence on the trigger.

Sinclair tugged his sodden gloves off, one finger at a time. "Why did you burn a building that has made you money for decades? What could be so important that you would personally shoot a man dead within yards of Federal Agents who are certain to check this car before they let it leave the parking area?"

The tiny click of a switch filled the old Packard with tranquil music. An eerie complacency settled over the fragile man, as if unholy forces had permitted him a glimpse of the future and he had seen that it posed no threat to him.

Figaro's second sight was perfect. Federal agents had abandoned their scrutiny of departing cars. They hurried traffic out the access road with impatient waves of flashlights. The reason made itself obvious on the two lane asphalt. Sirens welled up through a series of punishing crescendos as a convoy of fire trucks blew past. Headlights and red flashers left darkness in their wake.

The Packard became a prison of monotonous speed.

CHAPTER 26

Jackknifed into the foot well of the limousine with a pistol pointed at his head, Sinclair could only wait. The hum of the tires signaled a change in velocity when they reached the expressway. Headlights flashed occasionally in the window above Sinclair's head. Music droned. After a time they left the expressway. Rain blurred fragments of neon in the window placed the Packard on a boulevard in one of the chic suburbs. The intersection lights had gone to winking amber at that late hour. Preacher ignored them.

"Our traffic cover is gone, Doctor. We have only the Buick ahead of us, and another car well ahead of that."

If he expected a response, he was disappointed. Several minutes and several miles passed before he spoke again.

"The Buick has reached Rickenbacker Causeway, Doctor. The closure lights are flashing. The driver is using the emergency vehicle access."

"I'm afraid young Mr. Birmingham has forgotten where his loyalties lie," Figaro said sadly.

Wind hit the limousine full force as it passed onto the Causeway, hissing at the window edges. Torrents of spray cascaded over the car. There was a slithering sensation underneath.

Virginia Key brought relief from the spray. High wind cleared the glass and Preacher studied the mirror. He might have thought he detected movement far back along the Causeway. Or he might simply have been cautious. He said nothing.

Wind-driven spray hit them with redoubled fury on the short bridge to Key Biscayne, where the storm seemed to recede to a respectful distance. Lilting music became audible again. Surrounding vegetation rustled endlessly, like a fresh dead thing called back from the grave by the pulse of Voodoo drums. Fallen branches broke with the snap of old bones under the wheels. Eventually the Packard drifted to a stop. Preacher switched off the motor.

Figaro buttoned his raincoat at the neck. "I expect you know where we are, Mr. Sinclair."

"Earl Moncavage's house?"

"Circumstances force us to pay a call on the Congressman. You will, of course, be on your best behavior."

Preacher got out and opened the rear door. Sinclair climbed out and managed a couple of clumsy steps. Figaro got out and Preacher closed the door. The two men wore identical black raincoats and fedora hats. They traded guns. Preacher took the silenced .22 and Figaro took Birmingham's automatic.

Preacher started off and Figaro motioned Sinclair to follow. The three of them went single file, like a patrol infiltrating enemy lines. A paved service alley took them to the beach where flying spray kept them close to the sea wall. Preacher paused at the stairs that went up to Moncavage's. A cigarette glowed at the far end of the colonnade, back under the eaves. Light filtering through heavily draped French doors silhouetted a man. Preacher cat-footed up the steps alone, melted into the shadows.

A noiseless flash showed in the dark of the colonnade, so brief it might have been an error of perception. The cigarette fell. The silhouette dropped and lay still. Preacher emerged from the shadows and kicked the fallen heap. He kicked it viciously, more than once.

No response. He stepped to the French doors. There was a soft tinkle of breaking glass, almost musical.

Figaro touched the cold muzzle of his gun against the back of Sinclair's neck. "Ever so quietly now."

The main hall of Earl Moncavage's mansion offered a forbidding sanctuary. Faces in dark oil paintings were the ghosts of another generation's robber barons, half-seen and half-imagined, resenting any intrusion of petty ambition in the corridors of wealth and power. What had seemed considerable light from outside proved to be a single shaft that leaked through the slit between two pocket doors not quite drawn together. The drone of Moncavage's self-satisfied oratory came as the chanting of Litany.

"...the cocaine stolen and the processing equipment looted by Harvey Ricks," he could be heard to say over the quiet squish of wet footgear. "Your family should be very happy, Tonia."

"The whole scheme was never more than a monument to your own conceit," came the cultivated Castilian response. "Neither the volume of product moved by my family nor the price per unit would have changed in the slightest."

Preacher curled his fingers into a brass-lined recess in one of the pocket doors and waited for the next voice to cover any noise he might make opening it.

Scott Birmingham said, "Before you start feeling smug, Congressman, you'd better make sure David Sinclair was killed in that fire."

Preacher eased the door back on silent runners to reveal the lawyer slumped in a heavy old chair in a parlor the color of apricot. Water dribbled down from Birmingham's matted hair and washed streaks in the smoke smudges and plaster dust on his face. His parka and sport coat lay in a sopping wad on the Persian carpet. One bare white forearm was stretched out on a blood-soaked towel on an end table that had been drafted for the emergency. Cotton swabs soaked and shriveled by blood filled the glass bowl of a heavy floor ashtray. An open bottle of antiseptic tilted precariously.

Tonia had kicked off a pair of evening pumps and hiked up a form-fitting cocktail dress to kneel beside the table. She worked with the impersonal efficiency of a parochial Dona accustomed to dealing with random gunshot wounds picked up by the hired help.

"If you wanted this Sinclair dead, Mr. Attorney, why didn't you shoot him?" she scolded. "Instead of letting him shoot you."

"You couldn't kill him with a machine gun. That ambush of yours just put him on guard."

Tonia sprinkled a liberal dose of antiseptic and Birmingham stiffened in his chair. She glanced at Cindy Rivendahl, curious about her reaction to Birmingham's pain, and to the fact that another woman was tending him.

Cindy had curled into a nearby chair. Her coat was gone. Rain had left a blouse and slacks limp and clinging. She stared at nothing and ignored everyone.

Earl Moncavage stood protectively behind her chair. He wore a peach colored silk shirt and a paisley ascot, and held a snifter of brandy. Juniper logs burned lazily in a heavy grate behind him. He would have made a nice liquor advertisement.

"Scott," he said peremptorily, "if you hadn't chosen to sell your services back to Judge Picaud, Sinclair would have been testifying before a Federal grand jury to avoid prosecution for the murder of Captain Hewitt while you were comfortably ensconcing yourself in your new position at the bank."

"Sinclair wasn't that frightened or that stupid. And you can forget about burying me at a dead-end assistant general counsel desk while you float off to Nirvana on a river of cash. I want a piece of the action. And I want protection. From the Justice Department. And from Ruellene—" Birmingham stopped talking because everyone had stopped listening.

Sinclair stood two paces inside the half-open door, dripping water on the fringe of the carpet. His sodden clothing was filthy and torn. In a wet face, black from smoke, his eyes burned a malevolent red.

Preacher and Figaro stood behind him, one at each shoulder. Preacher put the silenced .22 on Tonia.

Figaro spoke in his dry, ethereal voice. “My apologies, Mrs. Cardenza, but after what befell Mr. Sinclair, I must insist on a personal search.”

Tonia stood without a word, aloof and taunting. She ran a zipper and shrugged. The cocktail dress fell into a limp circle at her feet. Dropping a camisole left her in sheer panty hose and a black lace bra. She stepped out of the circle of clothing and did a slow, insinuating pirouette, shedding the bra as neatly as an exotic dancer. She arched her back and let her shoulders squirm. Ample breasts took on lives of their own. When neither black rose to the provocation, she knelt and went back to work on Birmingham’s arm.

Preacher stepped forward with startling quickness. He kicked Tonia’s evening clutch across the floor. It hit the far wall with a thud. He stepped back behind Sinclair, didn’t bother retrieving the gun inside. Tonia scarcely seemed to notice.

When Moncavage saw no one was in immediate danger of being shot, he waved his glass in an extravagant gesture that forgave all. “It’s good of you to stop by, Doctor Figaro. In fact, I was planning to call on you in the next few days. Do come in. Sit down and be comfortable.”

Figaro shifted sideways, putting his back to the wall. “Thank you, no, Congressman. Though perhaps Mr. Sinclair would like to join his friends.”

“Friend,” Sinclair corrected.

Stiff legs took him behind Birmingham’s chair, where he would not cross Preacher’s line of fire. His shoulder brushed ivory drapes. The chill of outdoors penetrated one of the mansion’s big front windows.

Tonia paused her work on Birmingham’s arm to watch him pass, shameless in her nakedness and taunting in her expression.

A mocking grin played on Sinclair's lips. "Moncavage can't afford a butler, so the maid had to do it?"

Contempt glinted briefly in her eyes.

Cindy watched Sinclair's movements for signs of fresh injury. Birmingham's heavy leather case stood forgotten at her feet.

Sinclair winked at her and lowered himself awkwardly to the upholstered arm of her chair. "Swallow much of the gas?" he asked in a voice that tried to sound cheerful through clogged sinuses.

Cindy just shrugged. She offered him her glass of brandy, holding it up insistently until he took it.

"Don't get brave and bold," he cautioned. "The Doctor and his man have already killed two people tonight."

Figaro addressed Moncavage. "I must know the extent to which we have the house to ourselves?"

"My wife has taken a sedative. Labor Day is always hectic in politics."

Figaro let impatience show in his dry purr. "May I also have the number and posting of Mrs. Cardenza's sentries?"

"Please consider yourself under my personal guarantee of safe conduct, Doctor."

Figaro's smile could not have been smaller.

Moncavage made a convivial movement with his glass. "How can I help you? It must be something quite important to bring you all the way out here on a night like this."

"This may seem a trivial matter to a man of your standing," Figaro allowed, "but your scheme to ruin Judge Picaud has placed me in considerable jeopardy."

Moncavage blinked in confusion. "Perhaps if you could explain?"

"Correct me if I have misread the situation, Congressman, but to outward appearances you cultivated an association with young Mr. Birmingham, the Judge's former law clerk, whom he had managed to place in the State Attorney's office. At your behest, Mr. Birmingham approached the Judge with a scheme to import and distribute cocaine. When the Judge was sufficiently extended to be vulnerable, you alerted the FBI."

"Judge Picaud," Moncavage said emphatically, "was and remains the sole target."

"Tonight I was forced to burn Cutler house, a property I was loathe to risk from the beginning, to insure that no evidence of even my limited connection to the scheme remained."

"My apologies, Doctor. I will soon be in a position to make that right."

"Does Mrs. Cardenza's presence indicate you intend to shore up your overextended banking interests by laundering the cash from her family's narcotics wholesaling?"

Moncavage allowed himself a sip of brandy. "I am gratified, Doctor, that you appreciate the scope of my plans."

"I do not appreciate your persuading Judge Picaud to reject me after an association of forty some years and use your dupe, Mr. Sinclair, to establish a casino to provide cash for police protection and a location for processing."

"Sinclair was mine," Moncavage protested, "only in the sense that he was the one candidate my people could find on short notice who fit the requirements set down by Judge Picaud."

"Requirements?"

"Never married. No children. No known will. Experienced in casino and office building management. As you can imagine, working through Judge Picaud's former law clerk, I was in no position to question his reasons."

When Figaro frowned at Sinclair, he found only sharp, attentive eyes as eager for answers as he was. "If Mr. Sinclair was uniquely fitted to some set of qualifications, why did you have Mrs. Cardenza shoot him?"

"For your information, Doctor, Judge Picaud gave the order to have Sinclair killed."

"The Judge? Why?"

"I haven't a clue. He gave the order to an agent of mine. A hapless blowhard named Bernard Cohn, who was masquerading as part of a large New York drug ring. It was a matter of either making good or allowing Cohn to fall from grace. Fortunately Tonia had the resources and temperament to follow through."

"But Cohn did fall from grace," Figaro said. "The Judge personally ordered his removal. And the placement of his remains at a precise spot in the Everglades."

Moncavage smiled grimly. "Yes, I rather thought it must have been you who had Cohn killed, Doctor. The style was unique."

"At my age, any significant prison sentence would be tantamount to life. Murder is not a particular risk. Do you understand what I am saying?"

A voice as brittle as old parchment floated in from the dimness of the hallway.

"The young fool understands nothing."

CHAPTER 27

Judge Picaud stood in the doorway. A topcoat hung askew on his bowed shoulders. His hat sat with absentminded crookedness. He fixed smoldering eyes on Birmingham.

"I sent you to eliminate this man," he croaked, and leveled a knobby finger at Sinclair, "and here I find you in the company of scoundrels."

Roland Jardine appeared at Picaud's side. Water plastered his blond curls flat to his head, dribbled down his steely expression and glistened on his leather jacket. He directed a smirk at Sinclair.

"Did you really think you wouldn't see me again?"

"I didn't expect you to take up geriatric nursing. Who is the fossil?"

"I found the Captain's private address book. The one with the real connections. Then I staked out the casino. When I saw what went down tonight, I got on the cell phone. The Judge knew right where to come."

"Judge Picaud?" Sinclair stared at the frail old man.

Picaud ignored him to point at Moncavage and wail piously. "You are the cause of this trouble. You and your blind ambition."

"Greed was your undoing," Moncavage shot back in a voice made unsteady by mounting anger. "The greed of a drooling tyrant too stubborn to relinquish his grip on power. The greed of a hypocrite who punishes the slightest misdemeanor in public while he schemes in private to prostitute his trust and deal in drugs. Well, your scheme has failed. Your drugs and your equipment are gone."

The old Judge lowered his arm. "They will be returned," he said, and cackled with private pleasure. "Arrangements are already being made for the next shipment."

Tonia finished taping Birmingham's arm. "Your agent is dead," she announced casually.

Picaud's head moved in spasmodic twitches of confusion until his eyes found the kneeling woman. "Who are you? Why are you naked? Cover yourself."

Tonia retrieved her bra and put it on with tantalizing slowness, caressing each breast into its cup and arching her back when she fastened the clasp. "Your suppliers in Cartagena learned the FBI was waiting for their shipment," she said, using a sweet voice as sadistically as a lash. "Lewis Lloyd knew enough to get them extradited." She drew a finger across her throat.

Moncavage took a startled half step away from the fireplace. "Not Crofton Lloyd's grandson?"

Sinclair let out a note of malicious laughter. "No, Congressman. The Judge's grandson."

Every eye in the room fixed on him.

"The Judge, before he was a Judge, and Opal Lloyd, before her name was Lloyd, were a social item. A couple of hurricanes blew the props out from under local real estate and the nine years of depression wiped out any spare change the aristocracy had left over. Picaud had to practice law for a living. Opal went from playing Susie Spreadlegs on the cocktail circuit to providing the family comforts for Crofton Lloyd, while she stepped out with one of her old boyfriends on the side."

The Judge's voice cracked under the strain of saying, "Don't cheapen something you haven't the breeding to understand."

Sinclair addressed his audience confidentially. "Lloyd got a nose full of hydrocyanic acid on a train ride north, Opal wasn't about to dilute her winnings by marrying Picaud, but over time she acquired enough influence to promote him a judgeship so he could do her some good. A former hotel clerk who'd fixed them up with their love nests was shot dead during an apparent robbery to preclude any embarrassing revelations. In return, Doctor Figaro wound up with Cutler house, and a powerful friend on the bench."

Figaro pointed his automatic at Sinclair's head. "I shall require the pistol you stole from me."

"Desbrisay stole it from you," Sinclair corrected, "after he served a prison term for killing his father-in-law on your orders. You killed him because he knew you killed the hotel clerk with it. You sent his son to be killed in tonight's robbery, in case DesBrisay had told him. And you killed Vernon Granger when he put the clerk's death together with Picaud's appointment to the bench in the same year."

Judge Picaud took a shaky step toward Tonia. His voice faltered on its own strictness. "The truth, whore! Tell me my grandson is alive."

Tonia stood up, slipped into the camisole and retrieved her cocktail dress. She noticed a drop of blood on the tip of one finger and licked it off, slowly turning the finger against her tongue like an ice cream cone. A wisp of a smile savored the pain her silence inflicted on the old man.

"Doctor Figaro, shoot her if she fails to comply."

"Your Honor," Figaro cautioned, "we have not searched the premises. Mrs. Cardenza has certainly posted sentries."

"Your man killed the sentry. We saw him in the gutter beside Scott's Buick."

"Buick?"

Figaro's small pink eyes filled with alarm, but before either he or Preacher could react Harvey Ricks materialized in the doorway. Ricks was a gaunt apparition in a tan raincoat soaked brown across the shoulders. He touched the front sight of his .22 Colt against Jardine's ear to freeze the police officer between himself and Figaro.

"Only cops and amateurs tail from behind," Ricks told the fragile man in a derisive rasp. "I got out the back way and waited where the gravel road met the blacktop until I saw Birmingham's Buick coming. It was simple to lead the parade until Cindy made the Causeway, then hook on behind that rolling dinosaur of yours."

The memory of trailing headlights flickered in the eyes Preacher had shifted to the doorway. It was too late to bring the silenced automatic to bear. Ricks already had his Colt leveled. The gray stain of recent firing was evident at the muzzle.

"Lose the piece, Smoke. Center of the carpet. Where nobody can reach it."

Preacher smiled solemnly. He took the tip of the silenced .22 carefully between the thumb and forefinger of his left hand and released the grip so that it swung slowly, like a hypnotist's pendulum. He made a production of casting it away. As misdirection it was only a millimeter short of perfect.

A miniature automatic swept up in Preacher's right hand. Ricks faded half a step as the little gun cracked. Glass broke out in the hallway behind him. Ricks' pistol let off a couple of firecracker pops, like an abortive beginning to Chinese New Year.

Preacher stood with his gun almost pointed at Ricks and didn't do anything. The tiny automatic slipped from his hand and made a muffled thud through the carpet. Preacher died as quietly as he had lived. His knees buckled. Resiliency left his body and he folded down. He hit the floor and his fedora came off. A lock of his plastered hair fell loose. The acrid bite of nitrocellulose began to drift and mix with the tang of burning juniper.

Jardine's police training had him flat on the floor. He clawed under his jacket. Ricks stomped on his hand. An automatic squirted out onto the carpet. Ricks kicked it sideways into the hall and moved behind Picaud with his pistol leveled at Figaro. Blood seeped where

Preacher's bullet had cut his cheek going by. His eyes shifted warningly.

"Move somebody. Anybody. Just a little."

Nobody moved.

Gusting wind forced its way down the chimney flue and raised flares from the juniper logs. An intricate chandelier swayed from the center of the ceiling and flickered, threatening to plunge the parlor into darkness. Rain rattled against the window like thrown gravel. Cindy stiffened and clutched Sinclair's leg.

Jardine picked himself off the floor, rubbing his hand and glaring around with cold fury. Figaro let his pistol fall to the carpet. Ricks wasn't satisfied.

"Kick it. Center of the room."

Figaro kicked the pistol behind a chair, where he would have cover if he had to scramble for it. "I have my own agenda here," he warned Ricks. "I will cooperate only as long as it serves my interests."

"You do what you got to do," Ricks rasped, adding significantly, "after I've taken it on the arches."

"Have a pleasant journey to wherever you are going, Mr. Ricks. Just make sure you never return to Miami."

"I'm not leaving empty," Ricks informed him. "There's a quarter of a million of my money in that case. And I repoed the old Mercedes you stashed in your cadaver factory."

A sudden light of encouragement winked on in the depths of Figaro's eyes. "The money may be negotiable," he offered in his dry purr. "The car must be returned to me."

"My ride went up in that bonfire of yours," Ricks rasped. "I take the Mercedes, I take the cash. No negotiations."

Cindy reached down, wrapped her fingers around the handle of the leather case and came to her feet. She could barely manage the weight but her smudged face remained a mask of coolness and determination.

"I've got the money, Harvey. Shoot Figaro and let's get going."

Burning juniper disintegrated under its own weight and the contents of the fireplace shifted audibly, sending up a shower of glowing embers. It was the only movement in the room, and the loudest sound.

"Shoot Figaro," Cindy repeated. The cobalt eyes she fixed on Ricks were sultry and suggestive, unspoken hints of the possibilities once they were safely away together. She shifted Birmingham's heavy case so she could use both hands to hold it.

Birmingham tensed in his chair. "You don't have to go with him, Cindy," he said in the voice thickened by its own fervency. "Ricks won't shoot you. Stand your ground. He'll have to leave without the money. We planned this together. We can still bring it off."

"What am I supposed to do then, Scott? Hang around until you get lonely for Mom and Nicki and the kids?"

A combination of ardor and embarrassment brought him to his feet. "I told you that part of my life was over."

Ricks shifted his Colt. "Sit down, Hunkie."

The smell of death was still fresh in the room. The blood Birmingham had lost to Sinclair's bullet blunted his assertiveness still further. He sat down with the furtive, casual air of a man who caught himself lighting up after he quit smoking.

Cindy shuffled, trying to ease the weight of the case. "What are you waiting for, Harvey? Shoot Figaro."

The beading on Figaro's upper lip had to be sweat. The rest of his face was as dry as his voice. "Such a bloodthirsty young lady. Has it occurred to you, Mr. Ricks, that she may be employing you in an effort to save Mr. Sinclair? They do appear to be very good friends. And Mr. Sinclair was certainly right about what happened to Crofton Lloyd when he tried to buy domestic bliss."

Sinclair moved down into the chair Cindy had abandoned and settled back comfortably, as if to declare himself nothing more than a spectator.

Desire got the better of any suspicions Ricks still harbored. "Come on, Cindy. It's okay. Figaro won't try to stop you. Not while I'm set for him. He hasn't got the speed or the style."

Cindy hesitated on the verge of her first step. "You can't watch our backs and drive at the same time. Better throw me the car keys now, while you've still got everybody where you can see them."

The case tugged at Cindy's grip and she muffed the catch. She had to stoop by Sinclair's feet to retrieve the keys. When she rose, the key to Birmingham's Buick was pushed out of sight under Sinclair's shoe.

"Good-bye, David," was all she said. She made it sound final.

Moncavage put his brandy on the fireplace mantle and ran the tips of his fingers through his styled hair. "Doctor," he began in a stirring tone, "leaders like you and I must remain above these petty disagreements. We must concentrate on forming the political and economic coalitions that will foster growth; our own as well as that of the region."

"No thank you, Congressman. I have quite enough difficulty already without channeling my cash flow through a bank that is almost certainly under Federal investigation for irregular currency transactions."

Figaro stepped aside politely to let Cindy pass. She slipped behind Harvey Ricks with a tender smile and gripped the leather handle of the case with both hands. Ricks started to ease back. Cindy planted her feet and whirled like a hammer thrower in a field meet, swinging the case at the back of Ricks' head.

Ricks stepped into the full impact. His automatic emitted another firecracker pop. A gouge appeared in the upholstery beside Sinclair's head. Mortar dust puffed out of the fireplace facing an inch from Moncavage's elbow. Ricks sagged down.

Figaro and Jardine scrambled for their guns. Tonia's was across the room in her evening clutch. Her speed and agility were stunning. If it hadn't been for her tight dress and three-inch heels, Sinclair might have been too slow.

He caught the fluted stem of the floor ashtray and bolted to his feet, swinging it upward. The ashtray tumbled one revolution and crashed into the chandelier. Glass and sparks flew. Light sizzled away.

Sinclair dropped flat on the carpet. Gloomy shadows danced to the slow rhythm of burning juniper. He squirmed on his stomach to the nearest point where he could not be silhouetted by the firelight. That put him tight against the window wall, where heavy drapery tickled the baseboard. The situation in the room was as uncertain as if it had been completely dark.

Scott Birmingham's voice was a hoarse, vengeful whisper. "He's over by the window. Where the curtains are moving."

The idea filled Moncavage with alarm. "No more shooting! My wife—the neighbors! You'll have the police down on us!"

A heavy pistol filled the parlor with thunder. The bullet gouged the spidery leg of a side table and slammed through the window wall, inches above Sinclair's spine.

"David?" The voice was Cindy's. It rode a wave of latent terror.

Birmingham called her name, without getting an answer. "She's near the door. One of you get her. Sinclair won't leave without her."

She would be a seized in a matter of seconds.

Sinclair grabbed one leg of the table. "Cindy! I'll meet you outside."

Sinclair rolled onto his side, crashing the table against the drapery. Glass broke on the other side. Violent wind came booming in. Thick cloth whipped and waved in the shadows. Gunshots reverberated from both corners of the opposite wall. The ballooning drapery jerked spasmodically. The echoes died away. For a moment there was only the wind, and the steady bang-bang of the open front door of the house.

Birmingham's was the angriest of the voices that erupted in the room. "He got out the window."

"I got the bastard!" Jardine snapped back.

Tonia shrilled orders in a mix of English and Spanish. She sounded like she was preparing to defend the hacienda against a bandit attack, but psychotic insistence was not long in bringing order out of chaos. A lamp came on in the corner—fifty watts of a three-way bulb—and stabilized the shadows.

Only Judge Picaud remained standing. It was unclear what kept him erect. The smoldering glow was gone from his eyes, leaving them hollow and vacant. Palsy was evident in his stance. His lips worked in wordless confusion.

Sinclair worked the automatic out of his clothing and framed the glow of the lamp in the sights. His shot took the bulb out in a shower of sparks. He gained his feet and charged the pocket doors on wobbly legs, weaving like a drunken antelope. Shadows swooped and dove in the fleeting brilliance of gun flashes. The front door hung ajar where Cindy had gone out. Sinclair turned his shoulder and hit it without breaking his clumsy stride. The steps outside were slimy with rain. Sinclair's boots slipped going down. He managed to stop himself on the terrace, but put too much pressure on his injured leg.

"Cindy!" he hissed painfully.

Something that was not a shadow moved out of the shrubbery rustling against the house. Cindy thrashed through the flower bed and caught his arm to steady him.

"I thought you jumped through the window! Can you walk?"

Sinclair pushed himself ahead against pain shooting up his leg. Light dissolved into wind-harried shadows where the stairs fanned down to the drive. The dim form of a man stretched out by the rear wheel of Birmingham's Buick; face down in a shallow gutter. Long black hair straggled in the water that flowed around him like a stream around a fallen snag.

Cindy was careful to avoid stepping in it. "Did you pick up the car keys?"

"I didn't have time to fumble. We need distance now. We can worry about transportation later."

"I've still got the keys to that Mercedes."

"It'll be out on the road. Ricks is too cagey to have come into the drive."

Flood lamps came on under the eaves of the house, and bathed an arc of the drive in the fringes of their light.

"Go ahead," Sinclair urged. "Find the car and pick me up at the gate. I can make it that far."

Sinclair walked sideways, with one eye on the house. Wind driven rain hustled him along. Haste dropped him painfully to one knee. A motorized garage door made noise somewhere behind the great restless black of the oak trees. The mechanism stopped and left the soft purr of a car engine. Sinclair rose immediately, moving again with a fugitive's frenzy.

A white Lincoln Coupe materialized in the floodlights. It swept around the curve of the drive and came at Sinclair with its high beams blazing. He reached the end of the drive and used a gatepost for cover. The Lincoln swept past in a spray of water. Phyllis Moncavage sat bolt upright at the wheel. Her features were oddly composed and serene. Then the taillights were a redness that blurred away to nothing.

A second engine idled nearby, with the barely perceptible note of warm machinery. High beams snapped on and jumped forward. The Mercedes slithered to a stop on loose gravel. The passenger door swung out and started to fall closed again. Sinclair stepped quickly and painfully and caught it. More headlights moved behind the oak trees when he slid inside. Cindy accelerated down the dark lane. A speed bump jarred the undercarriage and sent shock waves through the car. She slowed to a safer pace.

Headlights and blue flashers came at them out of the storm. A siren burst warned Cindy to the edge of the road. A police cruiser went by. Sinclair twisted his head to watch it out of sight. The headlights of the cruiser found another car following them, running dark.

When the cruiser was gone, the driver turned on the lights. Cindy's eyes jumped to the mirror, horrified.

"Who is back there, David?"

"It's got to be Jardine. Driving with no lights is just the sort of juvenile stunt that makes policemen go all giggly inside."

A dark Trans Am drew abreast and went by like a stone from a slingshot. Its lights faded fast.

"Who is he chasing?" Cindy asked.

"Phyllis Moncavage left just ahead of us. Jardine likely didn't know she was in the house. All he saw was her car in the floodlights."

"He thinks she's you," Cindy realized. "He may kill her before he finds out."

"She grew up on Key Biscayne. She'll have friends here, and she'll know better than to risk the Causeway in this storm. We passed her already and never knew it. She's probably the one who called the police."

"What you said was true, wasn't it? This all started because Opal Lloyd had a son by Judge Picaud."

"Opal had a son, all right. And the son married and left Opal to raise a grandson when he and his wife were killed. The grandson sucked down a lot of drugs and probably sold enough to support his habit. I guess Opal thought that at forty something now, he could at least be a wholesaler if he couldn't do anything else to save the family fortune."

"The Judge certainly acted like Lewis Lloyd was his grandson."

"Because that's what Opal told him—she would have said that even if she knew otherwise—and because he wanted to believe it. If you want to make a total soap opera out of it, suppose Opal's daughter-in-law led the same lifestyle Opal did. The so-called grandson may not have been an actual blood relative of any of the people involved."

High wind and pounding rain smothered any chance of conversation on the Causeway. Flashing blue strobes waited at the end.

Impact had plowed a State Police cruiser into the middle of Highway 1 and welded the crumpled front clip of Roland Jardine's Trans Am into its rear fender. Struggling troopers in ballooning slickers were setting out flares.

Cindy eased through the shattered roadblock. No one yelled at them.

"Are we clear?" she asked.

"We bought a little time," Sinclair said, "but we still have to face the law."

CHAPTER 28

State Attorney Ruellene Kingman lived on a street where white stucco houses with red tile roofs spoke quietly and emphatically of old money. A heavy set man with twinkling eyes and a mane of white hair answered Sinclair's knock. A hint of brogue bared itself like teeth when he demanded to see Sinclair's identification. He led the way along a dim hallway to a high-ceilinged den with French doors open to admit a fragrant afternoon zephyr.

The room held two easy chairs. Sunny Tearoe occupied one. The white-haired man closed the door and took the other. Ruellene Kingman sat behind a Queen Anne desk. Tall and rangy, she had been in authority long enough for it to sit comfortably on her. She spoke in the pleasant, neutral voice of a teacher trying to draw out a reticent teenager.

"You've caused quite a fuss, Mr. Sinclair."

He helped himself to a straight, hard chair beside the desk. "I may have been present when other people engaged in disruptive activities," was all he allowed.

"I once saw a science demonstration in high school," Mrs. Kingman recalled. "Several powerful chemicals were mixed in a beaker. Nothing happened—until the instructor dropped in a handful of iron filings. When all the smoking and bubbling was over, everything had changed but the iron filings. They had touched off the whole reaction, but remained untouched themselves. It's a little like that with some people."

"What am I being charged with?" Sinclair asked. "Failure to register as a catalytic agent?"

The white-maned man stirred in his chair. "D'you think this is funny, Sinclair?"

Sunny Tearoe interrupted in her cool, clipped Radcliffe voice. "Excuse me, Mrs. Kingman. The question is appropriate, even though Mr. Sinclair's phrasing was unorthodox. The U.S. Attorney is concerned that he be advised promptly of all charges the County authorities wish to lodge against him."

Ruellene Kingman smiled patiently and addressed the white haired man. "Deputy Director McDougal?"

"Sinclair's a professional gambler. He murdered a law enforcement officer."

"You have no witness to the precise circumstances of Captain Hewitt's death," Mrs. Kingman reminded him.

"Sinclair was apprehended at the controls of an airplane in which three passengers were dead by violence."

"He was not apprehended, Mac. He landed voluntarily at Opa Locka and surrendered to Federal authorities."

McDougal tamped tobacco into a straight pipe. "Those same Federal authorities developed evidence that Sinclair established the casino where narcotics from the airplane were taken for processing." He applied a small butane lighter to the pipe. "If that doesn't make him an active participant in conspiracy under the felony murder statute, I'd like to know what it takes."

"Sinclair doesn't own the house in the Everglades. There is no official record that he leased it. Or owned the gaming equipment seized from the premises."

"We can't yet connect Sinclair with the front company that bought the gaming equipment," McDougal conceded, "but we can establish that he was the last and, in two cases, the only person to inspect it before the purchase order was sent. And casino money did go through that church account where Sinclair was trying to deposit money when he was shot. Of forty banknotes lost by an undercover investigator, six turned up in the church deposit within a week. That's pretty significant."

"Significant won't cut it, Mac. I need conclusive. Have you located Reverend Granger yet? You will need his testimony to establish Sinclair's authority over the church."

"He'll turn up. They all do. Sooner or later."

"It's already later, Mac."

The police official subsided reluctantly. The pipe calmed him only a little, leaving a look of great energy lying just below the surface.

Ruellene Kingman smiled at Sunny. "I understand you had quite a night, Mrs. Tearoe. I hope this visit isn't a strain for you?"

"Not at all, Mrs. Kingman. Thank you for asking."

"You were struck by a shotgun charge?" Ruellene Kingman's eyes held a mix of queasiness and concern.

"I received only blunt trauma," Sunny explained. "My armor absorbed the pellets." She dismissed the whole thing with a buoyant laugh.

"If this were a matter of filing charges," the State Attorney informed her, "I'd have my staff handle it."

Sunny's smile was apologetic. "I can only relay what the U.S. Attorney told me when he asked me to meet you and Mr. Sinclair here."

Ruellene Kingman nodded complacently. "Mr. Sinclair, is there anything you would like to add to the conversation?"

"I've not learned a great deal beyond what you told me when you came to see me in the hospital, Mrs. Kingman."

Silence was a tangible presence in the room. Ruellene Kingman's eyes met those of Deputy Director McDougal and Sunny Tearoe in turn. Her gaze was firm.

"Mr. Sinclair and I had a brief visit about two weeks ago," she revealed. "I was concerned that the authorities, both you in the Federal Government, Mrs. Tearoe, and we in the County, Mac, might be losing leverage on a serious situation. I thought Mr. Sinclair might be the key to reasserting our influence."

McDougal rubbed a sideburn with the tip of his pipe. "Sinclair was working for your office?"

"Never for a minute," the State Attorney said.

"Then he is concealing evidence in no fewer than six homicides," the white haired man declared. "Assuming he didn't actually participate in any of them."

"Who besides Captain Hewitt?"

"This New York lawyer Cohn that nobody wants to talk about. A taxi driver, no body and the only witness, his son, has recanted on the advice of counsel. The assistant manager of a mortuary, dead on a Congressman's carpet, and two South Americans with fancy guns in their pants, shot outside his house."

"Mr. Sinclair?" Ruellene Kingman asked.

"No comment."

"There isn't anything you want to share?"

"I learned nothing beyond what you knew from the beginning. In the hospital you gave me the impression you thought Harvey Ricks was fronting someone. You didn't say who because you thought I'd stir things up trying to find out, that enough evidence would surface as a result to prove it was Bernard Cohn directly, and Earl Moncavage behind him."

Ruellene Kingman shook her head. "It was the FBI Cohn contacted when the Bronx District Attorney was going to charge him on a related matter. The FBI doesn't talk to me."

Sunny smiled uncomfortably. "If there are no charges to be filed, Mrs. Kingman, will you need Mr. Sinclair and me for anything further?"

"Please don't take any of this personally, Mrs. Tearoe. The U.S. Attorney knows he's struck out, and he knows why. I expect he wanted someone else in the Justice Department to hear it from me independently. Thank you for stopping out. You, too, Mac. I'd like to talk to you, Mr. Sinclair, if you don't mind staying."

Sunny Tearoe came to her feet and gathered her shoulder bag from the side table. She tried to catch Sinclair's eye, without success.

McDougal stood up. "What do I tell the Director?"

"About what?" Mrs. Kingman asked.

"Prosecution of Sinclair. He really did lay it on the line."

"I'll call him at home this evening."

McDougal nodded grudging comprehension. He held the door for Sunny, but paused on the verge of following her out. "We will see you at the house on Sunday, Ruellene?"

She leaned back and smiled broadly. "Wouldn't miss it, Mac. Just give me a little slack on the snacks. Those high octane dips of yours are a hundred calories a chip, and I'm past the age where I can make it through a whole exercise tape."

McDougal laughed heartily and left. Another door opened and closed and then there were no more noises in the house.

Ruellene Kingman stopped smiling. No feature of her face changed more than a millimeter, but she was a different woman—cold, incisive, relentless. She put on a pair of metal-rimmed glasses, opened a manila folder and began to make notes.

"Tell me how you got involved in this."

Sinclair did not reply.

The State Attorney looked up sharply. "I am being far more lenient with you than my oath of office or my sense of justice would normally allow. That can change, if you prefer not to cooperate."

Sinclair acquiesced with a minute smile. "My job as controller of a large hotel and casino in Atlantic City was eliminated in a reorganization. One of the dancers in the main floor show introduced me to your deputy, Scott Birmingham. He was the one who made the casino proposition."

"Let's focus on Lucinda Rivendahl for a minute. I'd like to be clear as to her exact role."

"Cindy was the roper. I think that's what they call it. She had her pick of the field, where men were concerned. A four-eyed bookkeeper was an easy target. Neither she nor Scott told me Earl Moncavage put them up to it. Nor that the ultimate objective was to lure Judge Picaud into a drug smuggling scheme which would then be exposed to Federal authorities."

Ruellene Kingman looked up from her writing. "Why you, Mr. Sinclair? If, as you say, Lucinda Rivendahl had her pick of the field, why were you chosen?"

"Judge Picaud wanted someone who could get the Lloyd Building back on track financially. Commercial real estate had been my specialty when I was an auditor."

"You were given full title," Mrs. Kingman pointed out.

"Probably to make sure I put forth my best effort. I was single and without heirs, and I took title from Opal's grandson. As long as I wasn't around to argue, it could be said that I duped an irresponsible party in the transaction. Once I had everything running profitably, I was to die under circumstances unconnected with the building. Opal would file a smoke screen action in Picaud's court, and be reinstated in ownership."

"What did Judge Picaud gain by this?"

"He was given the idea that Opal's grandson was his own blood."

Ruellene Kingman did not write that. "At what point did you learn that the FBI was running one of their notorious scams on Earl Moncavage?"

"I wondered if maybe they weren't, though no one would actually say so. If you'd care to tell me about it, I'll corroborate what I can."

"As far as I was able to determine," Mrs. Kingman said, "the FBI operation began with Bernard Cohn in New York. Cohn's law practice consisted of charging cut rates to mid-level drug dealers for strutting around various courtrooms to mollify underlings who had been promised a legal defense if they were caught. The authorities were flabbergasted when he turned up in a major money laundering investigation. Before the Bronx District Attorney could formally charge him, he went to the FBI.

"Cohn and Earl Moncavage had waited tables in the same college town restaurant twenty some years earlier. Moncavage was a student at Princeton. Cohn was barely holding his own in a local diploma mill. Moncavage married into Florida banking and made a name for himself. Cohn gravitated to New York and ingratiated himself into a lower level of society. With his bank on the brink of collapse, Moncavage contacted Cohn and asked him to use his contacts in the drug trade to channel cash flow through Moncavage's bank. Cohn went from bit player to the big time, and Moncavage's plans grew more grandiose. When Cohn told the FBI about Moncavage's scheme to destroy Judge Picaud, it put the Bureau in an ideal position. If they could find and corroborate a witness against Picaud, they could develop two high impact prosecutions with one investigation."

"I was their choice for a witness," Sinclair confirmed.

"You were to be the first domino," the State Attorney corrected. "The FBI would raid the casino to obtain evidence which would embarrass my office into prosecuting you for gambling conspiracy. Your conviction would force you to testify against Hewitt and Scott Birmingham, and theirs in turn would force them to testify against Picaud and Moncavage. The raid failed miserably. They neither caught you nor recovered the payoff envelopes, which would be essential to corroborate your testimony of corruption. All they could do was turn the equipment over to the Dade County Police and keep the pressure on me in the hope that a second raid would succeed."

"When you came to see me in the hospital," Sinclair wondered aloud, "were you hoping I'd uncover evidence, or torpedo the Federal investigation?"

Ruellene Kingman permitted herself a meager smile. "No County prosecutor has incentive to spend limited resources supporting an FBI operation that will undermine the credibility and effectiveness of her office long after the Justice Department has taken its bows and gone on to greener pastures."

"Are you hoping to use me to prosecute anyone?"

"Cooler heads prefer that Judge Picaud retire and leave public confidence in the courts intact. Once he is gone, police investigation can build a case against Bastien Figaro. You may draw whatever conclusions you want about my decision to let Scott Birmingham return to private practice, which he was never in."

Sinclair considered the woman shrewdly. "Then I don't understand why you've bothered talking to me."

"Do you know what was on the tape recording Captain Hewitt took from Cohn?"

"I saw Hewitt take the tape. I never heard it."

"It contains confirmation that Picaud had ordered Cohn, a Federal informant and provocateur, to murder you. It strongly implies that you were ambushed and shot as a direct result. If it became public knowledge that the Bureau had lost control of Cohn, their procedures could come under severe scrutiny. Federal investigation and prosecution could be seriously hampered."

"Which is what gives you your standoff with the U. S. Attorney," Sinclair realized. "But your stalemate is only good as long as the FBI can keep its dirty laundry out of sight. So I'm to forget I was shot as a result of Federal incompetence and you'll forget the charges against me. Is that the deal?"

Ruellene Kingman closed the manila folder with a delicate finality. "I don't know what Maureen Lefkowitz has been filling you full of, but there is no deal. The decisions resolving this matter have been taken to produce the greatest long-term gain for the criminal justice system, and for no other reason. You were shot as a result of your own greed and stupidity."

Sinclair grinned wryly. "I guess I had that coming."

"This whole scheme turned on how big a fool the schemers could make of you," the State Attorney pointed out. "Most men would see some form of retribution as normal and necessary." Sharp scrutiny demanded to know where Sinclair stood on the issue.

"No one can be duped unless he cooperates to some extent in the process," he said. "If I look a fool, then I'd better take responsibility for being a fool."

"You're taking this more casually than I expected." Her tone of voice wondered why.

"Casual is the last word I'd use," Sinclair said. "I've been popping antacid all day. My stomach is still churning at the thought of facing Cindy."

CHAPTER 29

Sinclair returned home to find Cindy on the patio in back. She sat in a white plastic chair in white shorts and an abbreviated white top that allowed the cool breeze off the canal to play on her tanned midriff. She had a portable television perched on the umbrella table and she was engrossed in the early evening news.

The video showed a gutted building with fire crews prowling among a few blackened supports. A sodden, subdued crowd watched a gurney disappear into the back of a flashing ambulance. Voice over, an unseen anchor woman:

"Football fans and University officials were stunned by the news that Henry DesBrisay, a promising linebacker widely mentioned as a candidate for all-conference honors during the upcoming season, was shot and seriously wounded during an FBI raid on what is now known to have been a casino operating in the historic Cutler Mansion. Gunfire during the raid claimed the lives of two men and left two FBI agents with blunt trauma injuries. Both dead men had police records."

Sinclair wandered to the edge of the canal. He buried his hands in his pockets and stood staring down into the water. The evening sun cast shadows on the surface and speckled them with highlights that shone like tears. He listened absently to the obligatory interview with a witness, who was sufficiently inarticulate to make a youngish reporter sound urbane by comparison.

The anchor woman came back. "When we return, an analysis of our top story; the surprise withdrawal of incumbent Earl Moncavage from the Congressional race to attend to pressing issues at his family's bank. Stay tuned to learn what this could mean for all of us."

Cindy unwound herself from the chair and shut it off. "What's in the box?" she asked.

"Excuse me?"

She glanced at a shipping carton at the edge of the patio. "The truck driver wheeled it around so I could sign for it."

He took out a small pocket knife.

She watched him cut the strapping tape, watched the sides fall away to reveal its contents. "It's that dumb old jukebox Harvey Ricks was working on."

Sinclair peered through the open back of the Wurlitzer. "Well, it looks all right."

"Why would he send it to you?"

"Peace offering?"

"If I were Harvey Ricks, I'd want to blow your brains out. Yours and mine both."

"That Harvey Ricks is a Halloween mask he wears to fool people into thinking they're dealing with an intellectual no-show. The real Harvey Ricks doesn't want me noising it around that he's planning to blanket Wall Street with shrink-wrapped snow. The jukebox is probably meant to remind me he knows a few things I wouldn't want to reach any official ears."

Worry robbed Cindy of a little color. "How did you make out with the State Attorney?" she asked in a voice braced for the worst.

"She also wants me to keep my mouth shut."

Cindy thrust her hands into her pockets and called him a liar with skeptical cobalt eyes that spoke more forcefully than words. "I want to know what she really said."

He settled stiffly into a chair and recounted his interview with Ruellene Kingman. Cindy listened intently. Every so often a flicker in her eyes would suggest that he had explained something she had wondered about.

"It's just stupid," she decided when he finished. "Why would Earl Moncavage go to all that trouble to get rid of a Judge who couldn't have lasted more than a year or two longer?"

"Moncavage has spent his life reaching for more. He wanted the power now."

"What about that woman who tried to kill you?"

"Maureen has been listening to the jungle drums. Word is that law enforcement is very interested in a Falcon 10 that took off from Opa Locka for Mexico City at four-thirty this morning and refiled for Cartgena in mid-flight. The prevailing theory is Tonia Cardenza was on-board."

"Isn't anyone going to be prosecuted?"

"Laws are enforced at the convenience of the people doing the enforcing. In this case, it wasn't convenient."

"Just tell me yes or no. Forget your cynical take on things."

"You're not an officer of the court yet. Some people who are have decided how things will be. The situation could have turned out a lot worse."

Cindy stood perfectly still. A breeze came off the canal and toyed with the ends of her hair. That was the only movement until her lips parted to speak.

"I went to register for law school today," she said quickly and softly. "New student orientation is the eighteenth."

Sinclair could not contain a sheepish grin. "I guess that's when the present and future guardians of order and justice check the class for good looking chicks with no wedding rings."

"No, David, you're not listening. You're free. You have your building. You have what you wanted out of this, and I'm glad for you. I really am. You're getting out luckier than you know."

"I don't think you'll mark me for any more Amazons with machine pistols, if that's what you mean."

Cindy's determination cracked apart like old plaster. Her eyes took on the wild, senseless quality of a runaway nightmare. "How long—how—how long have you known?"

Sinclair rose from the chair and stepped close to her. "It bothered me from the start. Neither Vernon nor Scott knew I rode without a convoy of shooters. The way the ambush was set, whoever planned it almost had to know."

"You knew!" Hurt brought moisture to Cindy's eyes. "And you never said a word?"

Sinclair looked down at the toe of his shoe. He pushed it around a little, making scuffing noises on the patio. He looked up into Cindy's damp, accusing eyes.

"I guessed. I didn't know about Moncavage then. I don't know now what he was to you. I'd like to think he was just the fast track to the top. Someone with the power to make you the person your mother wanted you to marry. If it was something else, I guess I don't ever want to know. But I had to have a pretty solid idea what was behind the shooting before I said anything. You were too important to me to risk guesswork. You are too important."

"It was just supposed to be a holdup; something to scare you away," she began quickly, and then fell shamefaced. "That sounds pretty lame, doesn't it? I never saw him again after that. Earl Moncavage, I mean. Until Scott told me to go there last night and I couldn't think of anyplace else we could run."

Sinclair grinned fondly. "You stuck your neck way out last night. First to get me out of the house, then waiting around for me outside. You could've taken off with the money any time."

"No." Cindy shook her head in a movement that wasn't more than a shiver. "That wasn't me, David. That was a scared, tired woman who let her guilt get the best of her."

"You're a better liar than that. Want to take another run at it?"

She touched Sinclair's sleeve. "Let me just walk away, David. Pack my things and leave. You can keep the money and we'll say it just didn't work out between us."

"I couldn't say that. I'm not that good a liar."

Cindy dropped her hand and stared at him. For a brief instant her eyes flirted with hope. Then it was gone.

"David, I made a fool out of you," she said dully. "That might not matter to you this minute, but it will when you've thought about it awhile. And forever after."

"It matters now," Sinclair said in a voice as gentle as Indiana springtime. "And you may be right about forever. I'm not as smart about those things as maybe I should be. But I am smart enough to know that it wouldn't matter if I didn't care. And if it matters forever, then I'll care forever."

0-595-22434-2

CPSIA information can be obtained
at www.ICGtesting.com
Printed in the USA
FSHW011959150321
79536FS